CORPSE PATH COTTAGE

CORPSE PATH COTTAGE

MARGARET SCUTT

ROBERT HALE

First published in 2018 by
Robert Hale, an imprint of
The Crowood Press Ltd,
Ramsbury, Marlborough
Wiltshire SN8 2HR

www. crowood.com

British Library Cataloguing-in-Publication Data
A catalogue record for this book is available from the
British Library.

ISBN 978 0 7198 2582 8

Typeset by Chapter One Book Production, Knebworth

Printed and bound in India by Replika Press Pvt. Ltd.

CHAPTER 1

MRS COSSETT WADDLED AROUND the corner of the road, saw that her bus awaited her, and heaved a grateful sigh. She was laden not only by the weight of a swollen shopping bag but also by that of the heavy coat which she had donned when she set out under the impression that the cold spell was continuing. On the little toe of her left foot a corn which, with more pleasing things, bloomed in the spring made its presence felt like a diabolical familiar. For half the morning she had stood in queues, obtaining as her reward little which she could not have purchased in the general shop of her own village. She would not have missed her Saturday trip to town for worlds.

The bus, a battered affair which had once been red but whose acquaintance with paint went back to the distant past, was one of three which served the villages within a twelve mile radius of Lake, and was fettered by none of the slavish allegiance to timetables shown by the town services. It was not due to leave for another half hour, and that it should leave on time was neither usual nor likely but already the heads of five or six occupants showed through the dusty windows. All the heads were female, and all their owners were hot, tired and as loaded as Mrs Cossett. They observed her with sympathetic interest as she heaved her considerable bulk up the steps, wedged herself into a seat, placed her bag on the floor beside her and heaved a sigh of relief.

'Thank God for a seat,' she observed, her voice slow and heavy like an underdone cake. 'My feet be killing me.'

'Ah, and so be mine, too,' said a thin lady in a knitted hood, which gave her the appearance of an elderly pixie. 'Outside Pinwell's I stood for three quarters of an hour, by the High Street clock – and time my turn came, two buns was all they had left. Currant buns,' she added, with a bitter laugh, 'if such you can call 'em wi' the currants so scarce as snowflakes in hell.'

There were groans of agreement. The bus, which served three villages beyond Mrs Cossett's own, held no-one at the moment known to her by name, but the camaraderie of the queue still held its sway – and indeed, this was the joy of the Saturday morning shopping expedition, in which perfect strangers might and did exchange intimacies of the most surprising nature. For this, if they would admit it, had they spent a morning of bodily discomfort. The social atmosphere of a club was theirs; Mrs Cossett leaned back and absorbed its pleasure.

'I could stand if 'twern't for my carns,' said a deep voice from the back seat. 'Do what I will for the varmints, carve' 'em out or burn 'em out, back they come – and wuss than ever in the spring.'

'So do mine,' said Mrs Cossett, with mournful pride. 'Fust change in the weather, and don't I know it! This I feel now be on my little toe, and a proper devil. I don't 'low as no-one wouldn't scarcely believe it, but I feel it this very moment. Yer,' she added, raising one forefinger and pressing it to her brow with a dark, dramatic gesture. 'Right up in my head.'

Far from being disbelieved, it appeared that all her hearers had experienced a like phenomenon, of which all were ready and anxious to give details there and then. A conversation which might have been entitled 'Corns I have known' continued for some moments.

'But 'tis these queues as finish me,' said Mrs Cossett, her flat voice dominating and silencing the chorus like a steamroller, slow but inexorable. 'Week after week, I say I won't come never no more, for tain't never worth it. And then I think, well, this time I mid just strike lucky – and God knows we get little enough.'

The blast of agreement was deafening. Every woman had her particular grievance to air, and none waited upon her neighbour. The bus resounded as to the outcry of a flock of starlings.

'Money gone afore you can turn round, and what can you get for a pound note? What the government be thinking of … This stuff they call cooking fat – about so fat as our tomcat … Points here, and kewpons there …'

Into the rising babble poked the enquiring head of a stranger. Peace fell as seven pairs of eyes fixed themselves on the first male to set foot on the bus that morning, summing him up with ravenous interest.

'Is this the bus for God's Blessing?' he asked generally.

'She be,' answered Mrs Cossett, giving the vehicle no more than its due since the name 'Flossie' was stencilled on the dashboard. She added, for good measure, 'She goes out at twelve, that is if she'll start.'

'All things,' replied the stranger, 'are with God.'

He glanced at his watch and stepped onto the bus, revealing himself as a tall, broad shouldered man who might have been anything between thirty and forty years of age. He wore an ageing sports coat with bulging pockets and brown corduroy trousers, and carried an obviously weighty rucksack. A slight but sinister cast in the left eye disfigured a face which needed no handicap. A black spaniel of far more aristocratic appearance than its master followed him with decorum.

'Talks like a 'Vangelist; looks like one o' they there hikers,' said Mrs Cossett to herself. ''Nor no oil painting, neither, though he mid look as if he thought he owned the bus. My God!' she added aloud, leaning forward in deep agitation.

Her voice was echoed by a muttered and unevangelistic oath. Over her bag, a good half of which projected into the aisle, the stranger had tripped. Before her horrified gaze like a horn of plenty, it now poured forth a stream of assorted merchandise. A toilet roll trundled merrily to the back of the bus; a bag of cakes burst open and scattered its contents, followed by a wire saucepan cleaner, a soggy newspaper parcel and various oddments. With an anguished squeal, Mrs Cossett bent to retrieve her property. The stranger bent at the same moment. Their heads met with a dull thud.

'Of all places to leave a bag!' said the culprit, evidently deeming the best defence to be attack.

'Eef,' retorted Mrs Cossett, her normally high colour deepening, 'you was to put yourself about to find my cuke, you mid do better than blaming others for your own faults. Cukes is cukes, if only half a one, and a wicked price to pay, and if folks had more sense than to look where they be planting their great feet –'

The hiker glared around him with a vague impression that an instrument of music was the missing article in question. At that moment, a small female who had been burrowing under a seat emerged with her hat on one side, triumphantly brandishing half a cucumber, very much the worse for wear.

'Here you be, dirt and all. Old Webby hasn't swep' out his bus since afore the war, I should say.'

'Which war?' enquired a sepulchral voice from the back seat.

The bus rocked happily with the exception of the hiker, who was picking up cakes and dissuading his dog from looking on them as manna from heaven, and Mrs Cossett, who was not amused. She received her battered goods with hauteur, repacked her bag and lifted it with an ostentatious effort to her lap.

'That's better,' said the stranger, seating himself behind her. 'Out of harm's way now.'

''Tis to be hoped so, I'm sure,' said Mrs Cossett distantly.

The spaniel crawled beneath its owner's seat, flopped, yawned, and laid its head on its paws. The stranger drew a newspaper from his pocket and became lost in it. The women behind him began talking again, but Mrs Cossett remained majestically silent.

A tall thin woman in a tall black hat shot into the bus, startling the spaniel into a short bark.

'There be mackerel in Brown's,' she announced.

'What!' exclaimed Mrs Cossett, forgetting her woes and sitting bolt upright. 'They never had a thing but stinking saltfish, and that young toad in there, God forgive him, said there wouldn't be nothing all day. Lucky to have that, he said—'

'Be there much of a queue?' interrupted a wistful voice.

'Queue! They be from Brown's to the Odeon, and springing up like mushrooms every minute.'

'Ah, well,' said Mrs Cossett, sinking back resignedly, 'they must have 'em as can. Mackerel nor no mackerel, my feet won't take me down town again.'

'Terrible tiring today, Mrs Cossett,' assented the newcomer, settling her angular form beside her. 'I've had about as much as I want my own self by now. And how be the world using you?'

'Mustn't grumble, Mrs Hale, mustn't grumble,' replied Mrs Cossett sorrowfully. 'Heard the news?'

'I don't never hear nothing. What?'

'Jimmy Fairfax have got himself a housekeeper. This be she coming now.'

They both watched with interest the arrival of a thin, neatly dressed woman in black, with a nondescript pale face and mousy hair dressed in a bun which pushed out her felt hat at the back. She passed on to a seat near the back. A pretty dark haired girl followed, who greeted the two ladies pleasantly and looked at the stranger with a faint gleam of interest. The bus filled steadily but the seat beside the one male remained vacant until a small woman bearing the invariable shopping bag and looking tired and nervous placed herself at his side. He adjusted

8

his bulk to make room for her and returned to his paper. Beneath the seat the spaniel lay still.

Mrs Hale glanced around, satisfied herself that the new housekeeper was some distance away, and turned to her companion.

'Talking of Jimmy Fairfax, I suppose you heard as Corpse Path Cottage were sold?'

'No!' exclaimed Mrs Cossett. 'Well, if that don't go to show! Baldy Lovejoy, the liar, told me as Jimmy had put a reserve of 900 on it. Nine hundred!' repeated Mrs Cossett, laughing heartily. 'Even wi' prices as they be – that be hanged for a tale, I said to un.'

'It weren't, though,' said Mrs Hale.

'What!'

'Mrs Cossett,' said Mrs Hale, wagging her head. 'Jimmy Fairfax did put that reserve. And what's more, he got it.'

'He never!'

'He did. Mrs Plummer, she dropped in at the sale, wanting to know what they cottages over to Fairmile made, and she heard it with her own ears. She said the auctioneer hisself was took aback.'

'And well he mid be! Housing shortage nor no housing shortage, that beats all. Why, those 'vacuees they put in from London never stayed more than a week. Sooner be killed in comfort, they said. The whole place be falling to pieces – and stuck in the middle of a bog whenever the rain comes.'

'Well, God knows if Jimmy don't die a warm man 'twon't never be for want of trying.'

'And with him as he is – no chick nor child to leave it to. Only this vinegar faced housekeeper—'

'Housekeeper!' echoed Mrs Hale with a coarse laugh. 'How long do you reckon 'twill be before if you holler "Fire!" in the night, two heads'll come out of one winder?'

'Lord, yes.' Mrs Cossett dismissed the love life of Mr Fairfax and his housekeeper. 'If Corpse Path Cottage be sold, Miss Faraday will be having a neighbour.'

'Sh! Just behind. Next to that strange feller.'

'Hope he don't tread on her toes with those great feet,' muttered Mrs Cossett, recalling her wrongs. 'For pity's sake, when be this bus going to start?'

The bus was now full of humanity and a strong smell of fish. At five minutes past twelve, the conductor strolled up, his fingers linked with those of a blonde damsel from whom he appeared reluctant to part. A few minutes later the driver was seen to emerge without haste from an adjacent snack-bar, wiping his mouth. He moved to the driving seat and pressed the starter twice without result.

'Now then, Perce,' he called amiably to the conductor, 'break away, there.'

'Why,' said Perce turning slowly, as one coming back from a far country, 'won't she have it?'

'She won't. Come and give her a swing, if so be as you can spare the time.'

Perce passionately pressed the hand of his love and obeyed. The engine gave a shattering backfire, causing an old gentleman who was dozing on a nearby seat to leap into the air, and broke into asthmatic life.

'Don't sound too good,' said Perce, shaking his head.

'Ah well,' said the driver philosophically, 'we must live in hopes.'

The conductor took his place, leaning out for a last glimpse of blonde curls. Vibrating horribly, the ancient vehicle set off.

'Fez, pliz,' said Perce morosely, and moved down the aisle.

The hiker folded his paper, placed it in an already overcrowded pocket, and sat back. He observed Mrs Hale and Mrs Cossett bouncing and quivering before him and thought with satisfaction that the noise of their progress might serve to drown their voices, which had a peahen quality not soothing to the ear. In this hope, however, he was disappointed. Halfway up a long gentle slope, about two miles from the town, the engine began to cough and balk like an unwilling horse. The driver clashed his gears despairingly; they moved forward in a series of jerks and finally stopped dead.

'I knowed it,' said Perce, in the tone of a justified soothsayer.

A chorus of advice, some facetious, all resigned to misfortune, was showered upon him and the driver as they lifted the bonnet and peered earnestly at the mysteries within. The passengers settled philosophically to conversation. The spaniel crawled from beneath his master's feet and yawned loudly. The other occupant of the seat jumped.

'All right,' said the hiker, 'he's perfectly quiet.'

'Oh yes, I'm sure. It was only that I didn't know he was there.'

Amy Faraday felt herself blushing, thought with bitterness that it was idiotic to do so, and nervously touched the smooth black head. The spaniel wagged politely, but with the air of inviting no further advances.

'... I do assure you, Mrs Cossett ...' the voice of Mrs Hale rose impressively.

'Mrs Cossett took a posset,' murmured the stranger dreamily.

'I – beg your pardon?' stammered Miss Faraday, thinking with some reason that her ears misled her.

'Not at all,' replied her companion graciously. 'Merely a poetic fragment. Listen.'

He jerked his thumb in the direction of the unconscious pair before them and learned forward unashamedly. Miss Faraday's tired eyes widened, and she shot him an apprehensive glance. The stranger's lips twitched.

'... Corpse Path Cottage!' said Mrs Hale, in accents of bitter scorn. 'Corpse Path Ruin 'ud be nearer the mark.'

'True enough, true enough,' agreed Mrs Cossett, 'but who were the loony as bought it – man or woman?'

'Man. Endalott or Bendalot, or some such outlandish name. Whatever it be, the feller must be out of his mind.'

'Not necessarily,' said the stranger, leaning forward.

There was a moment of incredulous silence. Both ladies started violently and turned surprised faces on the speaker. Miss Faraday, feeling for their discomfiture, smiled feebly and wished herself away.

'P-pardon?' stammered Mrs Hale.

'I said, in answer to your somewhat sweeping statement – not necessarily. The gentleman, far from being a loony, might have good and sufficient reasons for his behaviour. To take only one supposition, he might be a fugitive from justice. Thief – blackmailer – forger – murderer. You pays your penny and you takes your choice.'

Mrs Hale giggled nervously. Mrs Cosset recovered her breath.

'Stuff and nonsense,' she said.

'Not at all,' said the stranger, to whom the entire assembly was now listening with deep interest. 'I myself have not yet seen this cottage with the intriguing name, but from your most interesting conversation I gather that it would be an ideal place for a man with a secret. Tumbledown, isolated ...'

His voice was drowned as, with a shattering reverberation, the engine came to life. He sat back with a satisfied smile, met Miss Faraday's gaze and winked. She looked hastily away, feeling the foolish colour dye her cheeks again, and wishing devoutly for the end of the journey. She kept herself as far removed from her companion as the seat would allow, pointedly refraining from looking at him again, and was yet uneasily conscious of the pleased grin which creased his face.

The bus, moving more easily now, like a horse approaching its stable, swept along a woodland road, turned a corner and stopped.

'God's Blessing crossroads!' intoned Perce.

Mrs Cossett, Mrs Hale and Miss Faraday rose. The stranger did likewise, bumped his head sharply, and followed them. The spaniel came briskly after him. The bus moved away.

The stranger looked about him with interest. God's Blessing, no flaunting village, did not display all its attractions to the first casual glance. Three very ugly cottages and a small general shop were in sight, while across the road a school built of bricks which had once been red peered at him from narrow windows of an ecclesiastical appearance. Before him he saw with pleasure a village green – a rough triangle of grass on which an enormous sow and a number of piglets were rooting happily. At the end of the green, a group of splendid elms looked down with well-bred disdain on a long and hideous building of corrugated iron. The stranger sighed with complete satisfaction, turned, and met the concerted gaze of three pairs of eyes.

Miss Faraday blushed hotly yet again, murmured a fluttering farewell to her companions and was gone. The two matrons, built of sterner stuff, held their ground. This man had broken into their conversation, had contradicted them, had filled their minds with raging curiosity. No power on earth should move them until they had seen his going.

'Nice weather,' said Mrs Cossett to Mrs Hale.

'But hot for the time of year,' said Mrs Hale to Mrs Cossett.

With maddening deliberation, the stranger filled a blackened pipe and swung his rucksack to his back.

'Can you,' he said politely, 'tell me the shortest way to Corpse Path Cottage?'

There was a heavy pause.

'Corpse Path Cottage?' echoed Mrs Cossett in a hollow voice.

'Corpse Path Cottage.'

'Follow that lane,' said Mrs Cossett, pointing. 'Past the white house on the corner, to your left through the next field gate. But ...'

'But what do I want with Corpse Path Cottage? Well,' said the stranger pleasantly, 'my name is Endicott. Not Endalott, or even Bendalot. Just plain Endicott. I am, in fact, the loony—'

Mrs Hale uttered a hen like sound.

'—and Corpse Path Cottage, for good or ill, belongs to me.'

Chapter II

AMY FARADAY PRANCED ALONG the lane, not from haughtiness of spirit but from mortification of the flesh. The sudden heat conspired with a pair of new and unfriendly shoes to give her pain. And apart from these bodily pangs, her face still burned with embarrassment. Recalling the way in which she had so lately gaped at that impossible stranger, she wondered at herself. A school girl could not have stood more unashamedly at gaze; not that school girls did such things any more, she reflected, wincing as a particularly virulent stab assailed her suffering feet. They moved, these children, straight from infancy into a devastating assurance and poise. She had never known what it was to have poise, she reflected sadly; she looked back on a dreary procession of years through which she had dithered and tripped over her own words, agonizingly conscious of appearing as foolish to others as to herself. But even she should have known better than to stare at That Man as she had. Mrs Cossett, Mrs Hale and herself; three idiotic faces all in a row, like three cows staring over a hedge. No wonder he had grinned in that supercilious way. No wonder.

Above the meadow to her right a lark mounted, singing as it went, a dancing brown speck against the blue. Miss Faraday thought suddenly that it was folly to trouble her head over a man whom it was unlikely that she would ever set eyes on again. Here she was, missing the beauty of this perfect spring day, partly through her own folly, partly through these accursed shoes. The past she could not recall, but with the shoes, at least, she might deal. Pausing, in a dark and secret manner, she looked over her shoulder. No fearful fiend did close behind her tread; she saw only the lane, sun dappled, fringed with green, and empty. She limped to the grass verge, set down her bag, seated herself and removed her shoes.

Like prisoners all unused to freedom, her feet in the first moments of release protested more violently than before, then the pain receded in a wave and a heavenly relief took its place. She stretched out her legs and wiggled her toes. The shabby tweed skirt rucked itself in an abandoned manner above her knees. Overhead the lark still sang.

She thought how her mother's heart would have been gladdened by such a day as this. The first unfolding of spring she had always taken as a personal and delightful gift; it was a joy which had never forsaken her, even when the time had come that she could no longer creep around the garden to discover the first daffodil – the grape hyacinths, patches of heaven against the grass. It was said that you ceased mourning for the dead, thought Miss Faraday, with desolation closing coldly around her heart – that time must needs bring the balm of forgetfulness. Yet how could this be, when the simplest sight, sound or scent held power to remind you of the past so vividly that each time you lost them all over again? She had not wept in the presence of others when it would have been fitting and right to do so; at her mother's grave she had not shed a tear. Now, because the winter was past and a lark sang, her eyes pricked, and the scene before her became a blur of green and gold.

She put her knuckles to her eyes in a childish gesture and called herself to order. It was time that she ceased sitting at the roadside like a statue of melancholy and put on her shoes. Delaying for a space the evil hour, she regarded them coldly – ugly, stout and serviceable, and wondered as she had often done before at the malign fate which made shoes all yielding comfort in the shop yet allowed them to change from Jekyll to Hyde once money was paid and the die cast. Well, pain or no pain, their proud spirit must needs be broken, since even in God's Blessing one did not go barefoot. She bent forward.

With a sudden mighty crackling of twigs, a black dog burst through the hedge and uttered a loud bark almost in her ear. Surprised and confounded, Miss Faraday sprang to her feet. This, as she instantly discovered, was ill advised. She trod on a sharp stone, sat down suddenly where the grass verge was not, and disappeared into the ditch. The spaniel, greatly disconcerted at such behaviour, and vaguely conscious that he had sinned, barked continuously.

'Quiet, you noisy devil,' said Mark Endicott, swinging along the lane. 'What the—!'

His astonished gaze had fallen on the shoes and the shopping bag at the roadside. As he stared, Miss Faraday, like Venus from the waves, rose and confronted him. Her hat was over one ear and decorated by a long trail of bramble. Her face was scarlet with anger and mortification. She recognized him, and closed her eyes as if in prayer.

'Good Lord, it's the rabbit,' said Endicott, moving to her assistance. 'There we go. Up she comes, like a daisy.'

Held under the armpits in a grip of steel, Miss Faraday did, indeed, come up. For this assistance she felt no gratitude; the bitter resentment of the meek filled her heart. To her inflamed imagination this redheaded lunatic with his squint, his rucksack and his spaniel seemed to pervade God's Blessing like a foul smell. A woman could not so much as rest without his appearing, it seemed, and first inciting his dog to deeds of violence and then calling his victims names. Rabbit, indeed. I would like to bite him. Hard, thought Amy, and after a backward glance, seated herself in majestic silence and waited for him to remove himself.

'What happened?' asked Endicott, apparently all unconscious of offence.

'I was resting. That dog came bursting through the hedge. I was startled.'

'And base over apex she fell, eh?' Endicott laughed heartily. 'You aren't hurt, I hope? And fortunately the ditch was dry.'

'I am not hurt. And the ditch, as you say, was dry.'

'Well, I can only say that I'm sorry it happened. If there is anything I can do—'

'Nothing, thank you.' Only for God's sake take yourself off, she added furiously to herself.

'Not give you a brush down, or help you on with your shoes? Pinch, do they?'

The much tried Amy folded her lips tightly and shook her head.

'I could never understand women wearing tight shoes,' said Endicott conversationally.

'Mine,' said Amy in a suffocated voice, 'are not tight. I twisted my ankle a little way back.'

'Oh, bad luck. Which one?'

'Both. That is, it was not so much a twist as a slight sprain. It is better now.'

'Sure? Then I'll say cheerio. To our next merry meeting!'

'Goodbye,' said Amy.

She waited until man and dog were out of sight before wrestling with her shoes.

'It's all your fault,' she told them bitterly. 'And, of course, it would be

15

that – that oaf, and his mad dog.' She tied up the laces, tugging them ferociously. 'What possessed me to tell those idiotic lies? And I believe he was laughing like a hyena the whole time.' She stood up, shaking herself vigorously to remove the vegetable matter which clung to her. 'Rabbit! At least, thank God, I've seen the last of him!'

Mark Endicott, continuing his way with the source of Miss Faraday's discomfiture pacing virtuously at his heels, recalled their encounter with pleasure. The lady, so meek and insignificant as his companion in the bus, had worked up quite a healthy anger on their second meeting. It was difficult to appear dignified when draped like a bacchante with clinging vines, especially when the shoes which did not pinch had been cast aside, but the effort, reflected Mark critically, had been highly praiseworthy. His name, as far as she was concerned, was most undoubtedly mud. He wondered how near a neighbour of his she was likely to be, and looked inquisitively at the house he was now passing. No Corpse Path Cottage bought by a loony here; prim and white, it stood back from the lane, the patches of flower-bordered lawn before it veiled demurely by hawthorn hedges, and only visible from the green wicket gate. The spotted muslin curtain twitched to no enquiring fingers; no peering eyes looked forth to see the passing of a stranger. He called his dog and passed on. And around the bend, he came upon a decrepit field gate hanging from one hinge, which told him that if Mrs Cossett and Mrs Hale had directed him truthfully, he was in sight of his journey's end.

Before him was a large field, hummocky and thick with thistles. A deeply rutted track led across it to a hazel coppice which beckoned pleasantly enough to a weary traveller, hinting of drifts of bluebells, and the clean scents of spring. Endicott did not heed it, he was looking at the depth of the ruts, and imagining what the clay soil would be like after rain. Well, he had wanted solitude – had, in fact, paid through the nose to get it – and must expect some slight drawbacks in exchange. Nor had he a wife to shudder at the habitation he had chosen.

A few yards to his left, the chimneys of his purchase, apparently sprouting like fungi from the soil, were all that told of the glories awaiting him. He marched purposefully along the rutted patch, and looked down upon his domain.

Corpse Path Cottage might well have been named Toad in the Hole. Why any man had been moved to build in the depression so oddly dimpling the surface of the field was a mystery; unless the answer lay in the fact that he had utilized the piece of earth most difficult to cultivate. Not that the rest of the field showed signs of having paid for working; Endicott was country born, and looked on it with a knowledgeable eye. A miserable patch, he thought, with a grudging, miserly air – not that it was any affair of his. Corpse Path Cottage and the saucer in which it stood was the extent of his purchase. And quite enough too, he thought, as he walked towards it, half moved by a boyish excitement, half wondering at his own folly.

The cottage was surrounded by a hedge, straggling and neglected, but proudly flaunting its new spring finery. The wicket gate had once been green, it checked under his impatient hand, and he was forced to lift it over the weed-strewn gravel. The spaniel shot ahead of him, quivering with excitement; Endicott walked slowly up the few feet of path which led to the front door, pausing there for a moment. And once again in his heart, he paid tribute to that redoubtable pair Mrs Cossett and Mrs Hale, who, whatever their failings, spoke no more than the truth.

The cottage was constructed with great simplicity in the fashion of a child's drawing, and with as little regard for straight lines, since the solid mud walls had bulged ominously under the attacks of sun and rain. There were two minute windows up and two down, with a door and a decrepit ivy-covered porch between. The thatched roof was blackened with age and as dilapidated as a deserted bird's nest. The right hand upper window had lost two panes of glass out of four, the left swung raffishly on broken hinges. Endicott nodded pensively to himself and wandered around the house. He found the back to be less ornate than the front, possessing a door but only one window, and this was covered with perforated zinc. The flourishing patch of deeply-rooted weeds which the house agent, blessed with simple faith, had described as a large and well stocked garden, spread over the slope behind the house. Not far away stood a kind of wooden sentry-box, leaning slightly, as if the victim of repeated assaults.

'All the usual offices,' said Endicott with a hollow laugh. 'No, God help us, though – what about water?'

His search was rewarded when he stubbed his toe painfully on some hard substance masked by a luxuriant growth of nettles. He spoke shortly, and bent to investigate. The wooden lid moved with reluctance, but at length he gazed down on his own face, mirrored like an unbeautiful Narcissus in a dark circle. The well was surprisingly small, but the level of water was high. Endicott, rising with green stains on the knees of his corduroys, reflected that this was to the good, since he was apparently expected to dip out the water by hand.

Feeling in his pocket for the key, he made for the front door. The dog suddenly darted past him, barking loudly. A young man who was on his hands and knees beside the path leapt up, looking surprised and displeased.

'Well, well,' said Endicott, 'our first visitor.'

'Who the devil are you?' demanded the young man, scowling.

Endicott raised his brows. 'I,' he said, with simple pride, 'am the owner of this charming bijou residence set in surroundings of rural beauty, having large grounds, usual offices, and own water. Name of Endicott. What can I do for you?'

Under his quizzical gaze, the young man coloured. He was extremely good looking with a close ripple in his fair hair, and blue eyes matched, as Endicott did not fail to note, the blue sports shirt under the tweed jacket. His teeth were white and even and his lips very red. Endicott found a name for him and spoke it to his immortal soul.

'Er – as a matter of fact, it is what can I do for you?' said his visitor, who appeared to be remarkably ill at ease. 'We – that is, my mother – heard that the cottage was sold. Being at a loose end, I thought I might stroll round in case you'd arrived to see if we could lend a hand. Neighbourly, and all that.'

He gained confidence by the end of his speech, and smiled with a flash of white teeth.

'Neighbourly?' asked Endicott, rather apprehensively. 'Would yours be the white house at the bend of the lane?'

'Not that, no. That belongs to Miss Faraday – school-marm, very prim, meek and mild. We live farther on – my name is Marlowe, incidentally, Brian Marlowe – and our abode is beyond the village on the corner of the main road. If such you can call it.'

'Ah! Not close neighbours, then,' said Endicott, with unmannerly satisfaction.

'All part of God's Blessing, old boy. God's Blessing!' repeated Marlowe, his smile fading and his tone not a benediction. '"We few, we happy few, we band of brothers!" And how!'

'It would seem,' said Endicott, 'that God's Blessing does not meet with your approval.'

'It won't with yours,' said Marlowe, 'unless you happen to care for tittle tattle and petty scandal and peering eyes wherever you go. I don't know what brought you here and it's none of my damned business, but if your idea was to find peace and quiet – brother, you've had it! Quiet, perhaps, but the quiet of a dirty pool with nasty things creeping under the slime—'

He broke off suddenly and attempted to smile, but the too handsome face was twisted. The hand with which he smoothed back his hair was shaking.

'As bad as that?' observed Endicott placidly. 'A man can always get out.'

'How right you are.' Marlowe laughed. 'Sorry for the outburst. I had rather a thick night. Forget it.'

Endicott nodded. All very fine and large, but what was this matinee idol after? The line about a neighbourly call was scarcely good enough. In any case, he had seen quite as much as he wanted of Brian Marlowe for the time being.

'I must be looking over my domain,' he said.

'Yes. Sure there's nothing I can do? You're all fixed up?'

'All fixed up,' agreed Endicott.

'In that case, I'll leave you to it.'

'Cheerio,' said Endicott cheerfully, and turned to the door.

'Cheerio,' replied Marlowe dismally.

'"Parting is such sweet sorrow,"' muttered Endicott to himself and took out his key. Looking back, he saw with exasperation that his visitor still lingered.

'I've just realized,' said Marlowe, meeting his gaze, 'that you might be thinking the place was furnished. That old Fairfax wouldn't leave as much as a stick.'

'No? It doesn't matter. My furniture arrives on Monday.'

'Monday? Then you won't be sleeping here tonight?'

Endicott stared, half angry, half intrigued. The eagerness in the fellow's voice was unmistakeable.

He said shortly, 'Why not?'

The other flushed at his tone. 'No business of mine, naturally. But an empty house—'

'My dear fellow,' said Endicott patiently, 'your consideration for my wellbeing touches me to the heart but I assure you that I have slept in many worse places than an empty house. Also, as I may have mentioned before, I have with me everything I need.'

He turned back to the door, fitted the key into the keyhole and raised his brows as he removed it. When he looked around he saw that his visitor had gone.

'Thank God for that,' said Endicott piously, and opened the door.

19

He found himself in a brick-paved cell about four feet square and described by the agent as a hall. Facing him was a flight of stairs, narrow, precipitous, and thick with dust. To his right was a deal door, battered and in need of paint, but with nothing surprising in its appearance. To his left was one which appeared to have strayed from its normal surroundings, since only its lower half was of wood. Its upper portion was of glass on which was writ large and enticing the one word – 'BAR'.

Endicott blinked. Thirst had not misled him; 'BAR', however incongruous in this setting, was real enough. He wondered what his next discovery might be and pushed open the door, to find that the encouraging sign led to nothing more interesting than a stone paved kitchen with a rusty range and a sink of depressing appearance. A half open door disclosed a whitewashed larder. The back door was bolted top and bottom and, to make assurance doubly sure, secured across the middle by a solid wooden bar. This care for security seemed rather offset by the fact that he had opened the front door without needing to use his key.

He went back across the hall and into the other room. There he paused, his nose wrinkling. The kitchen had smelt, as was to be expected, of neglect and decay; obviously it had not known the warmth of human habitation for a long, long time. This room, too, was empty of any furnishing; cobwebs draped the walls and grime darkened the panes of the small window, but there was a different atmosphere here. It was not only the faint scent of tobacco, or that other fragrance, faint but clinging. Even without such silent witnesses, he would have sensed that the room had lately been occupied.

He walked across to the window, and the perfume came out in a wave, as if to welcome him. Instantly he was swept by the old blinding hurt. It was as if he had come there for the sole purpose of meeting her, that he might find himself lost and betrayed all over again. He had never conjured up so vivid a picture of her as now, when it was of all things the last he desired.

'You can't get away, can you, Mark? It's no use … you'll never get away …'

He brushed a hand across his eyes and jerked the window open. The air came sweetly in, banishing alike the mocking voice and the reminiscent perfume. Anger shook him. Plain enough what had happened, but who the devil had been making free with the place? No village pair, he knew well enough. That stuff, even before the war, had cost the earth. It was diabolically out of place in Corpse Path Cottage. And the fresh air was vanquished now, he could smell it again, faint but insidious.

Frowning, he glanced around, and saw the light glinting on an object in the corner of the room.

He picked it up with reluctance, for this was the object from which the perfume came. He had been right enough; no village girl had dropped this shining toy. And as he stared at the object so incongruously held by his dark hand, he recalled his first glimpse of Brian Marlowe bending at the side of the path.

'You looked in the wrong place, my son,' said Endicott. 'And in future you may take your pleasures elsewhere.'

The spaniel, who had been exploring, now wriggled his way into the room. There was dirt on his nose and a few small twigs ornamented his ears. He panted loudly.

'Food and drink required?' asked Endicott. 'And not such a bad idea, at that. I will join you, brother.'

He carried the compact into the kitchen and laid it on the mantelpiece. Bending over his swollen rucksack, he began to unpack.

CHAPTER III

AMY FARADAY OPENED THE door of the white house, and its emptiness came coldly to greet her. Mother has gone, said the house; no mother to hear your silly little bits and pieces to take, with laughter, the sting from the trials and errors of the day. Not Mother and Amy, a partnership happy and complete any more. Just Amy. Amy, foolish, lonely and afraid.

She saw her face in the hallstand mirror and stood examining it, quite impersonally. The weary eyes gazed back at her – strange eyes, looking coldly from a stranger's face. There were so many such faces to see in the course of a day – on buses, in shops or queues, drab, hopeless, the faces of those who had lost the way, and would never find it again.

She said to the face in the mirror, 'I was pretty once,' and turned away. It was a mere statement of fact, uttered without emphasis or regret. It did not matter. Nothing mattered any more.

In the spotless kitchen she pulled off her shoes and put on a pair of slippers, down at heel and full of years. The action brought back the memory of her accident in the lane, and of the oddly-mannered stranger. She felt no anger now. She would never see him again, which was all to the good, but that did not matter, either. Her mother would have laughed at the whole affair and Amy with her. She could not laugh alone.

She filled the electric kettle and pushed down the switch. Tea here, since it would be less trouble than carrying it into the sitting-room. She laid a checked cloth on the white table, and set out a cup, saucer and plate. Two slices of bread and the last of the butter, the sad looking cake which she had bought that morning. She was measuring tea into the pot when she heard the plop of a letter on the mat. It was at this precise moment that Mark Endicott, rummaging blasphemously through the dark recesses of his rucksack, was forced to decide that beyond all peradventure he had left his tin opener behind.

Miss Faraday stood in the hall with her letter. She read it twice without comprehension. The third time she took it slowly and painstakingly, her lips moving like those of a child forming unfamiliar words. This time she understood.

'Oh, no,' she said aloud. 'It's too much.'

Her face crumpled strangely. The letter dropped to the floor. She began to laugh. The laughter grew and grew, dominating her, hurting her, forcing its way. She felt a sudden longing for air and, still making strange sounds, opened the door. Mark Endicott looked at her in some surprise.

Amy started violently, uttered a strangled whoop, and staggered back to the staircase, where she collapsed on the bottom step. The idiotic laughter still bubbled from her lips. She felt a hand on her shoulder, and wondered if she dreamed.

'I knocked,' said Endicott mildly.

Miss Faraday swallowed a laugh which almost choked her and pushed the hair back from her hot forehead. She said in a suffocated voice, 'What are you doing here?'

'I came to see if you could lend me a tin opener. Then I thought you might be ill. From the noise—'

Amy rose unsteadily. Her heart was racing from her late inexplicable outburst. She wished that Endicott had never been born.

'The wireless,' she said coldly.

'They put on some queer stuff nowadays,' said Endicott.

She looked at him uncertainly, met his interested gaze and blushed painfully. To her immeasurable horror, tears sprang to her eyes, and she turned hastily away. Endicott, to his own surprise, patted her clumsily on the shoulder. Instantly, as if overpowered by this touch of humanity, Miss Faraday cast herself upon his breast and wept.

'God save us all,' said Endicott with glazing eyes.

He continued to massage his companion's shaking shoulders, somewhat alarmed by the violence of her weeping. It seemed hard to him that a man who wanted nothing more desperate than a tin opener should find himself landed with a spinster in the throes of raging hysterics. He could scarcely walk out of this strange situation into the midst of which he had plunged all unasked, but what to do with the choking Niobe in his arms he had no idea.

'There, there,' he said, kneading her shoulder like a football trainer. 'I don't know what the hell it's all about, but there, there.'

Miss Faraday wept the more.

'A cry will do you good – I hope,' said Endicott. 'There, there.'

'I – never cry,' gasped Miss Faraday.

'You'd make a fortune,' said Endicott, grinning, 'imitating them as do.'

For some reason the words seemed to bring his companion to her senses. She removed herself from him, sniffed, and mopped at her ravaged face with a useless handkerchief.

'I don't know what came over me,' she said.

'That's all right,' said Endicott, much relieved. 'Cry on me any time you like. Good neighbours, and all that. What you want now is a nice cup of tea.'

Miss Faraday caught her breath in a reminiscent sob. 'I put the kettle on,' she said.

'I was never,' said the vicar's wife emphatically, 'I was never so taken aback in my life.'

She leaned back in her chair and awaited her companion's reactions, which were as satisfactory as she could have wished. The two ladies were seated in Mrs Stroud's drawing room, which the vicar's wife had entered five minutes before. In that space of time she had contrived to rouse Mrs Stroud's curiosity to fever pitch.

'But Miss Faraday, of all people! Though, as my husband always says, still waters—'

'Run deep,' said Mrs Richards, who had a habit of saving other people the trouble of finishing their sentences, and had been accused by those who did not love her of taking the words out of your mouth and turning them to suit herself. 'Yes, of course. But that quiet little creature, always completely absorbed by her mother and broken by her mother's death, and at her age – she must be close on forty if she's a day, though perhaps that accounts for it.' Mrs Richards drew a much needed breath. 'I said at the time and I say it now, she should have given up the house and gone into nice rooms in the town – or at least have found some respectable person to keep her company. It was strange the way that she insisted on remaining there alone. Though one cannot help wondering, now—'

'But what is it that's going on? You forget that you haven't told me yet. I'm consumed –'

'With curiosity. And well you may be. It was like this. I was calling today on Mrs Oliphant, and we got to talking about the Garden Fête which is to be on the 26th July, a month later than usual owing to the vicar attending the June Convention this year which he should do and must, although I have had a trial to persuade him – these men! However, where was I? – oh, I know! It occurred to me that it would be a kindness to ask Miss Faraday if she would help with the jumble stall. We are short there, and it would be a charity for the poor little soul. Her painful shyness wouldn't matter on the jumble, and it might take her out of herself. Or so I thought—'

She checked suddenly as a maid entered, steering in a trolley set out for tea. Mrs Richards, in one piercing glance, saw that the eatable part of the feast consisted of a plate of digestive biscuits, and was grieved.

'Okeydoke?' replied Betty cheerfully, and passed out.

'How long have you had her?' asked Mrs Richards, momentarily diverted.

'Three days,' said Mrs Stroud mournfully. 'It seems a long time.'

'She won't stay,' said Mrs Richards.

'Oh, no. They never do. But do go on with what you were saying.'

She poured a pallid stream of tea into a delicate china cup and passed her visitor a digestive biscuit, reflecting as she did so that it was long enough since any of the vicarage rations had passed her lips. Mrs Richards nibbled her biscuit, calculated the length of time it must have spent with her hostess to become so flabby and steeped in gloom and took up her tale.

'Well – over the jumble stall – I thought to myself, I will do it now, or with one thing and another it may well slip out of my mind. So off I went to the White House. Twice I knocked, and was rather surprised when she did not come, it being Saturday, but I thought she might be out, so I tried the door to make sure. It was unlocked so I stepped into the hall and called, "Miss Faraday! Miss Faraday!" There was no answer, but from the kitchen I heard the sound of a laugh. A loud laugh.'

'Miss Faraday? Miss Faraday laughing loudly?'

Mrs Richards paused for a moment.

'The laugh,' she said, 'was masculine.'

Mrs Stroud, her cup halfway to her lips, sat transfixed. Well pleased with the effect of her tidings, Mrs Richards nodded her head with such emphasis that her hat jerked itself forward and momentarily obscured her glittering eyes. She straightened it, and continued her tale.

'The first thought that crossed my mind when I heard that laugh – that low laugh—'

'I thought you said it was a loud laugh,' said Mrs Stroud, wrinkling her brow.

'It was. I mean low in the sense of vulgar. Common. Depraved. Almost a drunken laugh.'

'Good gracious me,' said Mrs Stroud. 'Do go on.'

Mrs Richards fortified herself with a sip of rapidly cooling tea, set down her cup with a faint shudder, and complied.

'As I was saying, the first thought which crossed my mind was that someone had broken into the house and was making free with it in Miss Faraday's absence. There have been so many cases of petty thieving lately – the vicar has been quite concerned.'

'So has the colonel,' murmured Mrs Stroud, glancing at her beautiful silver teapot.

'That being the case, and never dreaming that such a laugh could have been uttered in Miss Faraday's presence, it was my clear duty to investigate. My shoes, as you see, have rubber soles. I went softly through the sitting room and stopped at the kitchen door, which was open. And then I saw how greatly I was mistaken. For there they were.'

'They?'

'Amy Faraday and a man. A man of an appearance to match the laugh. A creature whom I should not care to meet in a lonely lane. Yet there he was with her. Alone.'

Like a mute Oliver Twist, Mrs Stroud leaned forward in her chair and asked for more. Pleasant excitement filled her plump breast. The word orgies sprang to her mind and found itself a welcome guest.

'I would never have believed it,' said Mrs Richards, rather meanly abandoning descriptive and returning to her early cry.

'But what were they doing?' urged the tantalized Mrs Stroud, her voice raising. 'Were they—?'

Mrs Richards leaned back in her chair. She spoke with deliberation, giving due weight to every syllable.

'She was in her slippers. Her face was flushed and her eyes strange and feverish. Her hair was wildly astray. I can only describe her as looking depraved. And,' her voice dropped a tone as she reached her climax, 'they were having tea.'

The wood, with the dusk coming softly down on it, was full of furtive movements and sleepy twitterings. Endicott strolled along, puffing at his pipe and waiting until such time as his dog saw fit to return to him. At the moment, crackling twigs and falsetto yelps told where rabbits enticed and eluded. Endicott grinned; he was in no hurry to take himself back to the hollow welcome of Corpse Path Cottage, and it was pleasant enough here. The years had fallen away from him; once more he captured the magic of a wood at dusk. He reached the gate at the top of the path and rested his arms on the top bar.

It was now so dark that he did not see the girl until she was beside him, and even then could not distinguish her features. There was a pale blur for a face, something pale and faintly glimmering surrounding it – a breath of disturbing perfume. Then, like a ghost, she had gone.

Endicott had knocked out his pipe. The peace which had enfolded him so snugly was gone, and he felt an angry frustration. Even here ... and he must know more of it. He whistled to the dog and turned to the field path which the shadowy figure had taken.

James came up the path, reluctant but obedient, and fell in decorously at his master's heels. He had caught no rabbit, but did not consider his time in the wood ill spent. James, at least, had no doubts as to the desirability of their present abode. Corpse Path Cottage had abounded in smells of charm and distinction, and the wood spelt heaven itself.

As they approached the hedge which enclosed the cottage, James suddenly stiffened, and uttered a low growl. Endicott looked up to see that a shadowy figure had detached itself from the shelter of the hedge. The girl of the wood, it appeared, had not covered much ground.

James growled again, and Endicott spoke softly. The plot was thickening. Someone was running across the field to meet the girl. He thought that, short as had been his stay in God's Blessing, he might hazard a guess at the identity of the hastening Romeo. The two figures met and halted. Endicott, one hand on the head of the quivery James, stepped into the shadow so lately vacated, and shamelessly listened.

'Darling!' The breathless voice was unmistakably that of Brian Marlowe. 'I'm terribly sorry – I ran into old Richards, and couldn't shake him off.'

'That's all right. Only if it's so much trouble for you to keep an appointment we'd better drop the whole thing. Is that what you want?'

At the sound of this new voice, sulky and provocative, the hand on the dog's head clenched. You fool, Endicott told himself, you're imagining it. Just because of a whiff of scent ... pull yourself together, and listen....

It was Marlowe who was speaking now.

'For God's sake! If you chuck me—'

There was a low laugh. Endicott felt the sweat start out on his forehead. He knew a bitter resentment against a fate which seemed determined to torment him.

He strained his ears, but the next words were too low for him to catch. Suddenly he tired of his position. He told himself that the love life of Brian Marlowe was no concern of his, and knew that it was an empty boast. It was strange that Corpse Path Cottage should have been chosen for this rendezvous – strange and no doubt a jest at which the gods might laugh. And suddenly he thought of the powder compact still on the mantelpiece where he had placed it that morning. Well, he could scarcely hand it over that night. He cursed the whole business, and called the dog, loudly and unnecessarily. He sensed as he went into the cottage that he had left a startled silence behind him.

'Who was that?' asked the girl sharply, after a moment.

'I suppose the fool who's bought the place.'

'Bought it? For heaven's sake, who?'

'Some lunatic. Endicott, he said his name was. Big ugly chap, with foul manners.'

The girl caught her breath sharply. She said, in a stifled voice: 'Did you say … Endicott?'

'Yes. Why, do you know him?'

'I knew a man once – years ago. How much do you think he heard?'

'Nothing, probably. We weren't shouting. God knows where he sprang from.'

'Probably from the wood gate. Some man was leaning over it as I came by.'

'Did he speak?'

'I didn't give him the chance. The gate was open and I thought it best not to pause for light conversation. Well, his coming puts paid to all this.'

'All this? You can't mean—'

His voice was muffled in her hair as he pulled her to him. She resisted him for a moment, then turned her face to his.

'I don't know what would happen,' he muttered, 'if you turned me down.'

'Would it hurt so much? Poor boy!'

'Don't laugh,' he said. 'I'm a fool, I know. You needn't rub it in. Sometimes I think you don't give a damn for me.'

'Do you? That's rather surprising.'

'But I never know – never have – if you aren't playing with me all the time. You're bored here – out of your element and I suppose my feelings offer you some form of distraction. Like a butterfly wriggling on a pin.'

She said mockingly, 'How touching. And not at all correct. Because I don't hold you in any way. You're free as air, my darling.'

'Free!' he said.

'You know,' she said, suddenly impatient, 'your trouble is that you dramatize yourself all the time. At the moment you are the tragic hero of an unhappy affair. Well, you needn't be. There's always the Morris girl, and a happy ending – yours for the asking.'

'Shut up,' he said.

'Oh? Mustn't I mention the pure girl's name?'

'Now you're being common.'

'Thanks very much. In that case, let's drop the whole thing. I assure you, it's becoming damned dull for me.'

'Only because you're tired of me,' he said bitterly.

'Oh, for God's sake! I come here risking everything to meet you – Ralph's temper is worse than ever lately – and all I get is the tale of your woes. Could you bear to think of me for a moment?'

The husky voice changed on the last words, murmuring an unmistakable invitation. His bewilderment and pain were vanquished, as always, by her nearness.

'I must get back,' she whispered at last. 'We are mad to stay here. That man may be peeping round the hedge all the time.'

'No. Look, there's a light in the cottage. I can see his shadow moving. I wish the fool had kept away from here.'

'So do I,' she said under her breath.

They moved off slowly towards the wood.

A moment after the linked figures had disappeared, a man came quietly to Endicott's door. His tap was answered by an explosion of barks from inside the cottage. Endicott, with visions of the tall slenderness of Brian Marlowe, and in no good mood, flung open the door.

'Evening to 'ee,' said the visitor affably. 'Mr Endicott?'

'That's my name.'

'Well, mine be Fairfax. You may ha' heard it,' said Mr Fairfax with a chuckle, 'afore.'

'Oh. The philanthropic gent who sold me the cottage. Come in, Mr Fairfax. I take it you know your way.'

'I do. I do indeed,' said Mr Fairfax cheerfully, and followed Endicott into the kitchen. In the light of the candle stuck to the mantelpiece by a blob of grease, he was revealed to be plump, bald and rosy – a Mr Pickwick without spectacles or gaiters. His blue eyes shone with childlike candour. Endicott recalled the price asked for his abode and reflected that the guileless countryman in excelcis stood before him.

'I can't ask you to sit down, I'm afraid. No chairs until Monday.'

'Quite all right, sir, quite all right. Stand and grow good, so they say. And how do you find yourself, Mr Endicott? You like the place?'

'It will suit my purpose.'

'Ah?' queried Mr Fairfax hopefully.

Oh no, said Mark to himself, that's not in the bargain and remained silent.

'Erh'r'm,' said Mr Fairfax, clearing his throat with surprising violence, 'if it suits you, it suits me. I'm sure. But speaking of chairs, I did have a few bits and pieces put by as I thought might be of use to 'ee.'

'Why,' said Mark cordially, 'that's very good of you. And, of course, that explains it.'

'Explains what?'

'The price you asked for the place. Furniture being thrown in makes all the difference.'

'Ha ha ha,' said Mr Fairfax, without conviction. 'I see, sir, as you like your joke.'

'I wasn't joking. However, I see that I was mistaken. You mean your furniture is for sale?'

'Well, there,' said Mr Fairfax, disparaging filthy lucre by his tone. 'You might call it so, but cheap – dirt cheap. As nice a table—'

'Very good of you, and I'll let you know later. I think I have all I need – except, indeed, stock to give meaning to the legend on the door.'

Mr Fairfax followed his gaze to 'BAR' and smiled, no whit abashed.

'A nice piece of work, that door,' he said. 'Last your time, I daresay. Picked it up at a sale. Surprising what you can pick up at sales.'

'I daresay.'

'But I mustn't be keeping you. I really came to ask if you would be wanting a woman.'

'A woman?'

'To clean and cook and wash, and such like. Unless your arrangement be made.'

'I might be glad of someone. I shall be alone.'

'I thought as much,' said Mr Fairfax obscurely. 'Well, my housekeeper, as good a woman as you would wish to have – her and me have talked it over, and she would be willing to oblige. Me being a widow man, and the house small, she finds time on her hands. I'll send her round come Monday, and you can arrange it between you.'

'Very good of you,' said Mark.

Mr Fairfax radiated kindliness, and the consciousness of a good deed done. 'Any eggs?' he said.

'Eggs?'

'I bought half a dozen on the chance. Two shillings to you.'

'That sounds fair enough.'

'You deal with me,' said Mr Fairfax impressively, 'and you won't go far wrong. There be folks out from town as would go on their bended knees to me for as many eggs as I could give 'em – ah, and at my own price. But what I say is, fair's fair. I'm content, and I ask no more – only keep it dark. There be those I could touch wi' a short stick as would take the bread out of an honest man's mouth, ah, and glad to do it.'

Honest, is it, thought Endicott, looking into the baby blue eyes. He might well have been giving away the eggs from the loving kindness which shone from the rosy face.

'By the way,' he said, struck by a sudden thought, 'how did you know that I had arrived?'

'Came by bus, I believe,' said Mr Fairfax simply.

'Well, well. You said two shillings, I think?'

'That's right, sir.'

Mr Fairfax, with the air of a benevolent conjurer, pulled a paper bag of eggs from a capacious pocket, and placed it on the mantelpiece. The operation took a long time.

'Here's half a crown,' said Endicott, rather impatiently. He felt that a little of the smiling Fairfax went a long way, also he was thirsty. 'Can you change?'

'I can, certainly,' said Mr Fairfax obligingly. Taking the half crown, he jerked his head in the direction of the mantelpiece. 'A pretty thing you have there, Mr Endicott.'

The candlelight glinted from the gold compact. Mr Fairfax absently pocketed the coin, picked up the compact and turned it in his hands.

'A very pretty thing, and costly, too, I should say. I have a brother with a nice little watchmaker's and jewellery business, and judging from his stock, I should say this cost a pretty penny.'

'I daresay.' Endicott took the compact and dropped it into his pocket. His tone did not invite further discussion.

'Ah, put her in a safe place,' said Mr Fairfax approvingly. 'The owner will be ready to give her pretty ears for that, I shouldn't be surprised.' He turned to the door. 'You'll be wanting the place to yourself, no doubt. You can be quiet enough here, if that's what you want.' He opened the door. 'All the same, there's a neighbour close at hand, if you should fancy company. A nice lady, too, though not so young as she used to be. But there, you'll have found all that out for yourself. Good night to you, Mr Endicott.'

The door closed behind him.

'Well, I'm damned,' said Endicott.

It was not until he was halfway to God's Blessing's pub, The Ring and Book, that he realized that Mr Fairfax had gone into the night, guilelessly omitting to give him his change.

CHAPTER IV

'... AND HAVE DONE THOSE things which we ought not to have done ...'

The meek voice of Miss Faraday faltered and failed. She felt that she had, indeed, done those things which she ought not to have done, and the burden of her sin lay heavy upon her. The feelings of a hunted criminal were hers; the bumbling tones of old Colonel Stroud just behind her, the deep bass of Mr Heron, the schoolmaster, alike accused her. Looking up, she saw the mild face of the Reverend Richards, and even that seemed to condemn her. As for his wife ... Amy felt her ears burn yet again. What she must have thought was beyond her. If she had been able to introduce her new neighbour by name it would not have been so bad. And even then, Mrs Richards did not know the worst. The tea party a deux with a stranger was nothing compared to that.

Strangely enough, for a moment she forgot her troubles to recall the feel of Endicott's coat under a damp face, and found that not only her cheeks were burning. It seemed a dream that she, of all people, should have behaved with such abandon – should have found a father confessor and a comforter in the peculiar stranger. And she could not but admit that he had been kind, amazingly kind. He had shown neither amusement nor boredom, though Heaven knew he might have been excused for either. Chide herself as she might, a little glow of pleasure strove for life, and would not be denied. She, never before the recipient of more than a polite hand clasp from any male, had literally thrown herself into the arms of a stranger, there to be petted and comforted. It was terrible and shameless beyond all words; she looked on herself with fascinated horror, yet the little glow remained.

Across the aisle, Laura Grey stifled a yawn with the tips of her gloved fingers and wondered what would happen if she rose and walked out. It was part of Ralph's general foulness, she thought resentfully, to drag her here. The manor womenfolk had always attended morning service … he would have to learn that times had changed. And apart from her boredom, she had been afraid to enter the church after what Brian had told her. Not that it was likely that Mark would be here, unless he was on her track. She felt a little shiver run down her spine and moved uneasily. Probably she was troubling herself for nothing – a mere accident that a man of the same name should make his way to the village. And she had enough to trouble her without that – Ralph, ever more jealous and exacting – ever on the watch to see that she was doing her duty as his wife. Not yet, my dear, she thought, you may wait for what you want so badly.

Ralph Grey shot his wife a sidelong glance, and felt her beauty mock and hurt. It was strange that she, his wife, should look so virginal and remote. Or was it strange? He had never felt that she was truly his; it was that knowledge which maddened him, making those dark fits of anger more frequent, widening the gap between them. His marriage had been an act of sheer folly, he knew well enough – a man with his background and a girl twenty years younger. And such a girl; and, for the matter of that, such a man. A cripple.

Well, cripple or not, she had married him, and even now it might be possible to pull something out of the ruins. If she had a child that would solve so many problems; only there was no sign of a child – instead unmistakable signs that she was looking for interest elsewhere. That at least should not happen. Unloved he might be, but not betrayed. Betrayed. The stained glass window over the altar swam in a crimson mist. It faded, and once more he glanced at his wife. Her lashes lay on the soft curve of her cheek; her black hat accentuated the dazzling fairness of her hair and skin. He thought, if she could love me a little … only a little … and found that the palms of his hands were wet.

Mrs Richards thought that Mrs Grey was wearing another new hat, and wondered what she had given for it. Far more like a film star than Ralph's wife with that hair, undoubtedly bleached, and those scarlet lips. Theatrical. Naturally, since she was on the stage when he met her. Well, she would give that marriage another three months at most. Whatever had possessed Ralph Grey, when he could have married anyone – but all men were the same when it came to women like that. And he was mad about her, he made that plain enough. Poor fool … and not even a child. Well, it was to be hoped that she would cause no scandal in the village. George had such a hatred of scandal. It was worse for him, since he would never believe ill until the unhappy moment when it was forced upon him. He is too good for this world, reflected Mrs Richards, looking up at the unconscious face of her husband, and feeling, as always, a blend of affection and exasperation. And talking of scandal – she glanced across the aisle at the bent head of Miss Faraday. Unbelievable, had she not seen it with her own eyes, and a queer business, however George might think fit to belittle her fears. Of course she was just the age to make a fool of herself over some worthless man. It would be necessary to have a word with her.

Jimmy Fairfax in the suit of sober black reserved for church, weddings and funerals, joined in the responses made by his rigid housekeeper and was well content. A good 'ooman and a working 'ooman, he reflected, and with no nonsense about her. She had not turned a hair when he made his suggestion about Corpse Path Cottage, though he had expected signs of annoyance, if not a flat refusal. If that foolish newcomer wished to help him, James Fairfax, to keep down his household expenditure, so much to the good, for if Mrs Shergold was doing part time work for another, she would certainly not get so much from himself. And money apart, Jimmy was one who, if not precisely loving his fellow-men, had certainly a lively and insatiable interest in their affairs. With Mrs Shergold visiting Corpse Path Cottage, it would be strange if he could not discover much of interest concerning its inhabitant. Rising to join lustily in hymn, Mr Fairfax smiled.

The sermon, vague and scholarly, came to a decorous conclusion. The congregation stirred and rose, with furtive movements to pockets and handbags. Mr Richards gave out the closing hymn.

'For-tee days an' for-tee nights,' mourned the choir. The collection plopped into the bags and was carried to its destination. Walking in beauty side by side, Mr Heron and Colonel Stroud returned to their seats, on their serene faces consciousness of a task well done. Mr Richards pronounced the blessing.

On the heels of Miss Faraday, murmuring nervous greetings and scuttling across the churchyard, came Mrs Richards with a purposeful glint in her eye. Miss Faraday glanced back at her, smiled politely, and pressed on. Mrs Richards called her sharply by name. Miss Faraday shied like a spirited horse but halted obediently.

'Did you want me, Mrs Richards?'

'If you could spare the time to walk up the path with me, I should like,' said the lady ominously, 'a little chat with you.'

'Oh dear,' said Amy feebly.

Mrs Richards stared. 'I beg your pardon?'

Amy passed a hand across her forehead, causing her hat to rise, thus giving herself a slightly inebriated appearance. She looks half-witted, thought Mrs Richards. She said not sympathetically, 'Don't you feel well?'

'A headache. It's nothing. What were you saying, Mrs Richards?'

'I had not said anything as yet,' replied Mrs Richards with some asperity. 'If you would kindly not race up the path like an Olympic runner I might find breath to do so.'

'I'm sorry,' said Amy meekly, slackening her pace. 'I wasn't thinking.'

'Ah, now, that's it.' Mrs Richards rather cleverly seized her opportunity. 'I'm so afraid, my dear, that just lately you have not been thinking. Or shall we say that you have been a trifle thoughtless?'

'Thoughtless?'

'It is only that you have not quite realized how careful a woman living alone should be. Your dear mother—'

'Would you mind,' said Amy speaking in a voice which Mrs Richards had never heard from her before, 'saying what it is that you have to say? I am in rather a hurry.'

Mrs Richards actually gasped. If a worm on the path had reared itself on end to defy her she could not have been more taken aback.

'I don't think you can be yourself. To speak to me – me! In such a tone!'

'I am still waiting,' said Amy stonily.

'Well,' said Mrs Richards, two red spots appearing high on her cheeks, 'as your vicar's wife, I thought it might not be out of place for me to give you a word of advice. Of course, if you take it in this way ...'

She paused. Amy clasped her hands tightly before her, and was amazed by the violence of the anger which shook her. She fought back an urgent impulse to slap Mrs Richards's affronted face.

She said clearly, 'When my misdeeds are laid bare before me, Mrs Richards, I shall know whether I should apologize or not. In the meantime, may I say that I am no child to be intimidated by hints or insinuations.'

The words rolled out grandly. In the midst of her anger, Amy felt a glow of pride, mingled with a dreamlike wonder that she, of all people, should be capable of uttering such a speech.

'You are certainly no child,' agreed Mrs Richards. 'That, at least, I did not insinuate. But even a woman of your age lays herself open to the loss of her good name when she behaves as you have done.'

A group of belated choirboys now coming past were intrigued to see their vicar's wife and Miss Faraday facing each other in the middle of the path, one lady very red and the other very pale.

'Minds me of our two turkey cocks having a fight,' said one observant youth under his breath.

'Naw,' said another contemptuously, 'wold Mother Faraday hasn't gump enough for that.'

They passed on, losing interest. Mrs Richards met Miss Faraday's gaze and spoke again.

'I was surprised at what I found going on in your house yesterday. You, alone, and with a stranger – your mother—'

For the second time she had made an error of judgement. Amy's face, already crimson, fairly flamed.

'My mother,' she said clearly, 'has nothing to do with it. When she was alive, she would not have peeped or pried or thought evil. But then, she was not a malicious interfering busybody.'

Mrs Richards took a step backwards. Her large face quivered like that of an affronted child. The pure rage which had animated Amy at the mention of her mother faded and died. Suddenly conscious of the enormity of what she had said, she pushed her unhappy hat farther back and sought to mend what was irretrievably broken.

'I'm sorry. I should never have said that. Oh dear! Of course you meant well, and it must have seemed strange to you – my not knowing his name, and all. I can't tell you ...'

Against the stony barrier of Mrs Richards's offence, her voice quavered and failed. She said uncertainly, 'I was terribly rude.'

'You were indeed,' said Mrs Richards in a suffocated voice.

'I think,' said the unhappy Amy, 'that I had better go.'

'Yes,' agreed Mrs Richards, 'I think you had.'

The choirboys, lingering to search for a nest in the hedge, saw Miss Faraday pass swiftly by, looking neither to the right nor to the left.

'What have she done wi' Mrs Richards?' enquired one youth casually.

'Murdered her, and pushed the bleeding body in the ditch, I shouldn't wonder,' suggested another.

'Good riddance to bad rubbish, if you ask me.'

'Best send for Dick Barton.'

Laughing happily, they went on with their search.

CHAPTER V

BRIAN MARLOWE CURSED SOFTLY and jammed on his brakes. The girl he had overtaken smiled widely as he pushed open the car door.

'Life saver,' she remarked, settling herself beside him. 'I laddered my last decent pair of stockings, and saw the bus go by.'

'You're in luck,' said Brian, keeping his eyes on the road. 'This is the only morning I've been able to run her this week.'

'No petrol? You should keep in with the Black Market, my lad. They tell me there are ways and means—'

'Principally means. That's the trouble.'

Dinah Morris glanced at the handsome, sulky face, and her heart began to move queerly. In the small car his shoulder touched hers. She thought with bitterness, he scarcely knows I'm here.

'You're extremely glum this morning,' she said lightly.

'I'm not chatty first thing in the morning. Didn't you know that?'

'I haven't seen enough of you lately to know anything at all about you,' said Dinah.

He did not answer, but she saw his hand tighten on the wheel, and was miserably conscious of his annoyance and her own folly. Of what use to wear a bright, carefree mask if, at the first meeting you flung it aside, exposing the hurt and foolish creature beneath? She hastened to repair the damage.

'I hear Mrs Oliphant has a new poem for the next meeting.'

'Three hearty cheers,' said Brian.

'Will you be coming?'

'Like a lamb to the slaughter.'

'We get quite a crowd now,' persisted Dinah.

Brian grunted. The conversation died. She sat watching the hedges slip by. In another ten minutes the journey would be over, and he had not so much as looked at her yet. A lump rose in her throat. Hold on to yourself, you fool, and have a little pride … it was no use.

'Brian,' she said.

'Yes?'

He did glance round at her at last, but his blue eyes held nothing to please her. She cleared her throat.

'Tell me what's wrong.'

He jammed down the accelerator and shot out to pass a lorry. An approaching car swerved wildly, and the driver leaned out to show a red and furious face. Brian ignored the incident.

'My God,' he said, between his teeth, 'must you start a scene at this hour of the morning?'

She flushed painfully. 'Who was starting a scene?'

'You asked what had gone wrong between us. The classic opening remark.'

'I did not.'

Brian laughed unpleasantly. 'What, then?'

'You needn't flatter yourself unduly. I merely asked what was wrong with you.'

'Nothing, to my knowledge. And if there were would it concern you?'

The car swerved as she gripped his arm.

'Don't do that,' he snarled.

'Then stop the car!'

'The good girl steps out? For God's sake, don't be such a fool.'

'You heard what I said. Do you think I'd ride a yard with you after that?'

He met her furious eyes and shrugged his shoulders.

'Just as you like,' he said, and drew up.

Dinah was out of the car almost before it stopped. She was humiliated to find that she was shaking. Holding the car door, she looked in at him.

'I think,' she said, 'that you are a despicable worm.'

He raised his brows. 'Forgive me if I say that I couldn't care less.'

'And there's one more thing.' She paused, and drew a deep breath. 'I should be careful, if I were you.'

'Careful? My good girl, can you be warning me against yourself?'

'No,' said Dinah, 'against Laura Grey's husband.'

She saw his face for a moment, no longer bored and indifferent but roused to fury, then the car shot away. It was a bitter enough satisfaction to know that she had moved him at last. He had looked as if he hated her.

She walked on mechanically, holding her pretty head high, trying to force back insistent tears. A breeze sent her pleated skirt swirling, and a passing lorry driver leaned out to whistle his appreciation. Dinah plodded on, oblivious. The world was a desert. She would never be happy again.

By the end of his first week at Corpse Path Cottage, Endicott felt himself at home. His furniture, a motley collection enough but sufficient for his needs had arrived and been duly installed. He had called at the local food office, registered with the local grocer and milkman, arranged with the butcher from Lake to call once a week with his minute allowance of meat, and altogether coped with most of the petty tribulations surrounding modern life. He discovered that, in case of need, a meal could be supplied at the Ring and Book, where the beer, if not reaching a pre-war standard, was not to be despised. And, true to the word of the benevolent Mr Fairfax, on two mornings a week Mrs Shergold arrived to do the housekeeping for him.

The housekeeper was a woman whose predominant colour note was grey – pale grey hair strained back from a pale grey face, pale grey eyes with a habit of blinking rapidly behind pale grey lashes. Her lean and angular body was clothed in garments as drab and unattractive as her face. She might have been any age from thirty-five to fifty-five, and could have posed for the caricature of a middle-aged spinster, grimly repressed and utterly without appeal, despite the mute evidence of the gold ring on her left hand. To Endicott's relief, she had not the conversational powers of her employer. A shadowy figure she appeared, worked with almost speechless speed and efficiency, and returned to the place from which she came.

The room to which Mark retired daily held no inducement to sloth. Its furnishings were merely a solid table bearing a battered typewriter and an array of papers, a wastepaper basket, and an upright chair. In these austere surroundings, Mark set about the work which had brought him to Corpse Path Cottage, and here he rapidly gave birth to two chapters which filled him with surprise and admiration. The third chapter, however, refused to see the light of day. Mark walked for miles, the pleased James ranging at his side, worked in the neglected garden, and returned to his typewriter hoping for the dawn of inspiration, all in vain. Something had come between him and his work, pushed into the background by the creative excitement of those first easily born pages, now looming all too large to be ignored. And the whole trouble seemed, ridiculously, to be concentrated in the gold compact pushed into the pocket of his sports coat. There was more to it, of course – the vague and tormenting perfume – the sight of a girl slipping past him like a ghost, the sound of a low laugh in the darkness. But all these things were bound up in the discovery of the compact that first morning in the cottage.

On the Friday morning he came to a decision. The thing might or might not belong to the woman who had deceived him and disappeared; if the former, it was a dirty enough trick on the part of fate, but not one which should conquer him. He had come to Corpse Path Cottage to forget, and to write; if remembrance must needs be forced upon him, at least his writing should not be ruined by the woman who had ruined so much. And to that end, the compact should go. Brian Marlowe, presumably, had been searching for it – in God's name, then, let him have it. Endicott wanted no part in it.

He took it from his pocket, and looking at it critically agreed with the judgement expressed by Mr Fairfax. Here was, indeed, a thing and a very pretty thing, and a pretty penny had indeed been paid for it. There were initials engraved on the back, so flourishing and so intricately entwined that it was beyond him to decipher them. Probably an L, with a C, an O, or a G, he could not determine which. And here he was, wasting precious time over it again! But returning it was not so easy. He could hand it over to the village policeman, but against this course there were obvious objections. No, best to hand it to the beautiful youth remarking casually that he had found it, and to ask if Brian had any ideas as to the identity of the owner. If the fellow had the brains of a louse he could take over from there. And it would be interesting to see his reaction.

Through the still spring evening, therefore, emerging from their hollow into the dizzy whirl of God's Blessing village, the two new inhabitants took their way. Decorously they paced by the respectable stone house of Mr Fairfax and his lady, the beautiful manor house which looked as if it had not changed for centuries, cottages with solid walls and sanitation as primitive as Endicott's own. Here and there, curtains twitched as he passed; one or two men working in their gardens returned his greeting with the reserve due to a stranger, and the curiosity due to a man who had spoken strange words on the bus. By the vicarage, the stout lady whom he had last seen in Miss Faraday's kitchen looked at him with obvious dislike. Endicott gave her a courteous Good Evening and went his way.

Mrs Richards turned in at the entrance to the village hall slightly flushed. The man had looked at her in a subtly impertinent manner and his greeting, she was sure, had held more than a hint of mockery. That could only mean that Amy Faraday had told him of their interview, and he was glad to have an opportunity to show his scorn for her opinion. Amy had shown hers plainly enough. Mrs Richards had been unable to forget her words. A malicious busybody – malicious? It had an ugly sound. Surely, surely it held no backing of truth. It was hard to be so miscalled when only trying to do one's duty. Heaven knew the task was difficult enough. She wished that horrible man had not sneered at her.

The horrible man, who had not so much as set eyes on Miss Faraday since his one and only visit, and who had meant to Mrs Richards no offence in the world, walked on, all unconscious of his crime. The corner by the main road – ah, this would be it. When Irish eyes are smiling, hummed Endicott, reading the name Killarney, and pushing open the gate.

Killarney was correct in finding itself near the main road, with which it had far more kinship than with the rural joys of the village itself. A smug bungalow, white walled and with a green tiled roof, it stood back from the road all beautiful, paintwork gleaming and the strip of lawn before it green velvet. Awed by such perfection, Endicott spoke to James, who lay down obediently, his nose on his paws, his brown eyes watchful. Endicott walked up the smooth path to the door and gingerly touched the bell push, to be rewarded by a silvery chiming somewhere inside. The door opened almost at once, and he met the gaze of eyes as blue as Brian Marlowe's own. The resemblance went no farther. The woman in the doorway might once have been as beautiful as her eyes; the cruel hand of time endowing her all too bountifully with flesh that had blurred and hidden all. She was amazingly fat. The hand which rested on the door displayed sparkling rings, embedded in flesh. The lipstick on the carefully painted mouth emphasized its smallness in the vast expanse of her face.

'Good evening,' said Endicott. 'I came to see Mr Marlowe. Mr Brian Marlowe.'

'There is only one,' said the woman, in a slow, placid voice. 'My son.'

'Oh, yes. Would it be possible for me to see him?'

'I'm afraid he's out. At the Literary Society, you know. Was it important?'

'Not really. I happened to meet your son when I arrived in the village, and thought I'd look him up for a chat. Some other time.'

She looked at him with a faint gleam of interest.

'You're the gentleman who has taken Corpse Path Cottage?'

'I am,' said Mark with a grin.

'I've heard about you,' she said.

'There is nothing surprising in that. All God's Blessing has heard of me, it seems. I awake to find myself famous.'

'Well,' said Mrs Marlowe, smiling, 'if you will tell people tales of forgers and murderers and what not—'

'You heard that, too? My tongue runs away with me at times.'

'You gave Mrs Cossett something to talk about, at all events. She obliges me three mornings a week. Mr Endicott, isn't that right? I might have asked you in all this time.'

'Thanks, but I'll be getting along. I'm sorry your son wasn't in.'

'You could go to the meeting and see him there. It might give you a laugh, if nothing else.'

'Meeting?'

'The Literary Society. Every other Friday. All are welcome. You wouldn't get me there, not with a barge-pole.'

'As bad as that?'

'Oh,' said Mrs Marlowe placidly, 'it's all right for the clever ones, but I'm not clever, thank God. Now Brian, he is. Besides, I'm too heavy for the chairs in the village hall. It's more comfortable to stay here and be told about it when he comes home.'

'Well,' said Endicott, fingering the package in his pocket, 'I think I will take a look in, if you're sure I shan't be unwelcome.'

'Unwelcome? They'd ring the church bells if they thought a new member was on the way. And if you hurry you might hear Mrs Oliphant read her poem.'

'Would that be good?'

'You'd be surprised,' said Mrs Marlowe.

One eyelid quivered. She wished him goodnight, and closed the door.

'Literary Society,' murmured Endicott. 'Death and destruction.'

With the patient James, he turned his steps towards the village hall.

CHAPTER VI

THE MEETING OF THE God's Blessing Literary Society was proceeding in its accustomed style. Twenty members were present, some because they had failed to find a legitimate excuse for staying away, some because they found pleasure in what they described as dabbling in writing, some because of the opportunity given them to raise their voices in uplifting conversation. A retired bank manager from Lake had read a paper on Trollope which he had greatly enjoyed, and which had been followed by a discussion of the merits of the writer's style. In this Miss Margetson from the post office had joined with verve and aplomb. She had not actually read Trollope herself, but owing to activities on the part of the BBC, she was more than able to keep her head above water.

'His style is so smooth. It flows,' she concluded triumphantly.

'Flows is the word,' grunted Mr Heron, the schoolmaster. 'Reminds me of the brook.'

'Rupert?' queried Miss Margetson.

'Tennyson's. "Man may come and man may go, but I go on for ever." Too much talk, too many characters, too many words. At least, that's how he affects me.'

'Of course,' suggested Miss Margetson nastily, 'for those who prefer cheap thrillers—'

'Not so cheap,' said Mr Heron sadly, 'nowadays.'

'You know what I mean!'

'Surely,' broke in Brian Marlowe, in a tone of bored superiority, 'a weariness for the over-verbose Trollope need not necessarily point to a yearning for trash. There are modern writers—'

'So often, one regrets to say, modern purveyors of dirt.'

Mrs Richards settled herself in her chair and sniffed the scent of a familiar battle from afar.

'From the artistic viewpoint there can be no dirt. As you call it.'

'Well,' retorted Mrs Richards, 'I only know that such novels as I draw from the library are all too often returned unread. My husband and I are nauseated. Nauseated. Drink, immorality, vice – Trollope, at least, was pure.'

'It has been said that to the pure all things are pure,' murmured Brian Marlowe, looking up at the ceiling. 'And, as a relief from your moments of nausea, you can always turn to the romances of Annabel Lee. They tell me that you find nothing there to bring a blush to the most sensitive cheek.'

'For once I find myself in agreement with you,' said Mrs Richards.

'I doubt it. I doubt it very much. My own opinion—'

'Ow!' cried Miss Margetson, with a squeal of girlish enthusiasm. 'I love Annabel Lee's tales. They are so sweet, and so romantic. I read *The Duke's Quest* three times. Of course, I'm passionately fond of historical novels, and hers are my favourite of all. I wish she'd write another.'

'Very pretty stories,' agreed Mr Heron, a soft gleam in his eye. 'What do you say, Miss Faraday?'

Miss Faraday who had been sitting mute and inglorious in a corner gave a little jump.

'Oh, yes – yes, indeed. I think them charming. But my tastes are not highbrow in the least.'

'A most misused term,' said Brian Marlowe, closing his eyes. 'And surely one need not be highbrow to recognize highly-coloured nonsense at its true worth. Mrs Richards implies that dirt is dirt; might I add that trash is also trash, even when hidden by a dust cover depicting a maiden in distress?'

'Oh, surely,' said a lady in a purple dress, leaning forward to smile warmly on Marlowe, 'there is room for all tastes in our little circle? And I must confess to a teeny weeny weakness for Annabel Lee myself.'

She blinked several times and sat back. The chairman cleared his throat.

'We seem to have travelled far from our friend Trollope and along a rough and stormy path, ha ha!' he observed. 'But however interesting the discussion – and I, for one, have found much er h'r'm stimulation in it – *tempus fugit*. We have yet to hear from Mrs Oliphant. She knows with what eager anticipation we await her latest oblation to the Poetic Muse. Mrs Oliphant.'

The lady in the purple dress rose, turned, and faced her audience with a wide smile.

'Dear friends,' she began.

There was a loud creak and the door opened. The enquiring countenance of Endicott, like a morose Daniel viewing the lions, peered in. All eyes turned to him. Brian Marlowe scowled. Miss Faraday blushed, glanced round to meet Mrs Richards's pregnant gaze, and blushed the more.

'Excuse me,' said Endicott generally. 'I hope that I am not intruding. I was told that the meetings of the Literary Circle were open to all.'

'They are indeed,' said the chairman. 'Glad to see you, sir. Plenty of seats. No housing shortage here, ha ha.'

Endicott thanked him and turned to the nearest chair.

Discovering his neighbour to be Miss Faraday, he greeted her with a pleased grin.

'What might the long lady with the teeth be proposing to do?' he asked out of the side of his mouth.

'Read one of her own poems,' whispered Miss Faraday.

'Good God,' said Endicott.

The rustle of movement and comment caused by his entrance died. There was a hush of anticipation or dread. The chairman, Colonel Stroud, set his brick red countenance in a smile as determined as that of the poetess herself, and leaned back in his chair. Endicott looked cautiously about him, unobserved, since all eyes were fixed on Mrs Oliphant, who appeared to be going into a smiling trance. He saw scornful boredom on the face of Brian Marlowe, otherwise the faces were of those who awaited uplift, not happily, but in the spirit of martyrs to a cause.

'Drip!' thundered Mrs Oliphant.

The chairman started, pulled himself together, and smiled again, a trifle apprehensively.

'A thought, dear friends,' said Mrs Oliphant, speaking in prose and in her customary high pitched voice, 'suggested by a defective kitchen tap. I should have mentioned this before. Forgive me.'

'Not at all,' said Colonel Stroud courteously.

Mrs Oliphant bowed, dropped her head to one side, and began once more.

'Drip!' (she declaimed deeply.)

'The slow drops fall
Slow,

So slowly!
Yet inexorable,
Like blood, reluctant,
Welling from out a mortal wound
Or grudging charity, heavily bestowed
By an unwilling hand.
A-ah!
Ah, heaven!
The torture of it,
Monotonous, soul sickening, inhuman,
Until one screams aloud
For anything – for anything on earth
With power to bring relief
From the inhuman, soul sickening, monotonous
Drip ... drip ... drip.'

Mrs Oliphant's voice, gradually diminishing, died on a gasping croak. She drooped as if virtue had gone from her. Out of all the room she knew true happiness.

There was a stunned pause as her voice ceased, followed by a rattle of applause. Endicott clapped more loudly than the rest. Miss Faraday looked at him with surprise and suspicion.

'If I stamped on the floor,' he said, 'would she give an encore?'

Miss Faraday shook her head.

'Ah, well,' said Endicott philosophically, 'I suppose it would be too much to ask.'

Colonel Stroud rose and thanked Mrs Oliphant. The audience clapped again.

'Has any other member a contribution to offer?' asked the Colonel, looking warily around him. 'No? Ah well, better luck next time.'

'It couldn't be,' said Endicott under his breath.

'Which brings me to the announcement of our next meeting a fortnight hence. The guest speaker will be Mr Wilberforce Browne, the well-known critic, who has kindly consented to address us, his subject being the novel – then and now. Judging from this evening, his talk should give rise to an interesting and animated discussion. There will, I need scarcely say, be ample time allowed for original contributions by our members, in verse or prose. And that, I think, closes our proceedings for tonight.'

In the general move towards the door, Endicott found himself accosted by a pretty dark haired girl bearing a small notebook and with a purposeful glint in her eye. As he halted, Miss Faraday murmured a word of farewell and was gone.

'Excuse me, Mr...?' said the dark haired girl interrogatively.

'Endicott.'

'Oh yes. I'm Dinah Morris, and the Treasurer of this Society.'

'Of course. I must settle with you. Miss Morris. Just a moment.'

Brian Marlowe was passing them on his way to the door. Endicott touched his arm.

'Could I have a word with you?'

Marlowe favoured him with a hard stare.

'Strangely enough, I was hoping for one with you.'

Endicott looked somewhat surprised at his tone. Dinah glanced quickly from one man to the other.

'Right,' said Endicott pleasantly. 'I'll see you outside when I have made my peace with Miss Morris here.'

Marlowe nodded ungraciously and turned away. Endicott found the girl's eyes upon him.

'Is anything wrong?' she asked directly.

'Not to my knowledge,' said Endicott. 'I'm a stranger here myself, as you may have heard.'

She flushed suddenly. 'I must seem very inquisitive. But Brian sounded queer.'

'Friend of yours?'

'He was,' said Dinah briefly.

'Um,' said Endicott noncommittally.

The girl became conscious that she was giving herself away. She shot him an angry glance, and said coldly, 'What I meant was that I had seen very little of Mr Marlowe just lately. And in any case—'

'It is no possible affair of mine. You are perfectly right. But I can't think,' said Endicott plaintively, 'why everyone is so cross with me tonight. After I had enjoyed myself so much, too.'

Her eyes danced suddenly. 'The poem?'

'Yes, indeed. The poem.'

'Pooh! That was a weak effort. You should have heard the one on "The Frustrated Cat".'

'You open an agreeable field for speculation. How frustrated?'

'It's a long story. Mrs Oliphant would probably be delighted to read it to you.'

'Really? Blessings light upon her, so she shall.'

'You are an idiot!' said Dinah, laughing.

'That's better. Now you sound neighbourly. But what about this financial transaction of ours?'

'One shilling per meeting non-members, yearly sub ten and six. Will you be joining us?'

'Having sampled your quality, nothing would stop me. Here you are.'

'Thank you. Name and address, please, and I'll give you a receipt.'

'Now I must go,' said Mark, having complied. 'Mr Marlowe will think I shun him, and that would make him sad. Goodnight, Miss Morris. We shall meet again.'

Dinah watched him out, her face troubled. 'I wonder?' she said.

James, who took a dim view of the Literary Society, greeted his master with pleasure and fell in behind him as he strolled to the group of elms where Brian Marlowe stood waiting. He swung around impatiently as Endicott approached, and greeted him with a scowl.

'You've taken your time,' he said, without preamble, and with great animosity.

Endicott raised his brows.

'This flattering desire for my company—'

'You can cut that out, and get on with your dirty business.'

'Dirty business?' Endicott, who had been merely intrigued by the other's manner, felt the first faint stirring of anger. 'What the devil do you mean by that?'

'You know well enough what I mean. You wanted to speak to me, didn't you? Well, I'm here – what more do you want? Or do you find it easier on paper?'

Endicott stared, actually wondering if he held converse with a lunatic. He said, speaking mildly out of very bewilderment, 'My good fool, I haven't the vaguest idea what you mean.'

'Haven't you?' snarled Brian, pushing a white face close to his. 'Why did you want to speak to me? Would it be, by any chance, about a compact?'

'At last,' said Endicott with relief, 'you begin to talk sense. I've got the thing here.'

'Yes,' agreed Marlowe softly. 'I thought you had.'

Immediately upon the words, and without the slightest warning, he smote the startled Endicott with great force upon the nose. Endicott dropped like a felled tree, and blood streamed down his chin. James uttered a yelp which changed to a menacing growl and launched himself upon Marlowe. Endicott, struggling muzzily to his feet, saw the dog kicked aside, and was helped in his recovery by a wave of fury. He knew pure satisfaction as his knuckles connected painfully with Marlowe's jaw. Marlowe instantly took up the position which he had himself vacated.

Mark pulled out a handkerchief and mopped his injured nose, while James pawed at him in deep concern. Soothing him, Mark gazed down on his fallen foe, who looked very young and defenceless with the bitterness wiped from his unconscious face.

'You asked for it, you know,' said Mark, justifying himself.

'You've killed him!' said an accusing voice.

Endicott jumped. Dinah Morris, her eyes burning in her white face, stood beside him.

'Don't you believe it,' he said thickly but reassuringly. 'He's worth a dozen dead men yet.'

Dinah cast herself down beside the prostrate figure, took one of the limp hands and began to rub it.

'Can't you do something? Fetch a doctor—'

'I tell you, he doesn't need a doctor.'

'But look at him, poor boy! And you just stand there, bleeding all over the place—'

'My God!' said Endicott, stung. 'Is it my fault if I'm bleeding? He hit me first!'

'Then you must have given him cause,' said Dinah coldly. 'And see what you've done to him.'

'And what about me? For no reason at all he comes at me like a lunatic, busts me on the nose, skins my knuckles—'

'Brian skinned your knuckles?'

'Certainly. On his jaw. And furthermore you will be pleased to observe that your boyfriend with the pleasing manners is now opening his eyes and in five minutes or so will be ready to sock me again.'

He jerked his head towards Marlowe, who was now looking up with a glassy stare. At length he recognized Dinah with a slight and rueful grin.

'Hello, Dinah,' he said.

The observant Mark noted the glow which transfigured the girl's face and was moved to pity. So much wasted on this conceited pup, who could not give a snap of the fingers for her now, whatever he had felt for her in the past. A nice kid, too – he was glad to see Marlowe's hand move gingerly to caress his jaw.

'All right?' he asked gruffly.

Without replying, Marlowe scrambled to his feet. Mark shrugged.

'I take it our conversation will be resumed later?'

'It certainly will,' said Marlowe.

'Are you two going on like this again?' demanded Dinah, flushing. 'For two grown men I must say it seems pretty silly.'

'I couldn't agree with you more,' said Endicott. 'A tale told by an idiot, full of sound and fury, signifying damn all. If you don't mind my saying so.'

'I can't understand it,' said Dinah helplessly.

'And why should you? I,' said Endicott handsomely, 'am not completely clear in understanding myself, though I have played some small part in our drama. However, I will now make my exit.'

He removed the sodden handkerchief from his nose and looked sorrowfully upon them.

'Gooddight,' he said.

'Wait – your nose is still bleeding,' said Dinah. 'You can't go through the village like that. I'll get some water.'

The two men watched her run lightly back to the Hall. When she was out of hearing, Endicott turned to Marlowe, thrusting a hand into his pocket.

'You might as well take this now. You could have done it in the first place. And I may add that I hope never to be mixed in your damn silly affairs again.'

Marlowe looked at the compact in his hand, his brow creased with an almost stupid bewilderment.

'But – are you giving it to me?'

'Did you think I should make a charge?'

'I thought—'

'You can keep your thoughts to yourself. Here comes Miss Morris. And the next time I come, at great personal inconvenience, to return your baubles, kindly refrain from dotting me on the nose.'

Marlowe opened his mouth and closed it again as Dinah came up breathlessly carrying a jam jar full of water. Soaking her handkerchief, she set about her ministrations with business-like competency, Endicott submitting meekly. Marlowe looked on, the frown on his face no longer of anger but bewilderment. A faint rustle in the nearby hedge went unnoticed by all save James, who moved off to investigate.

'There!' said Dinah with relief. 'It has stopped now.'

'It's very good of you,' said Endicott. 'I don't know why you should bother.'

'This business is quite silly enough without you spreading the news of it abroad.' Dinah, who taught in the village school, spoke as if she stood before her class. 'The sight of you bleeding like a stuck pig—'

'Bleeding, I admit. Like a stuck pig? – oh, surely not! But I take your meaning. It is scarcely worthwhile to give our respected poetess material for another work.'

Marlowe's lips twitched. Under other circumstances he felt that he might have liked Endicott well enough. It was queer that he should have handed over the compact in the end. What in God's name was at the back of it all? Suddenly, standing here in the quiet spring evening, he felt lost and afraid. All that was sure in life was shifting of late, values fading, Dinah, looking at him with her wholesome face puzzled – he had been glad enough to see her when first he opened his eyes. In that moment he had recaptured the simple pleasure which he had once found in their companionship, but only for a moment. He looked back with a kind of wonder at the past. Had he indeed ever known the serenity of that uncomplicated relationship? At least, he would never know it again. Laura Grey had seen to that.

James, returning from his investigations, bustled cheerfully up to the group. It appeared that he had forgotten the varied incidents of the evening.

'Which reminds me,' said Endicott to Marlowe, 'just as a matter of interest, what the devil did you mean by kicking my dog?'

'Kicking the dog! Oh, Brian,' said Dinah reproachfully.

'Damn it, he bit me!'

'Good old James,' said Endicott.

Brian and Dinah watched him go before silently crossing the path to the road. The girl, glancing at the sulky, handsome face of her companion wondered what was passing in his mind, and reflected that she knew nothing whatsoever of his mental makeup. Who could have imagined that Brian, cold sober, would leave a meeting of the Literary Society to indulge in a vulgar brawl with a stranger? It would be mirth-provoking if it were not so utterly incomprehensible. And it had brought her into contact with Brian again, since here they strolled together through the cool evening. She had sworn to herself that she would have no more to do with him, and her vows meant so little that when he opened his eyes to give her that queer, unselfconscious smile, her heart had melted within her.

'Queer bloke,' said Brian suddenly.

'He seems slightly mad. But I think I like him.'

'I don't dislike him myself.'

'Well, I must say you show your affection in a peculiar way.'

'Yes. I suppose you are wondering what the dickens it's all about.'

'A vague curiosity had crossed my mind.'

His colour deepened. 'The thing is, you see, I had an anonymous letter.'

Dinah stopped to stare. 'Honestly?'

'You don't imagine I should invent it for your benefit, do you?'

'You mean you had a letter about Mr Endicott?'

Brian kicked savagely at a stone. 'Don't be silly. Naturally, I thought he had written it.'

'Oh.' Dinah digested this. 'You know,' she said frowning, 'I don't think he would.'

'As a matter of fact, neither do I. At the time I could have sworn to it. And even now – if not Endicott, who the devil could it be?'

'Does it matter? The only place for an anonymous letter is the fire.'

'That's easily said by people who've never received them.'

Dinah shrugged her shoulders. She opened her mouth and closed it again without speaking. What was the use, after all? Brian obviously did not intend to confide in her further, nor did she wish to hear more. No need to be told that the unspeakable Laura Grey was at the back of it all. A cold desolation enfolded her. It was all so nasty, so miserably sordid. And what would happen if the rising tide of gossip reached Ralph Grey? No anonymous letters from him! Murder, perhaps ...

'What's the matter?' asked Brian.

'I'm cold,' said Dinah sadly. But it was not the cold which had made her shiver.

'The hall was unbearably stuffy. All the hot air blown off in it, I suppose.'

'I wonder you bother to come if it bores you so much.'

'If I don't turn up, Mrs Oliphant is on the doorstep the next evening to know the reason why. The remedy is worse than the disease. And why this hot defence of our so literary evenings? Rather a change from you.'

'Oh, I don't know. They're pretty grim, of course. But you sounded so unbearably superior.'

He looked down on her, a little surprised.

'You don't like me much, do you, Dinah?'

She did not reply, and they walked on in silence. Dusk was falling, and it was very quiet. Dinah thought, for two pins he would begin talking about Her, and that would be the end.

'Goodnight, Brian,' she said with relief, pausing outside her own gate.

'Goodnight, Dinah. I'm not surprised, you know.'

She looked at him doubtfully.

'Surprised?'

'That you don't like me. It's quite understandable. I'm not precisely in love with myself.'

CHAPTER VII

JOHNNY COSSETT LURCHED INTO his ancestral home a few minutes before nine that evening. He was a youth of fourteen, short for his age and with a freckled countenance which should have worn an expression of vacuous amiability. Johnny, however, owned a deep admiration for the more rugged types of American manhood, as portrayed in the gangster films which his soul loved, and except in moments of forgetfulness, his face was disfigured by a scowl or sneer. The scowl was easy, but the sneer, involving a slight lift of one side of the upper lip, had needed practice before a mirror in the seclusion of his chamber. He spoke three languages – the broad Dorset which was his by right of birth, the form of English painfully imparted to him by his pastors and masters in the shape of Mr Heron, and the American of the films and comic strips. Mr Heron, who would be attached to him for another year, during which period he knew well Johnny intended to do as little work as he could whilst causing as much trouble as was humanly possible, looked on him with a resigned loathing. In his mother's eyes, he was fair, all fair, with no spot on him.

'Where you bin, Johnny?' she demanded as he entered, speaking in the querulous tone with which she cloaked her enormous pride. 'Yer Dad were looking for 'ee.'

'Let un look,' said the youth simply.

'You be a bad boy,' said Mrs Cossett, shaking her head. 'Off 'ere, there, and everywhere, and never thinking of yer mother. High time this schooling were finished.'

'You said it, Maw. What's for supper?' asked Johnny, seating himself and drawing a crumpled comic from his pocket.

'Supper. Oh, ah,' said Mrs Cossett. 'I mid ha' knowed 'twas yer belly as brought 'ee home. There's half a cold pie in larder, if so be that'll do for yer Lordship?'

'I wish,' said Johnny dreamily, 'as we lived in Lake.'

'Why?'

'Pictures twice a wick. And fish and chips for supper.'

'Stinking dear, and poor stuff at that,' said Mrs Cossett austerely. 'Nor they don't fry every night, neither.'

She laid down the pair of pants she was mending, rose heavily and went to the larder, returning with a plate containing the despised half pie and some cold potatoes. This she handed to her child, who accepted it without obvious gratitude.

'I see a fight tonight,' he observed, when the first pangs of hunger had been stayed.

'Fight? Barney Burden again?'

Johnny shook his head. 'Naw. Him from Corpse Path Cottage.'

'What!' exclaimed Mrs Cossett, instantly consumed by curiosity. 'Him and who else?'

'Brian Marlowe,' said Johnny, swallowing noisily.

'Now I know you be telling a tale,' said Mrs Cossett, picking up her mending again. 'You can try that on someone else, my lad. I knows better.'

'Oh yeah?' observed Johnny, pausing in his supper to give a perfect example of his sneer. 'Then you know what ain't so. I see 'em as plain as I see you, and Ken, he'd tell 'ee the same.'

'Where?' demanded Mrs Cossett, still sceptical.

'Outside the Hall. Ken an' me were birdsnesting on 'tother side hedge, an' they never knew we was there. Ha! I 'low they thought no-one saw 'em. Except her.'

'Her?'

'Teacher. Dinah Morris. Always after Brian Marlowe.'

'She be sweet on un, sure enough. But did they fight over her?'

'She never got there till he were down.'

'Down? Who were down?'

'Mr Pretty Marlowe. Don't I kip tellin' 'ee?'

'I can't make head nar tale o't,' said Mrs Cossett, marvelling. 'Not but what I'd believe anything o' that there Endicott. A bad un he be, if ever I saw one. But why did he set about young Marlowe?'

'I 'low,' said Johnny simply, 'as 'twere on account o' young Marlowe setting about he.'

Mrs Cossett's jaw dropped.

'Lord save us all! You don't never mean as he began it?'

'Course he began it. Blood! 'Twere like a pigsticking,' said Johnny, pushing away his empty plate and leaning back to savour his memories. 'Laugh! Ken an' me, we nigh busted ourselves. Young Marlowe was waiting, see, under this clump o'ellums just outside Hall. Wold Mother Richards, she come out, an' Pecker Heron an' whole lot more, but Marlowe, he was just there stood. Presently out come Corpse Path Cottage feller by hisself, and up to Marlowe. They was talking, and we never took much notice, till all of a sudden up comes Marlowe's fist and bam! he give t'other a proper buster slap on the snitch.'

'Gaw!' breathed Mrs Cossett.

'Feller went down like as if he were pole axed, and that black spannell, he went for Marlowe. Then up comes Endicott, an' whop! he gets Marlowe on the kisser! One up, t'other down. Laugh! I tell 'ee—'

Overcome by mirth, he rolled in his chair. Endicott and Marlowe, licking their wounds in the chaste seclusion of their homes, little knew the simple pleasure which they had given that night.

'What happened then?' demanded his mother.

Johnny wiped his eyes. 'Dinah Morris, she come running over to 'em like a hen in a fit. "Ow!" she says, "You've killed un," she says, an' down she flops by Marlowe an' starts rubbing his hands. Marlowe, he never knew nothin' about it. Dead to the world, he were. She up at Endicott, an' she says, "You bleedin' rogue" —'

'She never said that?'

'That's what it sounded like. That dame,' said Johnny, swiftly crossing the atlantic, 'was sure all burned up. Yes, sir! Endicott, he says, "I can't help bleedin', can I, an' anyhow," he says, "he hit me first." And she says, "If he did I bet 'twere your fault."'

'Ah, an' so it would be, sure enough,' said Mrs Cossett warmly. 'What do he want 'ere, getting up to God knows what, shut away in that wold cottage? What did he say to me the very day he came, and wi' his own lips? Thief, blackmailer, forger, murderer – them was his words, and Mrs Hale, she'd tell 'ee the same. *And* Miss Faraday – she were there sat, right next to un. Well, now, this be the start. Young Marlowe be the first, but who comes after? You answer me that.'

This Johnny was unable to do. With some justification he felt that his mother had stolen his thunder. He said sulkily, 'All the same, Marlowe started it. Can't get away from that.'

'That's as may be,' said Mrs Cossett infuriatingly. 'What happened in the end?'

'You know so much I should think you'd know that too, an' wi'out my tellin',' said Johnny, with awful sarcasm. 'I don't know nothing. I never sat in no bus to hear tell o' forgers and murderers. All I did was see it all.'

His mother became conscious of error. She said cajolingly, 'Now, Johnny, my dear, we know you saw it. Bain't that why I be asking 'ee? You tell yer mother, like a good boy.'

'Well, you listen, then,' said Johnny, slightly mollified, 'an' not be cluckin' like a wold hen. Miss Morris, she says, "you go an' fetch a doctor," an' Endicott, he says, "not likely."'

Mrs Cossett opened her mouth, met her son's eye and closed it again.

'Miss Morris looks at un like a spittin' cat an' goes on pawin' Marlowe, an' Endicott, he goes on dabbin' his nose wi' his bloody handkerchief—'

'John-nee!'

'Don't be so daft! That ain't swearing.'

'That's as may be. I don't like to hear it, none the more for that.'

'Well, anyway, he did. And then Marlowe sits up, and Miss Morris, she helps him to stand, an' she says as she'll get some water. An' when she be gone Endicott takes summat out o' his pocket an' gives it to Marlowe.'

'What? What did it seem to be?'

'I couldn't see what 'twere,' said Johnny, reluctantly admitting defeat. 'An' just then that wold spannel come sniffin' through hedge, so Ken an' me, we come away. We went back after a bit, but they'd gone, so we never see them no more.' He brooded happily for a moment. 'You 'pend upon it, 'twere good while it lasted,' he said.

Without speech, Mrs Cossett rose, laid down her neglected mending, and took a coat from its peg behind the door. Johnny looked up in surprise.

'Where you goin', Mum?' he asked.

'I just thought as I'd step round to Mrs Hale for a word or two,' said his mother, smiling. 'I won't be above a minute or so.'

'Oh yeah?'

'If I were you I'd get to bed afore yer dad comes in. Not too pleased wi' you, yer dad isn't.'

'So what?' muttered Johnny, turning gloomily to the stairs. Mrs Cossett did not hear him. The door closed behind her. Great with news, she passed into the night.

From Johnny to his mother, from his mother to Mrs Hale, the story spread, gaining colour and sensation on its way. By the following evening, there was not a soul in God's Blessing who had not heard some version of the affair. The village constable, who was the father of Johnny's friend Ken, made his way to Corpse Path Cottage, cunningly masking his curiosity by asking to see Mark's dog licence. This being produced and a few compliments having passed, PC Marsh took his leave, conscious that he would recognize the man of mystery if called upon to apprehend him at any future date.

All day long the noise of battle swelled, in shop, post office, or bus. Brian, returning from his day's toil at the bank, found, to his disgust, that his mother had joined the ranks of those who knew. Her placidity was unruffled by the surprising knowledge that her fastidious son had been involved in a brawl, but she showed a desire to be given details of the affair which he was not disposed to gratify. He told her simply that he had been drawn into an argument, in the course of which both he and Endicott had lost their tempers. It was all over, and he could not imagine what the fuss was about.

'Lor bless you, Brian, I don't fuss,' said his mother comfortably. 'You know that.'

'Yes.' He looked at her queerly. 'How do you manage it, Mother?'

'Manage what?'

'To go through life so smoothly. Nothing ever seems to move you. It's a kind of protective coat, I suppose. I wonder how deep it goes?'

'You're too clever for me. You always were, and your father was another. It's the clever ones who worry, and fret and fume. Not me! I must say I should like to know why this Endicott wanted to see you, and what the argy-bargy was about. But if you don't want to tell me – well, you know I shan't lose any sleep over it.'

'No,' said Brian, 'I didn't suppose you would.'

She looked at him, not anxiously, but with a glint of shrewdness in her eyes.

'You haven't got yourself into any kind of trouble, Brian?'

'Now, what should make you think that?'

'I just wondered. All this – it isn't like you.'

'I'm all right, Mother. I keep telling you, this means nothing. Endicott's a queer fellow. He's probably forgotten the whole thing by now.'

She sat in silence for a moment. Suddenly a spark of interest lit her face.

'Did you remember the fish?' she asked.

He nodded.

'What did you get?'

'Plaice.'

'Ah! Don't be late for supper.'

'I'm not going out.'

'I'll do some chips,' she said, with sudden animation. 'The fat will run to it. Thank God for those parcels from Canada—'

Looking up, she found herself without an audience. For an instant, a flicker either of resentment or trouble moved her placid face, and was gone.

'I'm glad he brought plaice,' she said, and went out to the kitchen.

Mark was blissfully unconscious of the sensation which he and Marlowe had caused. His nose was swollen and somewhat stuffy, and his knuckles reminded him painfully of their contact with Brian's jaw, otherwise, absorbed in his own affairs, he had put the matter out of his mind. It did strike him that an unusual number of loiterers crossed the right of way past Corpse Path Cottage to the wood, but this he innocently attributed to the call of spring, and went on with his work – or endeavoured to do so. The two chapters which had sprung from his brain with scarcely a birth pang had been a false dawn, followed by gloom and blasphemy. Page after page left the typewriter to be hurled aside in crumpled balls. Those who were privileged to meet the unhappy author on his walks abroad observed his disinheriting countenance and generally sinister appearance and nudged one another, leaning to Mrs Cossett's opinion of the stranger within their midst. Endicott, with his own nagging preoccupations, and tormented by his elusive muse, certainly looked capable of any crime.

'Don't see that there feller down to Corpse Path Cottage in 'ere no more,' remarked a visitor to the Ring and Book one evening.

'Did 'ee poison un, Joe, or what?'

'Company don't suit un, maybe.'

'Bad,' said a patriarchal gentleman, shaking his white head. 'I don't care for a man to drink solitary.'

'Best go in and help un out, Mr Garrett.'

Mr Garrett glanced around him benevolently.

'Ah!' he said. 'I mid do just that. I feel for the feller, shut away in that godforsaken place all alone by hisself. I call it agin nature.'

'Oh, I dunno.' A morose looking man sitting in the corner was moved to join in the conversation. 'He mid do wuss. A dog for company, nor no woman to mind his business for un.'

'Hark to Nabby, now!'

'Almost say as married life didn't suit the feller.'

'Bain't the bed o' roses, then, Nabby?'

The exchange became Rabelaisian. In the baiting of Nabby, who had lately been married to a local widow, the subject of Endicott was forgotten.

CHAPTER VIII

A COLD CHEERLESS DRIZZLE wiped the colour from the spring. Amy Faraday, moving furtively from her doorway and clasping a bundle to her breast like the heroine of a melodrama, felt the chill strike through to her guilty heart. She latched her gate, and turning into the lane, almost collided with a tall figure.

'Oh!' said Miss Faraday, uttering a mouse like squeak. 'Good morning, Mr Grey.'

Ralph Grey touched his cap.

'Morning, Miss Faraday. Afraid I didn't see you. Beastly weather.'

'Yes. Such a change.'

The parcel in her arms seemed to be growing larger. Thank heaven the label was hidden. She might have guessed that she would run into someone. Any other day, one could count with all confidence on the lane being deserted. She hugged her secret to her breast until the edges of the parcel caused her bodily pain.

'How is Mrs Grey?' she asked nervously.

'Very well, thank you. She is away at present, visiting friends.'

'How nice. Oh!'

From some little distance a gunshot had sounded, causing Miss Faraday, whose nerves were jingling, to jump and drop her parcel. It fell heavily in a puddle, causing quite a fountain of muddy water to spring up around it. Ralph bent and picked it up, his eye casually drawn to the brilliant publisher's label.

'You won't improve your books that way,' he observed, handing over the muddy parcel.

Miss Faraday clutched it feverishly. Ralph saw with surprise that her face was crimson, and wore an undeniably hunted look.

'Is anything wrong?' he asked.

Miss Faraday shook her head.

'They won't be damaged, you know, through that stout paper,' said Ralph reassuringly. 'I was only joking.'

Amy found her voice. 'Yes, of course. I must just tie them up again,' she added, on a sudden inspiration. 'I can't post them like this, can I?'

She was gone, popping inside her gate like a rabbit bolting into its burrow. Ralph limped on, somewhat intrigued. The mud-splashed label had borne, as he had noted in that one quick glance, the name and address of Miss Faraday herself, typed upon it. And Miss Faraday, when they met, had been heading in the opposite direction from the village.

It was half an hour before the unfortunate Amy ventured out again. This time, on the well-known principle of locking the stable door when the steed was stolen, she had removed the tell-tale label, and forced the parcel into a large bag. She moved with a pessimistic certainty that fate was against her, and was not in the least surprised to find the Reverend George Richards fumbling for the latch of her gate. Let them all come, she thought, and murmured a mournful greeting.

'Ah, Miss Faraday! I come at an inopportune moment. You are on your way out?'

'It's nothing of importance. I can go later. Won't you come in, out of the rain?'

'Thank you. Thank you indeed. Only for a moment. I fear that I shall drip ...'

Amy, with a sudden recollection of Mrs Oliphant, stifled a nervous giggle. She ushered Mr Richards into the hall, further than which he declined to go.

'No – no, my dear Miss Faraday. I will not keep you, damp and unwelcome guest that I am.'

He sneezed suddenly, and obscured his long mild countenance with a handkerchief. Amy thought he looked tired and ill, and forgot her own troubles in a momentary pity. The life of a country clergyman was not so easy, after all, especially when the pride and hope of that same clergyman's life had not returned from a night raid over Berlin. And with the thought she recalled the affronted face of Mrs Richards, seeing her no longer as an interfering busybody but as an unhappy woman, striving to continue the ordinary business of a life which had lost its meaning. Pity made her bold.

'Mr Richards,' she said.

Mr Richards removed his handkerchief and looked at her with courteous attention.

'I wanted to speak to you. About Mrs Richards.'

'Ha!' said Mrs Richard's husband, rather apprehensively.

'I was very rude to her the other day. At the time I was angry, and said more than I should have done. I see now that I was wrong.'

Mr Richards smiled, and was transformed from an elderly and undistinguished clergyman to someone tolerant and wise.

'My dear,' he said gently, 'that is a brave thing for anyone to say.'

'No. I was bitterly hurt and angry, but I am sure that she meant to be kind.'

'She does, invariably,' said Mr Richards. 'But even the kindest souls can, at times, tread on our favourite corns. And between you and me, the wife of a clergyman needs to walk more delicately than Agag, and to own qualities more than human if she is never to give offence.' He looked at her quizzically. 'You know, Miss Faraday, I have discovered that most of us, poor, simple souls groping in darkness, are actuated in the main by good intentions – and that despite the light which psychological novelists have shed on impulses which are hidden – thank God – from all, save them.'

He looked at Miss Faraday for her agreement, to see with surprise that her face was suddenly dyed a violent crimson. Somewhat disconcerted, the poor gentleman harked back mentally, lest he had inadvertently uttered words unfit for the ears of a diffident spinster. He discharged himself without a stain on his character.

Still scarlet, Miss Faraday said faintly, 'You do not approve of the modern novel?'

'Insofar as it portrays the lowest motives, giving no man credit for simplicity of purpose, I do not. Why set to work with a muckrake?' demanded Mr Richards, forgetting his hearer's discomfiture and sailing happily into the arguments which he had aired so often. 'Clever? Alas, yes, amazingly so. And to that end? To such base uses I – but forgive me. My tongue runs away with me, and I fear that you are not feeling well.'

'It's nothing,' said Miss Faraday faintly. 'I have a slight headache.'

'Dear me, dear me,' said Mr Richards sympathetically. 'Migraine?'

'I don't think so. Just a headache.'

'You look a little feverish. Aspirin and bed, if I may venture a prescription. Also quiet, which you will certainly not have unless I carry myself off. Now, I can see myself out. Please do not trouble to move.'

He looked at her with genuine kindliness.

'I am glad to hear that you are to have Miss Morris with you. A nice girl, and it is not good for any of us to live alone.'

Amy smiled faintly. Mr Richards pressed her hand, picked up his hat and made for the door.

'Ah!'

He pulled up suddenly, swung around and pointed a finger at her. Amy watched him with apprehension.

'I am a dunderhead. It has just dawned on me that I am leaving without having so much as mentioned my reason for disturbing you. It was about the fête.'

Miss Faraday, who had expected she knew not what, heaved a sigh of relief. Through a kind of mental fog she heard the vicar talking steadily on. When he left she was uncertain whether she had committed herself to help with the jumble, tell fortunes, or manage the treasure hunt. She put a hand to her forehead, which was by sharp throbs giving verisimilitude to her statement regarding a headache, and laughed mirthlessly. For the third time she took up her burden and sallied forth.

The way to Corpse Path Cottage was this morning at its worst. The little wood was hidden by the driving rain, the path itself a repulsive affair, with every hole full of brown liquid. Miss Faraday squelched along, her small nose reddened and with raindrops clinging to her lashes. Her head still throbbed, and she was heavily oppressed by a feeling of guilt. She turned towards the cottage, looked down on it, and saw the form of the Reverend George Richards standing at its door.

Miss Faraday lost her head. She turned and began to run madly for the shelter of the wood. Her feet skidded on the greasy surface and she sat down heavily, her hat shooting over her eyes and adding darkness to her nightmare sensations. She pushed it back with a trembling hand and looked cautiously around her. With a gasp of relief, she found that she was still alone.

With an ominous chill creeping through her skirt, she picked herself up and continued with more circumspection on her way. Back to her home she would not go with her errand still undone; from the shelter of the wood she might, unseen, espy Mr Richards returning from his ill-timed visit, and know that the coast was clear.

The idea was sound, but she had not realized the discomfort of the wood on such a day as this. As she stood, her feet sank steadily into black and evil smelling mud; every twig, laden with moisture, gladly discharged it upon her. With icy trickles making their devious way down her shrinking flesh, Miss Faraday realized yet again that the way of the transgressor is hard.

After an age of discomfort she was faintly cheered to see the figure of the vicar emerge from the hollow and trip it featly from tussock to tussock towards the field gate. When he was lost to view, she lifted her feet one by one from their resting place and made for Corpse Path Cottage once again.

Mark's morning had not been a good one. He had overslept and awakened unrefreshed and with all the symptoms of a bout of malaria clearly present. The range had showed its disapproval of the change in the weather by belching out sullen clouds of smoke as soon as he attempted to light it, and had continued to misbehave at frequent intervals throughout the morning. Mark knew well enough that in his present state he was incapable of work, and that the only sane course would be to dose himself and return to bed, but driven by an obstinate demon he determined to try. He had wasted four sheets of paper and was feeling a great deal worse when Mr Richards arrived.

Mark would not have been pleased to see his dearest friend at this moment, but he found himself unable to be rude to his visitor, who welcomed him to the village with disarming simplicity, and fortunately did not prolong his stay. His own cold was troubling him, and having done his duty he was glad enough to go. Mark saw him out and returned morosely to his typewriter.

Most unexpectedly, drifting from out of the blue, came an idea. He pondered for a moment, blinked to clear his vision which was somewhat muzzy and began to type. James, passing a restful morning on the rug, lifted his head and barked. Mark looked up with a scowl, and became conscious of a gentle tapping on the door.

With a loud oath he rose, staggering slightly, and went to see what new danger threatened his peace. The damp and disconsolate Miss Faraday met the fury in his gaze and blenched.

'I – I'm afraid I interrupt you,' she faltered.

Mark put a hand to his throbbing brow.

'God knows you do, but come in – come in,' he said.

Amy finished her tale and looked unhappily at her host, whose expression, to say the least, was not encouraging. She said timidly, as he remained silent, 'You told me you would help me.'

'Oh Lord, yes,' said Mark. 'The little friend of all the world – that's me.'

Amy's look of strain remained. Mark thought that she much

resembled a small dog which had gone sadly astray and had now crawled home, wet and miserable in search of pardon. Certainly his visitor, now looking her worst, was using no feminine weapons of beauty or charm to gain her ends. Her troubled countenance was hung by damp wisps of hair, and her nose was red and gleaming. She sat on the extreme edge of her chair, and the hands in her lap twisted and writhed. Mark thought with deep self-pity that his lot was hard. By now he was feeling extremely ill, and the last thing he desired was to share in another's burdens. His own, he felt, was quite enough for him. And here was this nerve ridden spinster ... He shivered, and rose to poke the sullen fire.

'What do you want me to do?' he asked, more curtly than he meant.

'Only have them here. I can't,' said Miss Faraday, with sudden emotion, 'have them in the house.'

'Oh, all right, all right – leave them with me, by all means. Though I think you're making a stink about nothing. You live alone—'

'In God's Blessing,' said Amy darkly, 'living alone doesn't mean that you can keep your affairs to yourself. And I shan't be alone much longer. Miss Morris is coming to live with me.'

'Is she?' said Mark incuriously. He put his hand to his head and shivered again. He said thickly, 'I'm afraid you'll have to go. I don't feel well.'

He blinked, trying to get the figure of Miss Faraday into focus. His head was swelling, and his whole body felt light, like a balloon. The hazy figure grew yet more indistinct, the creature of a dream, then faded completely. He slumped across the table, his face pressing into the litter of papers. James began pawing the still form, uttering little whines.

Miss Faraday, for one moment transfixed by amazement, the next realized that there was work for her to do. She crossed the hall to the kitchen, discovering with gratitude a brimming pail of water by the sink. She soaked her handkerchief and returned to her fallen host.

She thought as she bent over him that it was considerate of him to have collapsed in his chair, since it would most certainly have been beyond her to raise him from the floor. Watched with quivering interest by the dog, she gently lifted the fallen head until it rested on her arm, and began to bathe the temples. The dark strongly featured face looked unfamiliar with the eyes closed and all expression wiped away. She recalled another face which had looked thus the last time she beheld it.

With the memory came a stab of fear, causing her heart to beat unevenly. This collapse had been so sudden, and was lasting so long. If he did not recover, her own position would be a strange one. All the perfumes in Arabia cannot cleanse my reputation, thought Amy foolishly. Emboldened by fear, she thrust a hand under Mark's coat, and was rewarded by feeling an undeniable heartbeat. As if to underline the information thus given Mark stirred, groaned, and opened his eyes.

'Oh!' said Amy, almost hysterical with relief. 'You are alive!'

Mark spoke no word of agreement or dissent. Instead he shivered with such violence that only Miss Faraday's arm saved him from over-balancing. Apparently becoming conscious of her presence he looked up muzzily into her pink and anxious face.

'Hullo, darling,' he said faintly.

Amy started, and half withdrew her arm.

'It may seem funny to you,' she began stiffly, looked at the face still resting confidingly against her, and broke off. Mark Endicott was not speaking in jest. His eyes were open, but they were looking on some figure conjured up by his fevered brain. A wave of sympathy swept her. She tightened her clasp unconsciously, and felt his weak but instant response.

'I feel ill. Damned ill,' said Mark querulously.

'You should be in bed,' said Amy. 'Oh, dear, I don't know what to do.'

She looked wildly around her, as if seeking inspiration. Mark laid his hand on her arm.

'Don't leave me,' he said thickly. 'I can't lose you again – ever.'

'I won't leave you,' promised Amy. Her own cheeks were burning almost as fiercely as Mark's; even through her coat she could feel the heat of his touch. She began to feel seriously alarmed. To her troubled mind, Corpse Path Cottage seemed a desert island, far removed from any chance of casual assistance. There was no need of a thermometer to tell her the state of Mark's temperature, even had his attitude to herself not shown his condition. His hold on her was that of a drowning man.

'I must put you to bed,' she said, reaching a decision from sheer desperation. 'Can you get upstairs if I help you?'

He looked up at her, his eyes brilliant but empty of comprehension. He muttered, 'Feel foul.'

'Come to bed,' urged Amy, in the voice of a siren.

To her relief the words went home. Mark rose like an obedient child, and moved unsteadily towards the door.

'You come too,' he said plaintively.

Miss Faraday's cheeks burned with a yet fiercer glow. She buried

deep within her a sudden and disturbing vision of the countenance of
Mrs Richards and spoke soothing words. This undoubtedly sick man
must be humoured in his delusions, though the position was a trying
one for herself. It was entirely her fault, she told herself sternly, and
forgot her own affairs as Mark reached out his hand for her again.

'It's all right,' said Amy optimistically, steadying him with difficulty.
'I'll help you.'

'Darling,' said Mark, staring glassily ahead.

In Miss Faraday's troubled breast, like the unfolding of a flower,
something came gently to life. Until this moment she had scarcely seen
Endicott as a person. Vaguely sorry for him, definitely sorry for herself,
she had striven to help him partly because she could do no less, partly as
the quickest means of getting free from an embarrassing position. Now,
for the first time, impersonal pity was mingled with a warmer emotion
which, paradoxically, made her feel weaker whilst adding strength to
her arm. This fevered creature stumbling obediently up the narrow
stairs was utterly dependent upon her. It was true that he had confused
her with some unknown female by him beloved and for whom at that
moment she felt extreme distaste, but the unknown was heaven knew
where, whilst she, Amy, was steering him precariously to the haven of
his chamber, clasped by him and addressed by him (twice) as Darling.
The warm weakness at her heart grew and dominated her. Anything I
can do, thought Amy incoherently, anything, and felt that her strength
was as the strength of ten.

Before they reached the landing, Mark began to shiver violently.
Looking at him anxiously, she saw that the flush had left his face, which
was shadowed and grey. He stumbled at the last step and almost fell.

'There, my dear,' gasped Amy, staggering under his weight but
upheld by an almost maternal solicitude. 'Just one more – there! We've
done it.'

Panting but triumphant, she steered him through the open door to
her left, into a room furnished without vulgar ostentation by a single
iron bedstead and a very ugly washstand with a marble top. Amy
thought that the article might have been dragged from the dark recesses
of a junk shop, and in this surmise she was perfectly correct. Not that
she need pause now to consider Mark's taste in furnishing; the great
thing was that here was a bed. She led him to it, and he instantly and
obligingly collapsed, snuggled his face into the pillow, and appeared to
fall asleep.

Amy looked down on the dark rumpled head, and was momentarily at a loss. Her right arm and shoulder ached from the recent Jane Eyre and Rochester-like progress up the stairs; it was certain that she could not, without assistance, move him now. I came to Taffy's house, Taffy was in bed ... The foolish words jingled through her brain. And this Taffy was not precisely in bed, though there he most certainly should be. Well, she could at least remove his shoes before going, as she certainly must, for help. Be sure your sins will find you out, thought Amy dismally, kneeling to wrestle with stubborn laces. After all her foolish precautions, all her miserable sneaking across country like a thief in the night, her presence here must needs be made known. Not that it mattered ...

One shoe came off, disclosing a large toe peering nakedly from a hole in the grey sock. Maternal warmth again swept Miss Faraday, and a little smile crossed her anxious face. Men – so utterly self-satisfied and dominating, yet at bottom helpless creatures enough. She pulled off the other shoe and swung the dangling legs on to the bed. Mark did not stir; he was breathing comfortably and looked quite peaceful.

Amy tugged at the grey army blanket on which he lay, and succeeded after some difficulty in disengaging it. She covered him carefully, tucking in the blanket at the sides. As, being well trained, she began at the foot of the bed, the closing stages of this operation brought her face close to the unconscious one on the pillow. As if answering a signal Mark stirred and opened his eyes. He smiled, murmured something which she did not catch, and pursed his lips appealingly. Like a mesmerized rabbit, Miss Faraday drooped towards him. From the foot of the stairs, James uttered a loud and startling bark.

Amy sprang back, her heart thumping violently. Mark closed his eyes again with a look of fatuous contentment and fell asleep. Downstairs James continued to bark.

Poor Amy had already experienced the feelings of a discovered criminal; now a veritable scarlet woman moved down the stairs to meet the gaze of the world, which, in the person of Mr Jimmy Fairfax had opened the front door and stood on the threshold. Farther than this, James, who took his arrival ill, had not allowed him to come. There he stood framed in the doorway like a damp and inquisitive Father Christmas, his blue eyes taking in with the most lively interest first Miss Faraday's mud caked shoes, then her ankles, and so, by gentle degrees, the whole person of that harassed lady as she made her way down the stairs.

CHAPTER IX

DINAH MORRIS ROLLED UP the last pair of stockings, rammed them into a corner of her suitcase and sat back upon her heels to survey the room. Amazing how the removal of her few personal belongings had changed it; for three years, since she had come from college to instruct the infant population of God's Blessing, it had borne the impress of her personality, yet already it looked on her with a stranger's eye, cold and faintly unfriendly. Oh well, it was a poor enough room at that, thought Dinah, striving to fasten an overfull case; the thing was it had represented home to her since her parents had been buried in the ruins of their London flat in the closing stages of the blitz. Because of that gap in her life, she had come to cling to this poor little room, and was sorry enough that the time had come to leave it. A woman put out roots, it seemed, on the slightest provocation. Besides, she had been happy enough after the first shock of her loss had passed. Until the past few weeks, when another loss of a different kind had come to take the brightness from her days.

The stairs creaked to herald the approach of her landlady. Dinah scrambled to her feet, nailing a determined smile to her face. Mrs Hale was lachrymose enough at the moment without encouragement from her; already she could hear the mournful sniff which, she knew, foretold a lingering farewell.

'Here I am, packed and ready,' she observed brightly as the lean form of Mrs Hale appeared in the doorway.

'And I be sorry enough to see the back of 'ee. Never did I think,' said Mrs Hale with a rending sniff, 'that the day should come for me to turn 'ee from my door.'

'It couldn't be helped, Mrs Hale. Your sister and her little boy must

71

come first. You know I understand.'

Mrs Hale's eyes filled.

'I couldn't but let 'em come, could I? – and her a widder woman like myself.'

'Of course not. I wish you wouldn't worry over it.'

'Ah, but I do. A nice, quiet young lady like yourself, and that there Freddy were a limb of Satan at three, and what he'll be now at seven God only knows, and my sister wit no more sense to manage the young varmint than a louse, if you forgive me speaking the word, and my good meogony furniture as I've took such pride in...'

She broke off to draw breath, dabbing at her eyes with a large hand-kerchief. Here we go, thought Dinah, patting her on the shoulder.

'Cheer up, Mrs Hale – it'll all come out in the wash.'

'And plenty of that there'll be, if I know our Freddy. Still, here I am, running on about my troubles, and never a word for yourn; but there, you know how I feel.'

'I shall be OK. Of course I shall miss the way you've looked after me, but Miss Faraday seems a nice little person. Quiet, and very prim—'

'That's as may be,' said Mrs Hale darkly.

Dinah raised her brows, somewhat intrigued. Mrs Hale's red-rimmed eyes met hers significantly. Mrs Hale nodded slowly thrice.

'Don't tell me the little lady has gone astray!' said Dinah, laughing.

'How far she may have went, miss, I do not know,' said Mrs Hale with dignity. 'But one thing I do know; she be a long sight too thick wit that neighbour o' hers.'

'Mr Endicott? Never in the world!'

'I shouldn't be too sure o' that.'

Dinah, with a vivid recollection of Mark Endicott's countenance as she had last seen it reflected that if these extremes had come together, the lion did indeed lie down with the lamb. Why, Miss Faraday could not so much as speak two words at a Literary Society meeting without becoming covered in scarlet confusion, whereas Endicott, from what she had seen and heard, would be intimidated by none. Well, you never could tell, and good luck to Miss Faraday if there was anything in it, though this she doubted. A greeting exchanged with her neighbour over a hedge might well have started a train of highly inflammable gossip.

'You know I bain't and never was one to talk,' declared Mrs Hale, with a complete lack of truth, 'but when it comes to her in his bedroom, and that there cottage tucked away in the middle of a field wi'out no-one handy to see their goings-on ...'

'It seems,' said Dinah, 'that someone did.'

She had abruptly ceased to feel amused. No prude, she was yet young enough to know a definite revulsion at the thought of one so unashamedly middle-aged as Miss Faraday moving furtively to an affair with the newcomer. She felt confusedly, as youth has felt so often, that what might be excusable to her own generation was disgusting when allied to wrinkles and greying hair. Besides, if one must sin, for heaven's sake let it not be hidden by a cloak of mim-mouthed virtue. She became conscious that Mrs Hale was speaking again.

' ...naught but chance that he were there. But so it happened, and so Jimmy Fairfax 'ud tell 'ee wi' his own lips,'

'Fairfax! Oh,' said Dinah contemptuously, 'if that old scandalmonger started the tale then you can divide it by ten and still not believe it. But I didn't think there could be anything in it.' She spoke with warmth, being somewhat ashamed of her previous feelings. Poor little Faraday, besmirched by the tongues of those who saw evil where none existed! No doubt the explanation would be of the simplest.

'I only hope as you may be right, miss, I'm sure,' said Mrs Hale with extreme distance. Her underlip protruded ominously.

Oh Lord, now I've done it, thought Dinah.

She said placatingly, 'We all know what Mr Fairfax is, don't we? The biggest old scandalmonger in God's Blessing, and that's saying something.'

'No doubt,' agreed Mrs Hale coldly.

The grandfather clock at the foot of the stairs choked, cleared its throat and struck three.

'Heavens!' said Dinah thankfully. 'Is it as late as that? I must be ready for the car. Goodbye, Mrs Hale, and thanks a million for all you've done for me. I shall be coming round from time to time – don't think you've seen the last of me.'

'I'm sure,' said Mrs Hale, forgetting her grievance and weeping freely, 'a welcome for you there will always be. Never doubt it.'

A knock at the door broke into her sobs. The car from the inn had arrived to take Dinah and her belongings to her new home.

Mark and Amy received their letters on the same morning. Mark looked at his with surprise and a flush of anger, swore violently, and threw it into the fire. He was days behind with his work owing to his illness, and no anonymous filth should be allowed to hold him up now that he was himself again. But it was queer, all the same.

Miss Faraday, unfortunately for herself, was unable to be so strong minded. Again and again she studied the straggling capitals which composed her letter, until the green ink blurred before her affronted gaze. The address was not printed but written in blue ink, the hand a round careful one which might have belonged to a child. But no child had printed the words of the letter itself.

Amy went to her work that morning with the crude insults of her letter for company. Throughout her day's work the words shouted themselves to her aching brain until it seemed they must be known to all the world. Through the turmoil, false notes pinged on her eardrum and went unchecked. Mistakes in time and fingering were alike disregarded. Her pupils, uncomprehending but glad to take what clemency the gods offered, went their way. Miss Faraday's colleagues found her more dim than usual, if such a thing were possible. And, at last, the day passed.

Dinah, who had been shopping, came in at half past six to find Amy sitting at the table in the dining room with a brimming cup of tea before her. She looked, thought Dinah, utterly vacant, and she knew a pang of nostalgia for her old abode and for Mrs Hale who, whatever her faults, was human.

'Oh,' said Amy, starting, 'I was dreaming. I didn't hear you come in. Would you like some tea? Though I'm afraid it's cold by now.'

'No, thanks. I had some at the Copper Jug. In Lake, you know. I had my book to change and one or two things to do so I went in after school.'

'Oh, yes,' murmured Amy, staring glassily.

Heaven help us all, thought Dinah. She tried again. 'Are you coming to the meeting tonight?'

'Meeting?'

'The Literary Society.'

'Oh dear. Is it tonight? I'm afraid I had forgotten.'

'Well, tonight's the night. If you are coming we could go together.' (Must try to be friendly with this half-witted white rabbit of a woman if we intend to live together. But oh, what a prospect!)

'Yes – yes, of course. I suppose I might as well come.' (Anything rather than sit here with the words of that horrible letter for company.)

'Good. We'd better be moving, hadn't we? Can I help you to clear away?'

'No, thanks. You would like a wash, I expect. I don't know why I sat over my tea so long.'

Dinah did not insist. Her skirt whisked around the door and Amy heard her running up the stairs. Her own feet felt leaden in contrast as she cleared the table and poured away her untouched tea. Going to the meeting would not help much, after all. The question would still be there to torment her. Who? – and for that matter, why? Why pick on one so meek and completely harmless as herself? Mr Fairfax had come upon her that day at the cottage, and Mr Fairfax was a scandalmonger unsurpassed, yet somehow she could not fit him into this picture. Without rhyme or reason, she was coldly convinced that a female hand had done this thing.

She heard the door of Dinah's room slam – an alien sound in the cloistered stillness of her home – and became conscious that she was holding a dripping dishmop with which she had performed nothing.

'Ready?' called Dinah's casual young voice.

'Just coming,' said Amy, splashing feverishly.

She dried her hands, scurried into the hall, and pulled on a depressed felt hat. Beneath its unbecoming brim, her nose shone brightly; her tired eyes looked out, Dinah thought, like those of a frightened rabbit from a thicket. Frightened – yes, that was the word. Though who or what she had to fear Dinah could not imagine. A quiet and lonely spinster, whom all the good things of life had passed by – for surely there were no grounds for the outrageous tale put about by Mr Fairfax! Looking at her companion, Dinah was assured of it. A touch of pity moved her. Too grim to be middle-aged, utterly without interest in life, and a complete frump! She herself, whatever happened, would never be like that. She vowed it to her immortal soul.

'Would you like some powder?' she offered, still stirred by pity. 'Save you going upstairs.'

Miss Faraday took the proffered compact and dabbed awkwardly at her nose. In the mirror she saw her own face, weary and drab, with for background the vivid and youthful features of the girl. A most feminine pang rent her breast. For a moment she hated Dinah, herself, and all the world. Most of all she hated her hat.

'Thanks,' she repeated, handing back the compact. 'Now we shall have to hurry.'

'Bags of time,' said Dinah amiably.

They went out together, Dinah swinging along with her head well up and the breeze tossing her dark hair, Miss Faraday trotting apologetically at her side. Her feet hurt, and she felt a hundred years old.

'Lovely evening,' said Dinah, sniffing the balmy air.

'Lovely,' agreed Miss Faraday drearily. She wished this girl were not so killingly hearty.

Outside the hall, three cars formed an imposing array. From one of them Laura Grey was in the act of emerging, two admirable nylon-clad legs swinging out to be followed by the rest of her exotic person. She wore black, with a shoulder cape of silver fox; her white skin and pale blonde hair seemed even more dazzling than usual. Her husband, standing by the door and being addressed by Mrs Richards, looked tired and not too amiable.

Laura glanced at the approaching figures, vouchsafed them a faint nod, and sauntered to the doorway. Here, for a moment, she stood, as if posing for a battery of cameras, then was gone.

'Pippa passes!' said Dinah.

Amy looked up, faintly surprised at her tone. Dinah did not look hearty now; she did not even look young and vivid, as in the moment when Amy saw her reflection in the glass. It seemed that the sight of the beautiful Laura had brought no pleasure to her.

'Hadn't we better go in?' enquired Amy.

Dinah laughed, without mirth.

'What are we waiting for?' she said.

The hall, as the visiting speaker noted with pleasure, was more than half full. He was a man fortunate enough to be unfailingly delighted by the sound of his own voice, but he was nonetheless gratified to see the numbers about to share this satisfaction. He shuffled his notes and smiled happily. In the front row the poetess, a newborn work nestling in her handbag, flashed her large teeth in sympathy. Horse faced old cat, thought Laura Grey, glancing across the room. Would she be the one? How fortunate that she had taken up the letters before Ralph had seen them that morning. He had a damnable way of asking who her correspondents might be. With regard to this morning's epistle, his guess would be as good as her own.

Miss Faraday, deserted by Dinah who, by virtue of her office now took a seat at the table beside the chairman, found herself a chair at the end of a row next to the large Mr Heron, who nodded to her and continued a conversation with his neighbour on the other side. Amy reflected with faint satisfaction that she could not now be accused of reserving a space for Mr Endicott should that unpredictable gentleman be thinking of honouring the gathering with his presence. Fate, however, proved to be against her. Mr Heron, beckoned by a friend, lounged across the room to join him, the Chairman cleared his throat loudly and rose, and at the same moment Mark Endicott came in and took the vacant seat beside her.

Miss Faraday murmured a vague greeting and stared at the Chairman. Mark leaned back as comfortably as was possible and stretched out his legs. His corduroy trousers creaked, and his broad shoulders seemed to invade the territory occupied by the shrinking form of his neighbour. He doth bestride this narrow world like a Colossus, thought Amy resentfully; why, why the devil couldn't he sit somewhere else?

Her determination not to look at Endicott caused her to be staring directly at the front row of chairs, where the bright head of Laura Grey seemed to draw all the light to itself. As Amy diligently glued her eyes to the same spot, as if conscious that she was attracting notice, Laura turned lazily and glanced behind her.

For one moment Amy saw the beautiful face, insolent, faintly bored, as she had seen it many times before then amazingly, all was changed. The eyes widened, and seemed to darken; the scarlet lips parted as if on a gasp of fear. Yes, fear, thought Amy, utter, unreasoning fear. Later she told herself that she was wrong, and had imagined what did not exist. What cause had Laura Grey for fear?

It was over in a moment. Laura had turned back, swaying slightly towards her husband. Ralph bent his head to speak to her, the look of concern plain on his lined face. They rose together, his hand under his wife's elbow.

'No, nothing – a touch of faintness,' said Laura to Mrs Oliphant, who had sprung fluttering to her side.

'Better in the air,' said Ralph briefly. 'No – please don't bother.'

The couple came slowly towards the door. Amy, watching with lively interest, thought that she had been mistaken. Pale, fragile and appealing, but surely not afraid. She passed so close that a faint breath of perfume came to Amy; her eyes were cast down, and she did not raise them as she went out of the hall.

A faint buzz of sympathy or conjecture followed her exit. Mrs Richards bent towards Mrs Oliphant, and both ladies were seen to nod. Amy reflected with ungenerous satisfaction that her own affairs had been placed comfortably in the background, and turned for the first time to her neighbour.

'Aren't you well, either?' she asked involuntarily.

'Quite, thanks,' said Mark coldly.

Amy flushed. Nobody asked him to plant his ugly self beside me, she thought resentfully – on the contrary. And he needn't be so rude, for he had looked queer. Not that it mattered.

Colonel Stroud had been standing for the past minutes clucking like a sympathetic hen. He now decided that the show must go on, and flashed his gold tooth at the gathering.

'Well, ladies and gentlemen,' he said, with perfect truth, 'I am sure that you have not come tonight to hear a speech from me.'

He paused, smiled again, and spoke for ten minutes, after which he glanced at his watch, laughed heartily, and introduced the speaker of the evening.

Mr Wilberforce Browne, who had been drooping sadly over the table, uncoiled himself like a serpent and rose to a surprising height. He acknowledged the polite rattle of applause, waited for it to fade, smiled around him, and began to speak.

His voice was extremely high-pitched and seemed by some ventriloquial quality to come from far away. Miss Faraday, tired and miserable, found her attention wandering almost at once. She looked around her, reflecting that all were there, the old familiar faces, some wearing expressions of bright interest, some apathetic, one or two militant and disapproving. She did not look at Endicott again.

'And now let us ring out the old, ring in the new,' declaimed Mr Browne. 'I am proud to bring before your notice a novel just published, *How Does Your Garden Grow?*'

As if struck by electricity, every nerve in Amy's body thrilled. Still seated in her chair, she was under the distinct impression that she had risen to the ceiling and come down again. A wave of burning heat swept her. She thought, I must get away, and moved. Endicott's hand touched hers.

'Steady,' he said, out of the side of his mouth. 'Don't give the game away.'

She looked at him wildly, showing the whites of her eyes. His hand gripped hers between the two chairs.

'Listen, and don't be a fool. This should be good,' he said. Miss Faraday withdrew her hand and obeyed.

'... I have a copy here,' fluted Mr Browne, waving a volume in the air, 'and I may say that unless I am greatly mistaken, I hold a book which will make literary history. *How Does Your Garden Grow?* I repeat a title which in itself is provocative as I'm sure you will agree is no ordinary novel. The author is unknown to me, and I imagine there is little doubt Tom Pinch is a *nom de plume*, but I venture to predict that he or she will not long blush unseen.'

Endicott cocked an eye at his neighbour's scarlet countenance and his lips twitched.

'This author,' continued Mr Browne, leaning forward and sending hypnotic glances around the room, 'has taken a group of people, as it might be you and I, to delicately, mercilessly, and with an uncanny perception, dissect them, discover their most secret inmost being, and lay it bare before our eyes. This, you may say, has been done before. I reply that it may have been attempted; we have here an achievement. These figures live, breathe, and have their being. They suffer, hate, lust, sin, move through a darkling forest of frustrated emotion, all beneath the cloak of conventional everyday life. Take the rector's wife—'

Mrs Richards started.

'—who, to outward seeming a placid matron, as far removed from suspicion as Caesar's wife, is destroyed by her passion for the half-witted jobbing gardener – a longing which dates from a frustrated urge of her early childhood. The village schoolmaster—'

A slow smile creased Mr Heron's large face.

'—to all appearances the most respectable and placid member of society, yet tormented by a dark secret which, for all his sedulous striving, comes at last to light. The village postmistress who, forced unwillingly to attend church in her youth now practices devil worship, and draws into her net many villagers—'

'I never did!' gasped Miss Margetson, giving utterance to an exclamation, and not a denial.

'And so it goes on – one after another, each the victim of his own frustrated ego, working out their appointed destinies to the grand tragedy of the climax. *How Does Your Garden Grow?* is not a pretty book – heaven forbid that it should be so. It will not, in all probability, be a popular book. We have, may God forgive a generation which craves for trash, no bestseller here. Nevertheless, read it. I repeat, and I repeat with enthusiasm, read it. If it does not make a deep and lasting impression on you, I shall be amazed.' He glanced at his watch and raised his brows. '*Mea culpa*! I have used the greater part of my time on this one modern novel, yet why should I apologize? It is not every day that a swan is found amongst the ducklings, a jewel on the dust-heap. Read it for yourselves, and in the printed page you will, I trust, find my justification.'

He sat down, wiping his brow, the noble echo of his own words mingling pleasantly in his ears with the sound of applause. A hum of conversation, unusually animated, broke out.

'What's this private life of yours, Mr Heron?' asked his neighbour.

'Ah!' said Mr Heron, and slowly closed one eye.

Colonel Stroud rose and made himself heard with some difficulty.

'Ah, well now, ladies and gentlemen, I know I put your own feelings into words when I express our thanks to Mr Browne for his most able and telling exposition. I, for one, intend to put *How Does Your Garden Grow?* on my library list at once. What did you say was the author's name, Mr Browne?'

'Tom Pinch. And it is published by John J. Twitterton at nine shillings and six pence.'

'Thank you. And now, in accordance with our usual custom, we may put questions to the speaker. Prepare for a bombardment, Mr Browne.'

He sat down. There was a deathly silence.

'Don't all speak at once,' said Colonel Stroud, laughing heartily.

Mrs Richards rose. A faint murmur of anticipation ran through the room. Miss Faraday closed her eyes.

'Ha! Mrs Richards,' said the Chairman nervously.

'I have listened,' said Mrs Richards sternly, 'with deep interest to our speaker. Touching this – this work mentioned by him which I understand has just been published, I must admit one question leaps to my mind. May I put it to you, sir?'

'Do, do,' said Mr Browne, closing his eyes.

'It is this. Does the author of such a book stand in no danger from the application of the laws of libel?'

'Hear, hear,' said Mr Heron cordially.

'Touched schoolmaster on a tender spot, seemingly,' said a sepulchral voice from the back of the hall.

The remark went well. Most of the audience, including Mr Heron himself, were convulsed with mirth. Mrs Richards was not amused. She waited, unsmiling, until the last guffaw had died. Mr Browne leaned forward.

'Yais. Indeed, yais,' he said thoughtfully. 'Er – may I ask, madam, if you have read the book in question?'

'I have not,' said Mrs Richards frigidly. 'In fact, I had not known of its existence until today, and I cannot say that I feel any great desire to read it now. That, however, is surely beside the point. I should be grateful for an answer to my question.'

'Well, now,' said Mr Browne, gazing upwards as if in search of inspiration, 'there is a law of libel, yais indeed, and a very powerful and far-reaching one. But if you will forgive me for saying so, I see no reason in the world for your assumption that this writer has infringed it in any way.'

'One up to you, old boy,' said Endicott, under his breath.

His neighbour, lost in a trance of misery, neither moved nor spoke.

'I was going merely on your own description,' retorted Mrs Richards, her colour deepening. 'You spoke of a group of ordinary decent people put under a distorting mirror and shown to be foul and loathsome.'

'Butchered to make an author's holiday,' murmured Endicott.

'Shut up!' snapped Amy.

Mr Browne was pained. He looked at Mrs Richards reproachfully.

'Oh, really, I must protest. Surely I said nothing of the kind!'

'In that case I misheard you. As I understood your description I can only say that I – and not I alone – deplore this type of book. It has not even the merit of giving pleasure. As far as I can see it does no atom of good; it can easily do untold harm. I only trust the author may realize what he has done. Thank you.'

Mrs Richards sat down, quivering. Mr Browne smiled with sad superiority, but spoke no word. After a moment Colonel Stroud rose.

'No further questions? Then I will call upon the Reverend George Richards to propose a vote of thanks to our speaker,' he said.

CHAPTER X

DURING THE NEXT FORTNIGHT a certain James Joy, the proprietor of a small bookshop in Lake, was surprised and gratified to find that he had sold no less than fifteen copies of a book by an unknown author entitled *How Does Your Garden Grow?* Fourteen were purchased by a like number of the members of God's Blessing Literary Society, the remaining copy being snapped up by a holiday maker who had remembered the birthday of a horticulturally minded and well-to-do aunt, and who was misled by the flaming blossoms which decorated the dust cover. No critics, however, shared the fine careless rapture of Mr Wilberforce Browne; for any notice shown by them, the novel might not have existed. God's Blessing, on the other hand, or the section of it which read anything other than the Football Echo in youth or the *Farmer's Weekly* in maturity, was much intrigued.

'Have you read it yet?' asked Miss Margetson of a friend across the post office counter.

'Not yet. Both copies are out of the library, and I can't run to nine and six. I might get a book token for my birthday.'

'It's well worth reading, believe me,' said Miss Margetson impressively. 'Powerful. If you know what I mean. Makes you think.'

'What? That you'll study the practice of Whatsit like the postmistress in the book?'

'Don't be silly.'

'Well, I think a spot of black magic might cheer God's Blessing up. God knows it could do with it.'

They giggled together, somewhat taken by the picture of a witch's Sabbath attended by members of the village. Miss Margetson sobered first.

'You know, Milly, joking apart,' she said, 'there's one thing I did notice. The vicar's wife in the book—'

'Yes?'

'The way she talks, finishing off other people's sentences before they have a chance – it's Mrs Richards to the life.'

Mrs Richards closed her book with finality and a loud snort. Her husband looked up from his crossword with mild interest.

'Finished, my dear?'

'I have,' said Mrs Richards.

'Well, what is the verdict?'

'A horrible book – horrible. Oh, clever, no doubt, in its way, but perverse and altogether foul. As to the characters living and breathing as that ridiculous man said, well! Such creatures never were on land or sea. And as to the vicar's wife—'

'I was rather curious with regard to that lady myself,' murmured Mr Richards.

'You will be disappointed. A mere caricature, and not even an amusing one. I have become used to a clergyman's wife being the butt of writers, but this is beyond everything. I have met no clergyman's wife – nor the wife of any man, for that matter – who resembles her in the least degree. In the whole dreary concoction,' said Mrs Richards, giving the words the effect of a blighting curse, 'I found one solitary thing which struck me as being lifelike. You remember Mr Browne mentioned the village schoolmaster?'

'Yes, I remember that,' said Mr Richards, smiling. 'Heron was rather funny about it, I thought.'

'It's really rather strange. You know that habit he has of hissing a kind of rhythm in the intervals of a conversation? The last time I spoke to him he hissed 'Old Hundredth', until I could have screamed.'

'Why yes, so he does. A queer habit. Nice fellow, too. But what about it?'

'Well – the schoolmaster in the book does it too. He does it all the time.'

'I've read that tomfool book,' said Mr Heron to Brian Marlowe. 'Got it from the library.'

'Which book?' asked Brian, without showing much interest. The two were on their way to a Cricket Club meeting, having met at the corner of the green.

'The one that pansy bleated about at the last Lit Society – don't you remember? Sss-sss-sss-sss-sss-sss-sss-sss-sss.' Mr Heron absently gave his own rendering of the first line of 'Tipperary'.

'Oh, of course,' said Brian, momentarily shedding his superiority and grinning. 'The one with the wicked schoolmaster. It sounded pretty average tripe, I thought. Did you find a portrait of yourself?'

'Good Lord, no. A miserable little pipsqueak of a feller – off his head, if you ask me. Wouldn't have kept his job for a fortnight. But there's one funny thing – you know that damsel at the post office?'

'The new one? Miss Margetson?'

'That's it. She and her Trollope! Well, she's got a horrible habit—'

'Devil worship?'

Mr Heron hissed derisively. 'That I wouldn't know. The thing is, if she's sitting next to you, with every remark she makes she gives you a jab in the ribs with her damned pointed elbow. Like this.'

'She does, does she?' said Brian, wincing.

Mr Heron hissed a few bars to the effect that Greensleeves was all his joy, and who but his lady Greensleeves.

'She does indeed,' he said. 'And what is more, the postmistress in the book does it too.'

'You know,' said Dinah, 'you really must read this.'

Miss Faraday looked upon the flaming cover of *How Does Your Garden Grow?* and smiled a sickly smile. She said feebly, 'I read very little fiction.'

'Do you?' asked Dinah in surprise. 'I thought you were so fond of Annabel Lee.'

'Oh, I am,' said Amy fervently, with the sensations of one who, sinking in a morass, had reached a tussock which would for the moment uphold her weight. 'I think her writing is delightful. There is a kind of gaiety about all her books – a freshness, don't you think? I have often thought what a charming person she must be.'

'Um,' said Dinah.

'Oh. Perhaps her novels don't appeal to young people like you.'

Dinah, who privately considered the works of Annabel Lee to be pure escapism for the emotionally frustrated, picked her words with care.

'I do think they're a trifle adolescent, don't you? I suppose as romances they're good, and the writing is quite pleasant.'

Miss Faraday, feeling adolescent and slightly crushed, smiled uncertainly. Dinah continued her theme.

'Of course they are amazingly popular, and must have given a great deal of pleasure. But what I really meant was that a book being charming is not an indication that the writer must necessarily be the same. I expect Annabel Lee is completely hardboiled. Her novels are her bread and butter, and she's found the way to spread the butter good and thick. I bet my bottom dollar you would have the shock of your life if you were to meet her.'

'She hasn't published anything since before the war, and I don't suppose there is any likelihood of my setting eyes on her,' said Amy. 'So I may as well keep my illusions.'

'Just as well. Now, what does intrigue me,' said Dinah, picking up her book again, 'is the personality of this Tom Pinch.'

Amy slumped back into the mire.

'T-Tom Pinch?'

'The author of *How Does Your Garden Grow?* You imagine a tall man with black brows and a piercing gaze – a sort of ultra-perspective Mr Murdstone. Actually he's probably a retiring inoffensive little creature who wouldn't say boo to a goose.'

Drawn by a fearful fascination, Amy picked up the book and fluttered the pages. The sentences which met her eye struck her as being worse than even she had imagined.

Thinking that Dinah was looking at her with some curiosity, she stammered, 'Is it good?'

'I – don't know. Really it's rather a hotchpotch, with a queer kind of power running through it. The climax is too silly for words – all due respect to Mr Browne – but there's no doubt that you do become absorbed by the characters. I should say the psychological studies were amazingly good. And the funny thing is that the three main characters – the vicar's wife, the postmistress and the schoolmaster – might have been drawn from our own three here.'

How Does Your Garden Grow? had burst upon the world three weeks before suspicion fastened on the innocent, and it was Mr Richards, gentlest and least censorious of men, who first put it into words. For all his dreamy ways, his perceptions were keen enough. He read the book, which struck him as poor stuff, and was intrigued to notice likenesses in the small mannerisms of many of his parishioners, besides those of the three main characters. It was probable that he noticed this before other readers, owing to his total lack of interest in the more lurid developments of the plot. Those pages referred to by Miss Margetson and her friends as 'the spicy bits' he flicked over with faint disgust. On the other hand, when he read that the village sexton could not utter a sentence without prefacing it by the phrase 'I'm now agoing to tell you', he was moved to lively interest. The vicar, he was somewhat disappointed to find, was a complete contrast to himself, being large, forceful, and a preacher of the hellfire school. In the vicar's spouse, however, he saw clearly portrayed the idiosyncrasy of speech shown by his beloved wife. It was true that in her actions she moved wildly and unbelievably away from life, as did the unhappy schoolmaster and the sinister postmistress; yet, in the tiny habits so clearly set down, it seemed to Mr Richards that the long arm of coincidence had been stretched indeed.

He mentioned as much to Ralph Grey, meeting that gentleman outside the Manor when on a begging errand connected with the forthcoming Garden Fête. Thirty years of ministering to a parish had not proved time enough to harden Mr Richards's shell and asking for alms was still one of the least pleasant parts of his duties. Having on this occasion got it over, and with Ralph's promise not enthusiastic but not withheld, the reverend gentleman was glad to find a change of subject.

'You know,' he said confidentially, 'I am much intrigued.'

Ralph grunted. He was looking even more worn than usual, and his complete lack of interest might have daunted another speaker. Mr Richards, however, gently burbling on, noticed nothing.

'It is touching, this novel, *How Does Your Garden Grow?*. It was the theme of the speaker at the meeting which you and Mrs Grey were so unfortunately forced to leave. Have you come across it?'

'My wife had a copy, I believe. I've no time for reading novels myself.'

'Er, no. Well, the strange thing is that from various straws which point how the wind is blowing, I am of the opinion that it is written not precisely about members of this village, since the capers they are made to cut would be out of place,' said Mr Richards austerely, his mild features momentarily twisted by disgust, 'in Bedlam itself, but that our gathering has been observed by a satirical eye, and any little eccentricities of speech or bearing used—'

'Add verisimilitude to an otherwise bald and unconvincing narrative?"

'I would scarcely call it bald. Unconvincing, most certainly. But don't you see what this implies?'

'I can't say that I do.'

Mr Richards's eyes flashed. He leaned forward slightly, reminding Ralph with surprising vividness of a white rabbit owned by him in youth.

'It means,' he said, 'if I am right, that we have the author in our midst.'

He drew back with a pleased smile, and awaited Ralph's reaction. But Ralph was not looking at him. His eyes were on the house, and a figure which was emerging from it. Mr Richards, a trifle dashed, turned likewise, and saw Laura Grey coming towards them.

The reverend gentleman was content in his marriage, the few small indiscretions of his youth all but forgotten, yet even he felt a stirring of the pulses as she approached. The sun set her pale hair glinting; only the faintest smile touched her lips. 'Tis beauty truly blent, thought Mr Richards, pleased that the words came so trippingly to his tongue, and greeted her with his usual slightly old-fashioned courtesy.

'Where are you going?' asked her husband.

'To the post office. I'm out of stamps.'

'There are some in my desk,' he said.

'I think I'll go, all the same. I'm tired of the house.'

'You could come with me.'

She looked down at her smart shoes. 'Through hedges and ditches? I don't think so, thank you very much.'

Mr Richards, feeling faintly uncomfortable, stepped into the breach. 'Ah – we were speaking of the new book.'

'New book?' She raised her brows. With some interest he observed that they were surprisingly dark considering the colour of her hair. He mentioned this fact to his wife on a subsequent occasion, when her reply caused him to bewail the lack of charity shown by the best of women at times.

'I refer to *How Does Your Garden Grow?*'

'Oh, that. I thought there would have been more to it. It doesn't come up to—'

'The thing is,' Ralph broke in, 'Mr Richards feels that the author must have known this locality.'

'Really? In that case, who?'

'Young Brian Marlowe,' said Ralph, 'has literary ambitions. Or hasn't he?'

There was a short pause. Laura's colour did not deepen, nor did her expression change, but the visitor had the impression that she was suddenly on her guard. Had she been a cat, he thought, the fur would be rising along her back. And he rebuked himself inwardly, thinking that but for the ever-present voice of gossip, such an idea would never have crossed his mind.

'Well – has he?' she asked negligently.

'One would think so.' Ralph stopped, plucked a daisy which blossomed at his feet, and began stripping the petals from it. 'Judging from his spate of high-flown speech at the literary meetings.'

'Talkers are not necessarily writers,' Mr Richards pointed out. 'The only author I have known well – a most prolific and successful novelist – was taciturn to the point of dumbness in company. I do not think I ever heard him utter more than four consecutive words at any social gathering.' (And that finishes the topic of Master Marlowe, I hope.) He added, aloud, 'But what guesses have you at the identity of our mysterious writer, Mrs Grey?'

'I'm a stranger here myself. I've no idea. Unless it would be you, Vicar.'

Mr Richards laughed. 'I fear I must deny the soft impeachment.'

'Of course, there's always the fellow in Corpse Path Cottage,' said Ralph, a momentary smile lighting his dark face. 'He's a bit of a dark horse, I understand.'

'He's also a writer,' said Mr Richards.

'No! Really? How do you know?' demanded Laura, showing animation for the first time.

'I called there one morning and found him at his typewriter in the throes of composition. Apparently the muse was far from kind, for sheets of discarded paper littered the floor, but I imagine all writers strike such patches.'

'Well then, if he is an author, why look further? I suppose he came to that ghastly hole to write, and has been studying types ever since.'

'Not good enough, my dear,' said Ralph, throwing his stripped daisy aside. 'He's only been here a matter of months.'

'No,' agreed Mr Richards, 'it won't do.'

'He might have come here in secret – who knows? And anyway, how long does it take to get a novel printed?'

'Years, I believe. You'd better ask this Endicott.'

'I might, at that,' said Laura slowly.

Ralph frowned. 'If you don't want your head bitten off you'd do well to leave the fellow alone.'

'Don't be so intense, Ralph.' She looked at him coldly. 'I don't believe in getting my head bitten off by the mysterious Mr Endicott or anyone else. Goodbye, Vicar, nice to have seen you.'

'Where are you going?' asked Ralph sharply.

'I told you,' she said, speaking with patience, as if addressing a slow-witted child. 'I'm going to the post office. To get some stamps. Goodbye, my sweet, for now.'

Ralph grunted. Without looking at her disappearing figure, he took out his pipe and began to fill it. With deep discomfort the vicar saw that his hand was shaking.

'Who went by then?' asked Mr Fairfax, guileless interest lighting his rosy face.

His housekeeper, who was dusting the desk in front of the window, straightened her back. She said, without expression, 'Mrs Ralph Grey.'

'Oh, ah. Was it now,' said Mr Fairfax, with deep interest. 'And going towards the crossroads, too. I wonder where she mid be bound.'

'There's no bus,' said the housekeeper distantly, 'not for another three quarters of an hour.'

Mr Fairfax looked at her grey and indeterminate features with warm approval. Whether the doubts cast on their relationship by evil minded villagers were founded on fact or no, there could be no doubt of his satisfaction in this twin soul of his. Never had so bountiful a flood of gossip come his way. What he himself regretfully missed, Mrs Shergold was certain to make good. If he had been called to the back of his dwelling at the moment when one or other of the members of the village passed by, he might rest happy in the knowledge that the nose of this pearl amongst women would not be far removed from the front windows. Like Jack Sprat and his wife, they lived in amity, and between them licked their platter more remarkably clean.

'A tidy piece, Mrs Ralph Grey,' observed Mr Fairfax, his cherubic features creased by a bland smile. 'No doubt of that.'

Mrs Shergold dusted vigorously. After a moment she observed repressively, 'I daresay.'

'No better than she should be, for all her pretty looks,' said Mr Fairfax, gently rubbing his hands together.

'Her path,' said Mrs Shergold, 'leads down to destruction.'

'I shouldn't be surprised,' agreed Mr Fairfax happily. 'I think,' he added, 'I'll step out myself. My baccy's running low.'

'Dinner's at twelve,' said Mrs Shergold.

'I'll be there,' said her employer amiably, and ambled from the room.

CHAPTER XI

'WELL, WELL,' SAID MARK mildly. Spreading the flimsy sheet on the table, he stared down, as if by the frowning intensity of his gaze he might wrest its secret from it. The straggling block letters, once again, were green, the paper pink and common. The matching envelope was addressed in a round unformed hand, completely without character, this time in blue-black ink. The postmark was a Sandbourne one.

Mark put the letter back in its envelope and began to fill his pipe. Outside the cottage the morning was scented and beautiful, the hawthorn buds on his untidy hedge white balls on the verge of breaking. A lark tossed itself ever higher, casting back a glittering trail of song. Basking in the sunshine, James awaited the coming of his Lord.

'Oh, what a beautiful morning,' carolled Mark, not as melodiously as the skylark. The sentiment was sardonic, since for him the thing lying on his table had effectually blotted out the beauty of the day. Something was here which, for the life of him, he was unable to understand. The first anonymous letter he had tossed with contempt into the fire – a fine and level-headed gesture, but one which he now rather regretted. Taking the new epistle, he folded it, and carefully placed it in the wallet in his breast pocket. This affair, he felt, would pay for investigation. The local police, undoubtedly, should be approached, but this he did not intend to do. There were reasons.... He stalked out of the house, greeted by James, and wandered moodily across the field.

The first letter had surprised and disgusted him, but he had been able to put it at the back of his mind. This one, coupled with its predecessor, was quite another matter. He grinned without mirth as he thought of his motive for coming to God's Blessing. Peace, solitude, and forgetfulness – too much, it seemed, to ask. But who could have done this, and why? No ordinary anonymous filth was here. The letters were written with a meaning, their venom coldly considered, a means to an end. But what had he said or done during his sojourn in the village to put anyone on this strange trail? God's Blessing, remote, peaceful, dreaming away its blameless life – yet in God's Blessing a hand which had penned the words which tormented his mind. The voice of Brian Marlowe on the occasion of their first meeting recalled themselves to him – 'The peace of a stagnant pool with ugly things moving beneath the surface.' Perhaps Master Marlowe had not been so far out, after all.

'And, apart from the foulness of it all,' said Mark, kicking moodily at a tussock, 'it's playing merry hell with my writing.'

There, indeed, lay the crowning offence. He had risen from his chaste couch, pleasantly certain that a good day's work lay ahead. A tricky situation in his novel needed tackling, and he felt modestly certain of his ability to do so. But how the devil could a man settle to his work when a half-sheet of notepaper had sent endless questions jigging through his brain? It was no use; the first fine careless rapture was lost, and he felt darkly that it might never be recaptured.

He was passing the White House without thought for its occupant when a window was thrown up and a voice called his name. Without pleasure he saw Miss Faraday leaning out and nervously brandishing a duster. He paused enquiringly.

'Oh – could you spare a moment?' called Amy, appalled by the looseness of her behaviour, but conscious of a duty to be done. 'It's rather urgent or I wouldn't bother you.'

'Very well,' said Mark, by now resigned to all that fate might bring. 'Will you come out, or shall I come in?'

'I'm all alone—'

'I'll be good,' said Mark, with a diabolical grin.

Amy flushed. 'I was going to say, please come in,' she remarked coldly.

'Right,' said Mark, and opened the gate.

The window slammed, and the lady disappeared. And what now, he wondered. Surely this fluttering spinster could not be about to confess to the authorship of the anonymous letters; the mere thought of his neighbour cutting such capers was enough to restore his good humour. As well as suspect the mild Mr Richards of robbery with violence. Yet after all, should it be so completely out of the question? When all was said and done, Miss Faraday was a horse of surprising darkness.

The door opened, and the dark horse stood before him. She still clutched her duster, and was dressed in a gaily patterned overall, which suited her much better than her usual drab attire. Her soft hair was loosened and she was still flushed, either from annoyance or nervousness. He decided that she was younger than he had thought.

She took him into a neat sitting room, where James flopped on the rug, looking rather disgusted at this curtailment of his walk. Miss Faraday seated herself on the extreme edge of a chair; Mark leaned back comfortably, observing her.

'I suppose it's the book,' he remarked.

'How did you know?' asked Amy, surprised.

'I didn't imagine your strange desire for anonymity would last. The first sight of a printed page would kill it. I suppose you want those presentation copies to send round to your admiring friends.'

'Very clever,' said Amy bitterly.

'We strive to please.'

'Only you happen to be wrong. I want no such thing.'

Mark raised his eyebrows. 'You must be unique as an author.'

'I wish,' said Amy passionately, 'that the presentation copies and every other copy of the wretched thing were at the bottom of the sea.'

'Oh, come,' said Mark, regarding her with irritated curiosity. 'Don't you care for such mundane things as royalties? What the devil did you write it for, if that's the way you feel?'

Amy muttered something and stared at her feet.

'And besides,' said Mark magnanimously, 'the book might be worse.'

'Worse? It's vile,' said Amy, two spots of colour appearing high on her cheekbones. 'It started as a joke.'

'A joke!' echoed Mark, honestly taken aback. He had read through *How Does Your Garden Grow?*, moved both by surprise at its situations and by an unwilling admiration for the efficiency of the whole thing. He had not liked it; he had been at one with Dinah in considering the gloomy grandeur of the climax ridiculous, but the idea of anything in the nature of a joke permeating those sombre pages had never occurred to him. He looked at Amy with a new interest and respect.

Amy met his gaze without shrinking. She was far beyond caring what Mark, so strangely placed yet again in the role of her sole confidant, might think. In a spate of words, she unburdened her soul.

'It would never have happened if I hadn't attended a course of lectures on psychology. I used to come home and tell Mother about them – she was always interested in everything I did,' said Amy, her voice softening. 'She couldn't go out herself, and whatever I did I made a story of it for her, and she would laugh. We used to laugh a lot, just she and I. Mother was very good at seeing the funny side of things. When school was awful and everything went wrong, I knew that by the evening we should be laughing together over it.'

Mark took out his pipe and filled it thoughtfully. His hostess had fallen silent, a tender reminiscent smile lighting her face. She might have been a young girl recalling the sayings of a lover. Once again she had taken him by surprise.

He said, 'So she found the psychology lectures amusing? Fortunate woman.'

'It wasn't so much the lectures. They were the usual stuff – you know. The thing was, we got hold of a whole lot of books mentioned by the lecturer, and some of them were really – well, I should never have believed it. Such stuff!' said the student of psychology scornfully. 'You would never think that anyone led a decent, normal life.'

'And do they?' murmured Mark.

'Of course they do. Only I suppose these people have such tortuous minds that they simply can't understand simplicity when they meet it.'

'You may be right. Only I don't quite see how that attitude leads up to your book.'

'No,' agreed Amy dispiritedly. 'You wouldn't, of course.'

She fell silent, twisting her hands in her lap. Funny little devil, thought Mark.

He said encouragingly, 'Come on. Spill the beans.'

'Well … it sounds quite mad, but we began to make a sort of case history of people we knew, purely as a joke, of course, saying what their inhibitions and complexes and frustrations might lead them to do. I got quite good at it,' said Amy sadly. 'The more outrageous my ideas were the more Mother would laugh. Even when the pain had been bad, she would say, as soon as she could speak, "For goodness' sake, Amy, make a book of it. I believe they would take it. Not like those others."'

'Others?'

'Six. In my case. Upstairs,' said Amy, with mournful pride.'

'You mean six other novels?'

'Of course I do. I said so. They all came back. Oh yes, they came back!' An expression of bitter offence crossed the face of the slighted authoress. 'I write good clean romances that many a simple person would read with pleasure, and back they come. I've sent them to every publisher in England, I believe. You should see my letters of rejection.'

'You must show me some time,' said Mark.

'And then write this monstrous rubbish, this utter tripe, which makes me perfectly ill every time I think of it, and do they send that back? Oh, no! They take it. They take it right away.'

'For Pete's sake, why did you send it in if you feel like that about it?'

'I wanted the money,' said Amy simply.

'He does but do it for his bread,' murmured Mark.

'Pardon?'

'Nothing. Merely a plagiarism.'

'I don't know what you are talking about,' said Amy peevishly.

'Never mind. I'm frequently in that condition myself. But touching your troubles, I can't see what you're making all this fuss about. The book is published, and no-one will be giving it a thought a month or so from now. It's not half as bad as you imagine, and you got your money, which is what you wanted.'

A queer little smile crossed her face. She shook her head.

'Well, damn it, you said so yourself!'

'I wanted the money for Mother. If they had published it quickly I could have put up with everything. It would have been worth it all. There were little things that meant so much to her. And they accepted it, and then it went on for months and months, until it was too late.'

She looked across at him, smiling again. 'I suppose it was a judgement on me,' she said.

Mark recalled the sobbing creature who had come to his arms that first day, and began to understand.

'My dear girl,' he said impatiently, 'don't talk such utter nonsense. One would think you had committed the unforgivable sin instead of bringing off a damn capable piece of work. Pull yourself together, and don't get things out of proportion. You want a thicker skin than that if you intend to write. And with regard to the delay, did you never think of asking for an advance?'

Amy's face flamed suddenly. For a moment she looked the girl that he had called her. She said in a small distressed voice, 'I didn't know one could.'

'She didn't know one could,' murmured Mark, gazing up at the ceiling. 'Well, well.'

'But would they have given it to me?'

'You could have tried. But it's too late now.'

'Yes,' agreed Amy. 'It's too late now.'

He looked at her with some apprehension, but she was gazing

down at her hands again, showing no sign of emotion or distress. He felt sympathy mingled with exasperation. What a foolish unpredictable creature it was – and how in the name of goodness came he, Mark Endicott, to be caught up in her affairs? Looking back, it seemed that the stars in their courses had fought to bring the two of them together, from the moment of his arrival in God's Blessing. And even before that, had not her shrinking form shared his seat on the bus? Not so bad, to come here for solitude and instantly to find oneself saddled by an unhappy spinster – and not for the usual reason since, he would be prepared to swear, she did not look on him as a man at all. A sharer of her guilty secret – a kind of sexless Father Confessor. A peculiar position, to say the least.

He said, a sudden thought striking him, 'I never thanked you for being so good when I passed out on you that day.'

Amy came slowly back to her surroundings.

'It was nothing,' she said wearily.

'How the dickens did you get me upstairs?'

'You walked. I helped you.'

'I bet you did!' He hesitated. 'Much trouble?'

'I thought you would fall,' said Amy, considering. 'But you didn't.'

'I meant,' said Mark carelessly, 'did I say much?'

Miss Faraday's face became scarlet.

'Oh, Lord! Well, I'm sorry. Very foul mouthed, they tell me, at such times. No doubt your psychology books could explain it all satisfactorily. But I'm sorry you should have come in for it.'

'I didn't,' said Amy incoherently. 'That is, what I mean is, you weren't foul mouthed at all. Not in the least.'

'Oh,' said Mark thoughtfully.

He fell silent. Amy, blushing again, sought desperately for words. Bright remarks about the weather seemed somewhat out of place. She looked up at last, met Mark's gaze, and said, without consciously willing the words, 'I had an anonymous letter!'

At once she felt an extraordinary relief, as if a crushing weight had been removed from her. The unbeautiful countenance opposite her seemed momentarily to be that of an angel of comfort. Through this man she had suffered, yet in him, of all mankind, she was able to place her confidence.

'Good God,' said Mark, not unnaturally taken aback. 'You had one, did you? So did I. But I went one better than you. Two separate and varied missives.'

'Were they abusive?' asked Amy, curiosity mingled with amazement in her face.

'Neither was precisely a *billet-doux*,' said Mark drily. 'The queer part is they seemed to come from someone who knew of my life before I came here.'

'That's strange. Mine was – oh, horrible. It made me feel dirty.'

'It's a habit they have. Sandbourne postmark?'

'Yes. But that means nothing. It's easy enough to get to Sandbourne from Lake.'

'That's true. Was your letter by any chance connected with your visit to me?'

'How did you know?'

'I didn't. But the fact,' said Mark, leaning forward to knock out his pipe, and dropping ash on the shining hearth, 'opens a field for speculation.'

'Too wide a field.'

'What do you mean by that?'

'Only that Jimmy Fairfax knew I was there. And what Jimmy Fairfax knows today all God's Blessing knows tomorrow.'

'I see. Well, it's most incomprehensible.'

'And most unpleasant.' Amy opened her eyes resentfully. 'What have I done, to be treated like this?'

'"Be you pure as ice or chaste as snow,"' said Mark. 'Never mind. At the moment, unless we take our missives to the Bobby there's little we can do, except be bloody, bold and vigilant.'

'I couldn't show my letter to anyone,' said Amy, with decision.

'Well, my first I consigned to the flames, but I'm wondering now if I did right. This sort of thing may grow, you know. I don't like it.'

His tone was unwontedly serious. Amy saw that his mouth was grim.

'You mean, we may get other letters?'

'I wasn't thinking so much of you. Unpleasant though it is for you, your conscience is clear. All the dirt thrown at the two of us can't stick. All the same, I don't like it.'

'Who could?' said Amy.

'I know. But it's more than that. There's something here I can't understand.'

'Neither can I,' said Amy fervently. 'Ever since the wretched thing came I've asked myself, why, why, why? Why should anyone do such a thing? What possible satisfaction can they gain from it?'

Mark shrugged. 'Satisfaction of a personal grudge? Failing that, go back to your psychology lectures, my dear. Sexual perversion – sexual frustration. Whichever way you turn sex rears its ugly head.'

'I still don't understand it,' said Amy, flushing slightly, not, strangely enough, at the explanation, but at the casually used endearment.

'Why should you? Who are you – who am I, for that matter – to follow the workings of a mind diseased? Though the Lord knows,' said Mark, laughing, 'one would say there was little enough hidden from the author of your novel. You know, you really are a most amazing person. Talk about hidden depths! How on earth you did it—'

'I told you,' said Miss Faraday petulantly. 'I told you the whole thing.'

'Did you, by George! But letting that pass, and turning to the matter of your anonymity, weren't you asked for any publicity by your publishers?'

'They wanted a photograph,' said Amy gloomily, 'and the story of my life.'

'I bet they did. And what did you say?'

'I told them that I did not wish my identity to become known, and that I had no photograph. Ethel M. Dell,' said Miss Faraday triumphantly, 'would never have her photograph published, and neither would Annabel Lee.'

'And where they trod lesser mortals may follow. Good for you. But what about this end? Wouldn't the people at the post office notice anything? Bulky parcels, and so on?'

Amy shook her head. 'I was lucky there. In the old days it would have been different, but now the mail vans come straight out from Lake.'

'All completely impersonal?'

'Yes. And of course I never sent anything off from here.'

'Diabolical cunning,' said Mark absently. He thought, with a faint shock, that the anonymous letter-writer would seem to have followed a similar technique, judging from the postmark. All the same, he would not cast Miss Faraday in that unpleasant role, even had she not been a victim herself. Unless, of course …

He found that he was scowling at Amy, who was looking at him in some surprise. He pulled himself together.

'You seem to have covered your tracks very well, and I don't see how anything can possibly be traced to you. As I said some time ago, you have nothing to worry about. Sit tight, watch reactions, and when you feel like it, write another. That's my advice, for what it's worth.' He rose, glancing at the clock. 'And now, unless we wish to give our friend the letter-writer further material, I had better go. There seems to be in this village what a preacher of my youth called a Hi which never sleepeth – a Hi which seeth all.'

'Oh, there is,' said Amy seriously. She stood up, twisting her fingers together. Stammering, she said, 'I haven't t-told you yet why I called you in.'

'Haven't you?' asked Mark, in genuine surprise.

'No.' She looked up at him apprehensively. 'You will be angry, I'm afraid.'

'As bad as that?'

She gulped. 'People are beginning to think that it – the book – was written about God's Blessing.'

Mark, with some justification, felt that he had had enough.

'Isn't this where we came in?' he asked coldly.

'But you don't understand.'

'For God's sake, what don't I understand?'

Amy bowed her head.

'They think you wrote it,' she said.

CHAPTER XII

IT WAS HOT IN the wood. The air was full of the drone of insects, and the bracken, proudly uncurling, already encroached on the path. Laura Grey dabbed at her forehead with a faintly scented handkerchief and frowned. She had no desire to appear overheated, or anything but mistress of the situation. A cool and graceful poise, touched delicately by a shadow of regret – that would be the line to take. She followed the path, moving up from the trough where a tiny stream flowed, and reaching the space at the top where the hazel clumps grew less closely, paused, taking a mirror from her bag and examining her face with intensity. Her fears proved groundless; the heat had not so much as heightened her colour. The blue eyes gazed into the mirror and saw satisfaction reflected there.

She closed her bag, and smoothed down her pleated grey skirt. Her jumper was blue, matching her eyes, and high to the neck. Somehow the effect was as revealing as that of a low-cut evening gown. She waited for a moment, for all her poise breathing more quickly as she thought of what lay ahead, then she left the wood and crossed the path towards Corpse Path Cottage. Endicott, who was sitting in a patriarchal manner in a patch of sunshine outside his front door, looked up to see her standing with one hand on the gate.

For a moment he neither moved nor spoke. His eyes, fixed on the slender and charming figure, were expressionless. The girl looked at him, her lips parted in an appealing smile. She said, when he had made it obvious that the first move must come from her, 'Won't you ask me in, Mark?'

He rose deliberately, placing the papers which he held on the step.

With helpless anger, he discovered that his hands were trembling, and thrust them into the pockets of his disreputable trousers.

'Come in, by all means … Mrs Grey,' he said.

Laura opened the gate and came slowly to him, moving her head slightly to one side to avoid the branches of the old lilac bush which dripped its blossom across the path. When she was quite close to him, she paused, looking at him with a faintly troubled gaze.

'You are angry with me,' she said.

Mark laughed shortly.

'Well – aren't you? I know I deserve it,' she said.

'In the past,' said Mark, 'I have felt angry, as you so euphemistically put it, with you. I may even have felt murderous towards you. I am happy to say that those days have gone. I no longer feel anything towards you any more.'

'Nothing?' said Laura.

Mark became conscious that a little pulse was beating furiously in his temple. He turned his head, that she might not see it. He said thickly, 'Why have you come here?'

'I wanted to speak to you. To explain,' she said.

'You have great faith in your own powers,' said Mark.

She did not answer, and her silence seemed an accusation.

'Don't pretend to be hurt,' he said. 'It doesn't tie up with your behaviour. How long have you known I was here? Your desire to explain didn't move you very quickly. And couldn't you have brought your husband with you, to round off the whole affair?'

'Don't, Mark,' she whispered.

'I hurt you, don't I? My Lord, you're clever. Even now you can make me feel I've hurt you. And that's damned funny, after what you've done to me.'

She moved, as if he had touched her. 'I was afraid you'd feel like that,' she said.

'Like what?'

'Oh, Mark, my dear! You make it all so plain. I was wrong, I know – wickedly wrong – and I know how bitterly I hurt you. Believe me, I suffered, too, and I shall suffer for the rest of my life – but can't it be forgotten now? I can't undo the past, but surely we needn't hate each other. Isn't there anything left?'

The low voice broke on the ghost of a sob. She looked up at him half shyly, half appealingly, like an unhappy child.

'You're a good actress, Laura,' he said. 'A pity you left the stage.'

She remained perfectly still, and her face did not change. In the lilac the bees droned and drifted. He felt the old charm creeping over him, and cursed his own weakness.

At last she said gently, 'I can see it's no use. I shall never make you understand. I'd better go.'

'I don't know why you came,' said Mark.

As if the words were an invitation she swayed towards him, laying her hands on his shoulders, her face upturned to his.

'You wouldn't have said that – once,' she whispered.

Mark drew a quick breath. The colour came darkly to his face. 'You won't manage it, you know,' he said.

'Manage what?'

'To fool me all over again.' He took her hands from his shoulders and held her away from him, looking her over from head to foot. Under the pitiless scrutiny her eyes fell, but she did not attempt to move away.

He said reflectively, 'You haven't changed. You're lovely as an angel still. Only it doesn't mean a thing to me anymore. Do you understand that?'

Her lips curved faintly. 'You make it fairly plain,' she said.

'Good.' He released her hands. 'That being clear, perhaps you will tell me what the devil you want with me.'

'I came to explain. To tell you I was sorry.'

'Very good of you. I thought you'd done that already. Don't you remember? So delicately and neatly, too. The first letter I had when I reached home. Those years in the prison camp it was all I waited for – the thought of you, and coming back to you. Doesn't it give you a good laugh? That was what kept me alive – and then a note. A nice little note.' His voice thickened suddenly. He turned away, fumbling for his pipe, and did not see the glint of triumph in her eyes. 'God only knows why I must choose out of all England the place where I should run into you again. I never wanted it,' he said.

'If you feel nothing anymore,' she said softly, 'there's no need for you to mind so much. Is there?'

He looked up quickly at her tone, and met the half-veiled triumph of her glance. The blood drummed suddenly in his ears. Dropping his pipe, he took a step towards her. His fingers bit into her shoulders.

'Damn you, Laura,' he said.

Her head fell back, her eyes half-closed. He did not know which longing most tormented him, to kiss the lips which he had kissed so often, or to move his hands from her shoulders to her long white throat.

'I could kill you,' he whispered. 'Do you know that?'

'You don't want to kill me, Mark.' There was a hint of laughter in the murmuring voice. 'In spite of all I've done to you. Do you?'

He bent his head. A stick snapped sharply, as if under the impact of a foot. James, who had been dozing in the sun at the side of the house sprang up, barking furiously. The man and woman moved apart.

'Probably your husband in search of you,' observed Mark, picking up his pipe and breathing rather fast. 'And not before it was time, if you ask me. Now we shall have a few explanations, which might be interesting.'

'For God's sake, see who it is,' whispered Laura, her eyes dark with fear. 'If it's Ralph, get rid of him somehow. He mustn't find me here.'

'No – all things considered, it might be awkward. But you might have thought of that before.'

He called James and walked to the gate. There was no-one in sight. He strolled up the slope, finding the path, too, empty. As far as he could see the field was deserted. None the less, the interruption had saved him. He looked back on the past moments with a sardonic wonder. He had not thought that he, Mark Endicott, was so great a fool that the mere fact of her physical presence could bring even a momentary forgetfulness of what she had done to him. No wonder she had come to him, since her power was still so great. All the same, she should not have reason for triumph again.

But when he turned back he saw that her attitude had changed. Not invitation but fear was in her eyes; she was rigidly poised, and the hands clasped before her were so tightly flexed that the knuckles showed white.

'You must have led this husband of yours a pretty dance,' said Mark, looking at her without pity, 'to be in the state you are now. Compose yourself, my child; the devil looks after his own. You are not discovered yet.'

Her hands relaxed. She pushed back the hair from her forehead and smiled faintly.

'I'm not pretending, you know. Just now you said you could kill me. If Ralph had found us then he would have saved you the trouble,' she said.

She spoke entirely without emphasis, uttering a mere statement of fact. Mark saw that she was utterly convinced of the truth of her words.

'You might have stayed away if you believe that. You came of your own accord.'

She shook her head. 'No. I had to come. To know what you intend to do.'

'Ah!' said Mark. 'That's the question, isn't it?'

She came closer, so that he felt her breath, hurried and troubled on his face.

'You won't tell him – promise you won't! What good could it do now? I was wrong, and God knows I'm sorry for it – but I didn't know if you were alive or dead and I wanted to get away ...'

'Don't worry. I shan't tell him,' said Mark. 'I'm quite prepared to pretend I never met you, and I only wish to God it were true.'

'I did try,' she said 'but it was too long.'

He said in a curious voice, 'It seemed a long time to me, too.'

'Is it any use to say again that I'm sorry?'

'What do you think?'

'I can't help being what I am,' she said.

'No – that's the devil of it. You did that to me without thinking twice about it and now you've got this Grey you can't even pretend to be a decent wife to him. I wonder he hasn't already discovered your fun and games with young Marlowe, and you came here today quite prepared to pick me up where you left me, if that would help to keep me quiet. You're a thoroughly bad hat, my beautiful Laura, and if you don't watch your step, you'll come to a thoroughly sticky end.'

'I've already been warned. By an anonymous letter-writer.'

'What?' said Mark. 'You too?'

'Oh, did you get one? And Brian did. I only hope they leave Ralph alone.'

'You seem to take it very calmly, considering the volcano you're sitting on at present.'

She laughed. 'It's some miserable spinster who can't bear to see anyone with a measure of good looks. Don't worry; no-one in God's Blessing knows about you and me – except you and me. And I'm finishing with Brian. I should never have started if I hadn't been bored to tears. It's funny to think what a moralist you are, Mark. You never really approved of me, though, did you?'

'Probably not. I only loved you.'

'"Indeed, my Lord, you made me believe so."' For a moment all wronged and deserted womanhood sounded in the soft voice. 'You may not think it, my dear, but I loved you too.'

'Only you couldn't wait.'

'No. So when Ralph came along, I ... married him.'

'And lived happy ever after.'

She shook her head. Turning to the lilac bush beside her, she drew down a scented spray and held it to her cheek.

'I hate him. He frightens me,' she said.

The letter, this time without filthy epithets or embellishments, said simply: *Do you know that your wife visits Corpse Path Cottage, and has been seen there in that man's arms? This is not gossip or hearsay, but God's truth.*

Ralph took up the flimsy pink sheet and folded it in half then over again. He put the small square into his notecase and looked thoughtfully down at his plate. The early sun was pouring in at the window, picking out the silver hairs at his temples and mercilessly emphasizing the harsh lines of his face. A half empty coffee cup stood before him, for he had almost finished his breakfast before the post arrived. A fleeting thought came to him that this was just as well, since a hard knot seemed to have formed in the pit of his stomach, and he felt that it would now be a physical impossibility to swallow food. The letter was out of sight; the printed words were as clear before his eyes as if he still held it before them.

He said aloud, 'Impossible, of course. A damned dirty tissue of lies.'

Corpse Path Cottage – that man's arms – the whole thing was ludicrous, so utterly unlikely. Would Laura, out of the blue, visit a stranger in a tumbledown cottage, and then and there fall into his arms? Tormented as he too often was by jealousy concerning her, he was not so jealous a fool as to swallow that. And, since it was not, it could not be jealousy which was drying his throat and making his breath come fast, it must be anger. Though so contemptible a thing should not have power even to anger him.

He pushed away his plate and walked to the window, gazing with unseeing eyes across the neglected lawn, glittering with dew in the sunlight. Birds were singing all around; there was scarcely a breeze to stir the heavy blossom hanging from the white lilac and scenting the air. Away from his domain, the slope was thickly clustered with green where the wood led to the right of way past Corpse Path Cottage, secret and remote in its hollow. Corpse Path Cottage – a place for a meeting – a strange place for a stranger to choose for a dwelling. Unless, indeed, he had come here for any purpose of his own. Unless he had known Laura before.

It was out now, the secret thought. He felt the moisture on his forehead and took out his handkerchief, wiping it with a shaking hand.

If she had loved me, he thought, I should never have been like this; and with the thought the door opened, and his wife came into the room.

She wore a housecoat of emerald green, tightly fitting the upper part of her body, and very full skirted. Her face, innocent of makeup, met the brilliant sunshine triumphantly. She looked lovely as a dream.

'Oh,' she remarked, as he turned. 'I thought you had gone.'

'I'm just going.'

She strolled to the table, sat down, and helped herself to toast and marmalade.

'What I could do to a hearty English breakfast!' she said.

'I should think we could run to more than that,' said Ralph, looking at the minute finger on her plate.

'No doubt. The thing is, I can't. You wouldn't wish me to lose my sylph-like figure, would you, my sweet?'

She met his brooding gaze with a touch of defiance.

Ralph said slowly, 'There are more important things in life than looks, you know.'

'I'm afraid you forgot that when you married me,' she said.

The colour came up in his dark face. She nibbled her toast, conscious of a little pleasurable thrill. It was so easy to wound him, to flick that defensive pride of his on the raw. A good joke that he should make light of her looks, considering the effect that they had on him, even now; only, of course, he hated his subjection. She had soon realized that. Well, he was not the only one to be disappointed. A tumbledown farm, which proudly called itself the Manor – a struggling farmer, who had buried her in this godforsaken hole. Her own fault, no doubt, but none the easier to bear for that. And she knew what he wanted well enough, but there was time enough for that. If he knew everything he would not be so anxious for her to produce him an heir. Heir – to this! A pity, as he felt so strongly on the subject that he had not picked a wife elsewhere. Life in God's Blessing was grim enough at the best of times. She certainly did not intend to be tied there hand and foot by the demands of a child. Even if—

She looked at Ralph standing darkly against the light, and her heart lurched suddenly. She could manage him, yes – except on those occasions, more frequent of late, when his temper mastered him. It was a slow moving affair, but once it was roused she was, as she had told Mark Endicott, afraid.

'Is – is anything wrong, Ralph?' she asked.

'Why? Why should there be?'

His voice was normal, but she did not care for the way he was watching her. Oh God, another scene, she thought, and wished with all her heart that she had not taunted him.

'Oh, no reason,' she said lightly, 'only you seemed to be waiting about, almost as if you had something on your mind.'

'Your wifely consideration does you credit,' he said.

'Oh, well, if you want to take it like that ...'

She helped herself to another finger of toast, not looking at him, but unpleasantly conscious of his brooding gaze. The room seemed very quiet. She thought, with sick exasperation, will he never go?

As if coming suddenly to himself, Ralph glanced at the clock and started slightly.

'Good Lord!' he exclaimed, quite naturally. 'I was to meet Rawlings at nine. I must go.'

He limped to the door and paused, holding the handle. He said, 'By the way, I meant to ask you. Did you ever come across that fellow Endicott?'

Mark, when he called Laura a good actress, had spoken no more than the truth. In the fraction of time which passed between the question and her answer her brain raced, but her face did not change colour, and her expression was one of mild surprise.

'You mean the mysterious gent at Corpse Path cottage? No, I haven't had that pleasure. Why do you ask?'

'You spoke of going to see him – to ask if he had any hand in that ridiculous book.'

'Oh, that!' she laughed, immeasurably relieved. 'Of course I never meant to go. Just a feeble joke to amuse his Reverence. You said at the time he couldn't have written it, so naturally I had no reason to go.'

'None,' agreed Ralph, opening the door. 'Unless, of course, you happened to have known him before.'

She caught her breath. 'Are you suggesting—'

'Suggesting?' His hard gaze raked her. 'I'm suggesting nothing. You seem very upset, Laura. Surely my chance remark didn't hit the bullseye?'

'Don't be silly. I was merely a little startled. Naturally if I had known him I should have told you.'

She met his eyes with exactly the right degree of slightly puzzled innocence in her own.

'I must say, Ralph, I find your attitude rather peculiar. One would think I was in the habit of deceiving you.'

'Oh, no, my sweet. Not that,' said Ralph.

He was smiling, but his smile brought her no reassurance. Instead, the hand of fear closed coldly around her heart. It became an actual physical effort to hold her indifferent pose. Mark could not, surely, he had promised, and she had never known him break his word. She thought, if he does not speak I shall scream.

'Because,' said Ralph, still smiling, 'if you were in the habit of deceiving me I should infallibly discover it. And if I did discover it I should just as infallibly kill you.'

On the quietly spoken words he went out, closing the door behind him. She heard his footsteps cross the hall and crunch haltingly along the gravel of the drive. She sat quite still, looking straight ahead of her. She had not moved a quarter of an hour later, when the maid came in to clear the breakfast things away.

CHAPTER XIII

THE WEATHER FORECAST FOR 26 July, the day of the annual Church
Garden Fête, was unsettled to an infuriating degree. The long dry spell
was due to break, as Mrs Richards knew well enough, but she thought
in her heart that fervent prayers for rain might well be held over until
the fête was safely a thing of the past. It was bad enough for stalls to be
crammed into the suffocating atmosphere of the Sunday School hall, but
added to this rain would mean the death knell to many immoral and
lucrative sideshows, not to mention the children's sports and a display of
barefoot dancing by the pupils of a highly select school whose principal
was an admirer of the poetry of Mrs Oliphant. The opening ceremony,
too, graciously undertaken by Lady Bingham of Bingham Grange,
would be far more impressive on the green stretch of the vicarage lawn
beneath the great cedar tree than with Abraham and Isaac peering hide-
ously from the background. However, biblical works of art and all, if the
rains came, the Sunday School hall it would have to be.

From dewy morn the preparations began. Loaded females with
distraught expressions shot in and out of the vicarage, colliding in
doorways and generally getting in one another's way. Mr Richards
hovered around like a well-meaning ghost, not on lissom printless
clerical toes, since he was wearing new boots which hurt him considerably. He felt, subconsciously, the need for support from one of his own
sex, and was filled with gratitude when he saw Ralph Grey approaching
him, accompanied by Mr Heron, who was to be in charge of the sports
billed to take place in a neighbouring field. He was pleased to see that
Ralph bore his sheaves with him, in the shape of a couple of rabbits and
a white cockerel, all lately deceased.

'Ha!' ejaculated Mr Richards, smiling happily. 'Thank you, thank you, my dear fellow. We shall raffle these, I think – by far the best way of bringing in the shekels.' He laughed gently, rubbing his hands together.

'An immoral business, if you ask me,' observed Mr Heron, grinning. 'The gambling fever corrupts God's Blessing. I'll have a couple of tickets myself. I could do with a square meal by way of a change. The last beef we had, my wife and I sat speechless for twenty minutes. Couldn't chew the gravy.'

Mr Richards was not listening. For the first time, and with a definite shock, he had seen Ralph Grey's face.

He said diffidently, 'Forgive me, my dear fellow, but is anything wrong? You don't look yourself at all.'

'Nothing wrong with me,' said Ralph shortly.

'You certainly look a bit under the weather,' said Mr Heron, observing him with some curiosity.

'It's nothing, I tell you. Couldn't sleep, that's all. The heat, probably. There's thunder on the way.'

'If we were not in such urgent need of rain,' said Mr Richards, his eyes on the scurrying figures beneath the trees, 'I would say, heaven forbid.'

At eleven o'clock, a scud of rain set the helpers fluttering like agitated doves. By the time the fancy needlework stall had been cleared of its carefully arranged stock the clouds had cleared, and the sun shone brilliantly. Muttering but undaunted, the ladies set the stall again.

'The devil's in the weather,' grunted Mr Heron, for a moment presenting his face instead of his wide rear to the sky as he paused in his labours of marking out the course.

'Conjured up by Miss Margetson, no doubt,' said Ralph, who was assisting him.

Mr Heron hissed happily. 'Talking of that fool book, have you heard the tale that's going the rounds?'

'I don't think so. What tale?'

'That the man of mystery at Corpse Path Cottage is the author. And none too popular for it.'

'Pack of nonsense,' said Ralph shortly. 'He couldn't have done it in the time.'

'Not in the time he's been in the cottage. Naturally. But he may have passed this way before.'

'And not be noticed? In God's Blessing?'

'There are those who say he was noticed. And if you cast your mind back you can recall the days when God's Blessing was so full of strangers that one more or less would be lost in the crowd.'

'The camp?'

'Why not? It's possible, you know. After all, someone wrote it.'

This Ralph was unable to deny. They worked in silence for some moments, then Mr Heron looked up again.

'Author or no, there are some queer tales about the bloke.'

'Oh?' grunted Ralph discouragingly.

'Apparently he told the entire bus load on the morning of his arrival a pretty tale – something about a hunted murderer being glad to find a hiding place in that crazy cottage.'

'Tight, probably. Or pulling their legs.'

'Making game of the yokels? Could be. Only so-called yokels don't like that sort of thing, and I don't blame them. But however you look at it, it was a queer thing to do. And then he knocks young Marlowe down—'

'Good for him,' said Ralph.

'You may be right,' said Mr Heron handsomely, 'I can forgive him for that. But when it comes to leading virtuous females astray ...'

'What the devil are you getting at?'

Mr Heron jerked up his head in surprise.

'I say, hadn't you better come up to the house and rest? You don't look good at all.'

'Blast you!' snarled Ralph. 'Leave me alone, and finish what you were saying.'

Mr Heron was slow to anger, and Ralph, his chairman of managers, but his colour rose.

'I don't know why you should take that tone, Mr Grey,' he observed.

Ralph swallowed. With a great effort he regained control. 'Sorry. Shouldn't have spoken like that.'

'Granted. Though I was rather surprised to find you so worked up over Miss Faraday.'

'Miss Faraday?'

The utter incredulity of his tone brought enlightenment to Mr Heron. He hissed that his bonny lay over the ocean, cursed himself for a tattling fool, and wished himself a hundred miles away. And yet, how was he to know? To his knowledge, no word of gossip had linked Laura Grey's name with that of the newcomer, though there had been scandal enough muttered in another connection, God save us from pretty ladies, thought Mr Heron piously, and calling to mind the features of his spouse, was comforted.

'Did you say Miss Faraday?' repeated Ralph.

'Believe it or not,' replied Mr Heron, rallying. 'I don't wonder you're surprised. I was myself. Never would have believed it.'

'Is there anything to believe?'

Ralph spoke in his normal voice. Mr Heron, softly hissing 'Cherry Ripe', was relieved.

'Probably not,' he admitted, 'but it makes a good story.'

Ralph laughed, and anxious to bury the memory of his display of emotion, related another story, both apocryphal and unprintable, which went well. They finished their morning's work in amity, but avoiding any further mention of the name of Endicott. Mr Heron afterwards mentioned to his wife that there was more at the back of Ralph's sudden gust of temper than met the eye. Mrs Heron fully concurred, adding darkly that with such women as Laura Grey, all things were possible. Mr Heron facetiously asked if she were by any chance moved by jealousy, to which she replied that any woman so misguided as to desire himself might take him with her blessing. A few like compliments passed with the utmost good humour, after which they spoke of other things.

The day of the Garden Fête was to be long remembered in God's Blessing. The thunderstorm alone would have been enough to mark it since its like had not been known in the village in living memory. And yet, as Mrs Richards afterwards tearfully said, at the opening ceremony not a cloud was visible in the burning sky.

She spoke the truth. The sun, so coy in the morning, by early afternoon decided to show its mettle. Strong men sweated visibly, and without shame. Women who had prudently set out in costumes smiled sickly smiles, and looked on those in flimsy summer dresses with an envy which was truly burning. Ices were sold out in the first hour, and there was a roaring trade in tepid and tasteless lemonade. Every leaf hung heavy on the branches, and no breath of air stirred the bunting chastely draped from tree to tree. The airy muslins of the barefoot dancers clung lovingly to their forms, outlining them with a clarity not always kind. Laura Grey, drifting across the lawn in a filmy turquoise dress and toiling not, took note of the perspiring damsels, and a momentary sardonic amusement lit the boredom on her face. The husband of Mrs Cossett, on holiday and brought like a lamb to the slaughter, looked likewise and for the first time that day was seen to smile. Mrs Shergold, bolt upright on her chair, watched the curvettings of a plumply quivering damsel and smiled not at all.

In the sports ground, half an hour later, the heir of all the Cossetts held up a race by beating the starting pistol thrice, and was ordered off the turf. Naturally hurt by such treatment, he waylaid the winner, who was of a fragile appearance and demanded half his prize money with horrid threats. As the victorious youth took a poor view of this suggestion, Master Cossett advanced upon him, and was instantly butted in the stomach. Loud laughter rang unpleasantly in his ears as he clasped his middle uttering strange sounds, whilst the victor scuttled to safety at the side of his parents.

Miss Faraday, standing behind the jumble stall, felt every stitch she wore clinging to her body, whilst the ominous beginnings of a headache made her temples throb. The heavy garments which she was handling were offensive alike to touch and smell. On all sides, she was assailed by requests to knock down this or that article in price, a thing which she had been strictly forbidden to do during the first two hours of the sale. Mere instrument though she was, her refusal was taken ill, and with mutterings. Her own hat she had removed for a moment, when it had instantly been whisked away, thereby making it clear that some were present who meant to find bargains, by hook or by crook. A jumble sale, she thought, together with flower shows and amateur theatricals, roused the worst human instincts, and all were immoral affairs which should not be allowed.

'How are you doing?' asked Mrs Richards, bustling up.

'Not too well,' said Amy sadly. 'They all want reductions.'

'What do they think we're doing, giving the stuff away? The prices couldn't well be lower. Well, hold the fort. It's only half an hour before Miss Morris is due to relieve you.'

She nodded, gave Amy a smile without warmth, and bustled away. A moment later her voice was heard upraised in encouragement by the bowling for the pig. Amy felt a reluctant affection. Nobody could deny that she was a worker, and well meaning.

'Them trousis,' murmured an insinuating voice in her ear.

'Never worth five bob, they ain't. Got the moth 'ere – and 'ere.' The garment was stretched out, and indelicately displayed. 'Two bob I'd give but not a penny more.'

Sighing, Amy bent her head to the yoke.

At five, Dinah, reluctant but resigned, arrived to take over. Amy, whose headache was now an unhappy fact, made her way to the tea tent, where, in the atmosphere of an oven, she at length received a cup of tepid and straw coloured liquid together with a crumbling slice of slab cake.

'There's richness for you,' said a voice at her side.

She looked up with a start to see the surprising figure of her neighbour. In deference, she imagined, to the heat, he had changed his corduroys for a pair of grey flannel trousers. With these he wore a garment of white towelling, short-sleeved and far enough open at the neck to expose a very hairy chest. Despite this light and pleasing attire he was plainly very hot.

'What on earth,' said Amy faintly, 'are you doing here?'

'Ah!' said Mark, with a large wink.

He lifted the slice of cake from his own saucer, and observed it closely. 'No,' he said, and put it down again. 'What am I doing here, you ask? I am taking notes.'

Amy became conscious that their conversation too was being noted, and with deep interest.

'I don't know what you mean,' she said.

'I am thinking, you see,' said Mark, taking a gulp of tea, 'of writing a book on village life. Tense, powerful (whatever that means) and very perceptive. All, therefore, is grist that comes to my mill. There's a chiel among us taking notes, and saying he'll print 'em – always supposing,' he added carefully, 'that said chiel can find a publisher misguided enough to abet him in his fell work. Why does this so-called tea taste of mould and corruption?'

His voice was querulous. Amy felt that the question required no answer, though having tasted her own tea, she could not deny that the root of the matter was in him. She finished her cake and rose.

'Let me take that for you,' said Mark courteously. 'Anything else you'd like? Ah, well, I daresay you're wise.'

He carried the relics of their meal to the trestle table, where Mrs Oliphant, drooping over the tea urn, received them.

'Let's get out of here,' he said, rejoining his companion.

'I'm going home,' said Amy shortly.

'Home?' echoed Mark, in a rising tone of blended incredulity and hurt. 'But I've only just come!'

Amy saw that such heads as had not turned their way hitherto now did so. Mrs Richards, talking to a group of ladies at the other side of the tent, seemed to nod with deep significance. Oh well, she thought, with a sudden burst of most unwonted defiance, what did it matter, after all?

Let them look, the whole boiling lot of them. This man might talk like a lunatic when he thought fit, and appear in garb that was disreputable, but at least he could keep a secret. And, surprisingly, since his coming her headache had gone.

'Well!' said Mrs Richards, unable to control herself as the oddly assorted couple moved away. 'Did you see that?'

'And did you hear what he said? About a book—'

'There must be something in it, after all.'

The heads went together. The tongues wagged.

Outside the tent, and in a heat scarcely less breathless, Mark grinned cheerfully at his companion.

'Ready to show me the sights?' he asked.

'Why?' snapped Amy.

Mark halted and surveyed her, smiling to himself. Never, he thought, had he seen a woman who paid less attention to her personal appearance. Miss Faraday's hair, flattened by the departed hat, hung limply round her tired face. Her flowered dress, unfashionably short and skimpy, could not well have been more unbecoming in pattern or cut. She looked more than her age. All this Mark saw, and wondered at his own behaviour.

'What an ungrateful woman you are,' he said.

'I am far too hot and tired to answer riddles. And I haven't the remotest idea what you mean.'

'"When lovely woman stoops to folly",' began Mark, adding in a different tone, 'listen, and don't be cross.'

'Well?'

'Believe it or not, I'm only trying to help. Truly.'

'Go and help someone else,' said Amy rudely, turning away. 'I told you, I'm going home.'

'Just as you like. Only don't blame me.'

'Why should I? What on earth are you talking about?'

Mark moved a little nearer, and grinned into her unresponsive face. He dropped his voice.

'Anonymous letter-writers don't find their material in public meetings. You did me a good turn, and suffered for it. I thought if we promenaded here in full view of the community it might put a spoke in the wheel of our unpleasing friend. Now do you understand?'

'Oh,' said Amy vaguely.

She looked around her at the sweep of lawn dotted with figures, busy or bored. Strange to think that amongst their number might be the one who had flung anonymous filth at one so innocent of offence as herself; stranger still to think that the man beside her should trouble his head over her affairs. It was true enough that she had been ungrateful, and after he had dressed himself for the occasion, too. A smile trembled on her lips. It was rather a pretty smile, and Mark observed it with interest. It seemed that for once virtue might be its own reward.

'Come along,' he said persuasively. 'Give the so and so's something to talk about.'

'Very well,' said Miss Faraday meekly.

From the grisly recesses of the jumble stall, Dinah observed them pacing decorously side by side. A pleased smile crossed her face.

'Well, I'm blowed,' she said.

Sighing, she returned to her task.

'The weather,' said Mrs Oliphant, speaking in prose, 'will not hold out much longer.'

As she spoke, a gust of hot wind agitated the bushes bordering the lawn, sending a raffish collection of paper bags and ice cream cartons leaping and bounding across the patch where a few self-conscious couples revolved to the strains of a violin (Miss Margetson) and a piano (Dinah). Although barely eight o'clock, it was growing ominously dark, and despite the wind which had so suddenly arisen, the heat was still oppressive.

'Tired, my dear?' asked Mr Richards, appearing at his wife's side.

'A little. Mr Grey has gone, George. Some trouble with one of his special cows. And his wife will not be singing for us tonight. Her head is troubling her,'

'Dear, dear. Did she go with her husband?'

'No. The headache did not appear until after his departure. I must say,' added Mrs Richards, rather reluctantly, 'she certainly looked far from well. She was getting a lift home, she told me – with whom she did not say.'

'Oh, well,' said Mr Richards vaguely.

'Do you know, George,' said his wife, abandoning Laura Grey, 'I have a most peculiar feeling – as if something utterly dreadful is going to happen.'

'Nothing more dreadful than a thunderstorm, I trust. But that is most certainly on the way.'

As he spoke a flash of lightning pierced the sullen sky. A rumble of thunder drowned the music, and a second gust of wind sent the pianist's sheet of music gambolling across the grass.

'My friends,' intoned Mr Richards, stepping forward with uplifted hand. 'The clerk of the weather most unkindly puts an end to our festivities in the open. Dancing, however, will continue in the Sunday School hall. Before we adjourn, might I ask for helpers – muscular helpers – to return this piano to the vicarage? Thank you. Thank you so much.'

Four or five youths, greeted by cries of encouragement, moved sheepishly forward and laid hands on the instrument. The thunder rolled again.

In the Sunday School hall, with Old Testament worthies gazing reproachfully down, the festivities, as Mr Richards had merrily termed them, limped on. At the piano, Dinah found herself much hampered by the efforts of Miss Margetson, who, no brilliant performer at the best of times, was rendered positively appalling by her nervous dread of thunder. With every crash, now nearer and more frequent, her bow trembled more, producing a variety of wails and shrieks quite awe inspiring. Dinah muttered under her breath and ploughed on. The Sunday School piano was bad enough, without Miss Margetson's assistance. She crashed a final chord with vicious emphasis, and sat back with a sigh of relief. Her gaze wandered over the sparse gathering, and became focussed on a tall figure which had just appeared in the doorway. Brian Marlowe, as if drawn by her regard, turned his head and looked unsmilingly at her.

Dinah wrenched her eyes away, and found that her heart had begun to thump unevenly. I shall be as shaky as Miss Margetson now, she thought disgustedly; the next dance should be a riot. What had brought him here, anyway? Surely he had not expected to find Laura Grey treading the light fantastic amongst this gathering …

A crash of thunder which seemed completely overhead made her jump. There was a chorus of squeaks from the assembly, and Miss Margetson turned on Dinah a face of pale green determination.

'I'm going home,' she said in a trembling voice. 'If I don't I shall be sick.'

'Can you go alone?'

'My friend is here. He's got the car. Oh …'

She hastily put her violin into its case and made for the door.

'Gone, has she?' remarked the Master of Ceremonies, coming over to Dinah. 'Will you carry on, or what? Strikes me we might as well pack up. Not that she's any great loss. That last one was like a bee on a hot shovel.'

'Thunder upsets her,' explained Dinah.

'You're telling me!' said the MC.

He cast an eye over the hall, saw that two or three groups were making preparations to leave, and reached a decision.

'Last waltz!' he roared, in the voice of a bull. 'Take your partners, ladies and gents, for the last waltz.'

'Bit early, ain't it, Teddy?' objected a plaintive voice.

'Early enough if you want to get home with a dry shirt, my son,' the MC retorted. 'Now then – drum effects supplied by the elements. What more do you want?'

Mechanically, Dinah strummed out the waltz from 'Bittersweet'. The MC left her side, clasped a stout lady to his chest and revolved with her. The thunder crashed, and as it faded gave place to a new sound – the rattle of monstrous raindrops on the roof.

'Too late, Billy,' said a youth, laughing heartily.

'I might ha' knowed,' said Billy resignedly.

Dinah, pressing the well known chords, became conscious that Brian was crossing the room towards her. She played more loudly against the increasing clamour of the rain.

'Dinah,' said Brian at her side.

'I can't talk when I'm playing.'

'Very well. I can wait.'

He seated himself on the edge of the platform. She played on, conscious in every fibre of his nearness.

With relief, she repeated the refrain for the last time, slowed the tempo, and stopped. Responsive to the MC's nod she broke immediately into 'God save the King'.

She took her time over collecting her music and closing the piano. People were crowding to the door, looking out at the rain and uttering dismayed comments. Dinah and Brian were, to all intents and purposes, alone.

'The car's outside,' he said, when she could no longer delay turning to face him. 'I'll run you back.'

Dinah recalled her last trip with him, and thought bitterly that walking through the storm would be preferable.

'It's very good of you,' she said distantly, 'but—'

She broke off suddenly. For the first time she had seen him closely, and resentment faded in a shocked pity. A queer grey shadow hung over his face; his eyes were darkly ringed, and even his lips had lost their colour. The good looks remained; Brian could never appear other

117

than a matinee idol, but this was a matinee idol face to face with tragedy.

She said impulsively, 'Brian. What on earth's wrong?'

'Why?' He spoke, she thought, defensively, but without anger.

'You're the most peculiar colour. And you look half dead.'

'Thunder. I've a filthy headache, but I shan't pass out on you. Are you coming? Even my company should be preferable to a soaking.'

'Very well,' said Dinah. She added, after a pause, 'Thanks. It's very kind of you.'

'Yes, isn't it? For God's sake, don't bother to be polite. I know what you think of me, and I don't blame you. Let's skip it and go.'

She glanced at his altered face, opened her lips and closed them again without speaking. They went out together.

The violence of the rain had somewhat abated, and there was a general movement along the dark and narrow path which led to the road where Brian's car was standing beneath the dripping trees. The air was fresher, with a new scent rising from the drowned grass, and in the western sky another flash of lightning pierced the night.

They got in without speaking, while the thunder, farther off now, rumbled menacingly. As they started off, the rain, as if refreshed by its rest, poured down with renewed violence. Peering ahead, Dinah could see nothing but the torrent cascading over the windscreen.

'Damn,' muttered Brian. The car swerved, skidded, bumped on to the bank and down again, and was still.

'What's up?' asked Dinah, raising her voice against the clamour of the rain.

'Windscreen wiper out of action. It is all this dry spell. I can't see a thing. We were on the bank then.'

'I guessed that much. What will you do?'

'Hang on until the rain stops. It's only a storm. Sorry but I can't help it.'

'That's all right,' said Dinah.

There was a pause. Enclosed by the streaming darkness, she was again vividly conscious of his presence. Brian. Brian, who had brought her happiness and pain. The dark figure, so close that the warmth of his arm was communicated to her own, and she could feel every movement of his breathing. The bundle of emotions so securely enclosed that even here, in their close and complete seclusion, she could have no inkling of what his thoughts might be. Some inexplicable urge had brought him in search of her, after weeks of neglect; here they were, together again, as they had been so often in the past. Yet there was no happy communion

of the spirit. Their bodies might be warmly touching, but loneli-
ness enveloped her, so that she felt cold, lost, and afraid. She shivered
suddenly and felt tears prick her eyes.

'Cold?' asked Brian.

Without waiting for an answer, he turned and put his arm around
her, quite gently. Her head fell against his shoulder as if it belonged
there; for a moment the old and lovely sensation of utter contentment
was hers again. Then, like a dream, it had gone.

She stiffened, and pulled herself away. Instantly he withdrew his
arm.

'Like that?' he said, in a queer voice. 'Well – I might have expected it.'

'I don't know what you mean,' said Dinah untruthfully. Most
unfairly, she felt a sense of guilt. Brian had come to her, hurt and
unhappy, and pride had made her add to his hurt.

'Brian …' she began, throwing pride to the winds.

A crash of thunder drowned her voice. He started the car.

'We'll risk it,' he said in his normal tone.

They drove on unsteadily through the streaming rain.

The thunder passed over at last, but the rain continued. It filled the
ditches, so long dry, until they overflowed and made rivers of the lanes.
It found a weak place in the thatch of Corpse Path Cottage and made its
way through the ceiling and down the wall. Cruelly, by force of violence,
it beat down the standing corn. And it fell upon something lying limply
outstretched by the entrance to the little wood, washing the stain from
the pale hair, and soaking it into the ground.

CHAPTER XIV

'FIVE WICKS,' SAID MRS COSSETT gloomily, 'and what to do wi' you all that time I do not know.'

'If we lived in Lake—' began Johnny, morosely giving utterance to his theme song.

'Well, we don't, so for God's sake stop kippin' on about it,' snapped his mother. She spoke with unwonted asperity, for, dearly as she loved her son, to have him under her feet for the five weeks of the summer holiday was a severe test of her devotion. Johnny absent during the day made the heart grow fonder than Johnny on the spot – or than Johnny released from school and wandering free to find the mischief ever present for his idle hands to do.

'What school teachers want wi' these 'ere dratted long hollerdays beats me,' said Mrs Cossett, peevishly voicing the classic grievance of those who do not teach. 'Taint as if they worked – not to call it work – while they be in school. And for how long? Five hours a day! – and that's what we pay rates for.'

Johnny remained unmoved. He had no desire to take up the cudgels on behalf of his pastors and masters, but on the other hand he did not himself feel that a holiday of five weeks was a day too long. The holiday itself might not be all enjoyment, but its close meant a return to school, and this he anticipated without enthusiasm.

'Be you going to Miss Marlowe?' he asked.

'Course I be. 'Tis Thursday, bain't it?'

'Ah.' A gleam of pleasure lit Johnny's ruffianly countenance. 'Gimme sixpence.'

'What for?'

'Ice cream,' replied her son briefly.

Mrs Cossett opened her purse and found the sum required.

Johnny dispensed with thanks, placed it in his pocket, and lurched towards the door.

'And where do you think you're going?' demanded Mrs Cossett. 'Ice cream van won't be 'ere, not afore eleven. Taint no more than ten to nine now.'

'I know that, don't I? So what? I'm going round to Ken Marsh. Maybe,' said Johnny, sneering, 'him an' me can do somepun to liven up this joint.'

'Don't you get up to no nonsense,' said his mother warningly, 'else yer dad will leather the lights out o' you.'

'Oh yeah? Him an' who else?'

The door closed behind him. Mrs Cossett shook her head.

'Five wicks!' she murmured.

Putting on her coat, she set off for Killarney and her morning's work.

Johnny proceeded through the serene streets of the joint he proposed to enliven. At the bus stop on the corner, two figures were waiting, those of Jimmy Fairfax and his housekeeper. The housekeeper was carrying a small case and wore a black coat and hat. Mr Fairfax was in his everyday clothes, topped by a greasy and aged cap. As Johnny came up, the bus, punctual to the minute, arrived. He observed Mrs Shergold and her case board the vehicle, leaving Mr Fairfax behind. The bus clattered away, and disappeared on its journey to Lake. A moment later the figure of Mrs Hale, hot and breathless, hove into view. Mr Fairfax turned to regard her with benevolent interest as she galloped up.

'Mornin', Missale,' he said.

The lady was in no mood for greetings.

'That weren't never the bus, for God's sake?' she demanded passionately.

'Ah, 'twere. Missed un, have 'ee?' asked Mr Fairfax with a pleased smile.

'Well, may I go a sojer!' exploded Mrs Hale. 'Never have I knowed this bus less nor ten minutes late, and more often than not twenty. And this 'ere blessed morning he must needs go and be on time!'

'Punctual to the minute,' agreed Mr Fairfax. 'My housekeeper, she had to go off at short notice, and we only got it by the skin of our teeth. Must ha' got out o' bed afore they went anywhere this morning.'

'Ah, so they must. And now I shall have to wait till 10.30. I s'pose he'll be half an hour late, just to balance it up. Enough to make a saint swear.' She paused to mop her face, and disposed herself for conversation. For want of anything better to do, on the opposite side of the road, Johnny Cossett lingered too.

'Be Mrs Shergold gone for good?' she enquired casually.

'Oh, no, nothing o' that kind, I'm glad to say,' said Mr Fairfax, chuckling. 'Hopes to be back in a wick or so, at the latest.'

'No bad news, I hope?'

'Well, in a way,' conceded Mr Fairfax, smiling.

'Illness?'

'Her sister is an invalid. Chronic. Bedridden, poor soul, and has been for years. The young person who keeps care of her has just gone and got married.' Mr Fairfax became waggish. 'They will do it, won't 'em,' he said.

'Bad job if they didn't,' said Mrs Hale absently. 'Won't the sister be needing your lady for good, then?'

'Now, now, Missale,' said Mr Fairfax, wagging a fat reproachful finger at her, 'don't you suggest nothing of that kind. A pretty quadrant I should find myself in wi' no good 'ooman to do for me – and me a poor widder man, too.'

'There be as good fish in the sea,' said Mrs Hale, darting him a glance of surprising coyness. 'But I wasn't making no suggestion, Mr Fairfax.'

'I know, I know. Jus' my joc'lar little way,' said Mr Fairfax soothingly. 'Truth to tell, it's all arranged. Another 'ooman be engaged by the sister, and should be starting now, but she be held up for the time being on some personal matter. What it mid be I do not know, but be that as it may, Mrs Shergold is to hold the fort until such time as she comes.'

'Oh,' said Mrs Hale, digesting this budget. She said, with womanly sympathy, ''Tis rather hard on you, Mr Fairfax, to be left at such short notice. Anything, in a neighbourly way, as I could do ...'

'Well,' said Mr Fairfax hastily, ''tis far from convenient, that I 'oon't deny, but don't you trouble yourself. I shall manage – I shall manage.'

'Oh, well, if you want me you know where I'm to be found.'

'I do, Mrs Hale,' agreed Mr Fairfax, rather uneasily. Apparently feeling that the conversation had lasted long enough, he glanced across the road to the spot where Johnny Cossett leaned upon a gate, his features twisted in a Bogart-like sneer.

'That Johnny Cossett? Well, Johnny, how many races did 'ee win up at the fête?'

'None,' said Johnny briefly.

'Tck tck. Spry young chap like you, too. And now you be on holiday, for how long?'

'Five wicks,' grunted Johnny.

'Too long. Far too long,' said Mr Fairfax severely. 'Never like it in my young days.'

'Nor in mine, neither,' said Mrs Hale, shaking her head.

'Taint my fault,' said the goaded youth. 'I never asked for it.'

'I bet yer ma didn't, neither,' said Mrs Hale, laughing heartily. 'Be she home now, Johnny?'

'No,' said Johnny.

'Oh, of course. Thursday be her day for Mrs Marlowe. I forgot for the moment. Well, I s'pose I mid so well look in at shop while I be here waiting for that dratted bus.'

'I must be getting along, too,' said Mr Fairfax. 'If you want to earn a copper, my lad, you can come and help me lift my early taters. I could do wit some help.'

Johnny grunted noncommittally. He watched the two figures out of sight with scorn and disgust depicted on his countenance.

'Wold apple women,' he muttered, and slouched off in the opposite direction.

Ken Marsh lived in what might be termed the Civic Centre of God's Blessing – that is to say, midway between the church and the school, and two doors from the Ring and Book. His father was the village policeman, and Ken had not only won a scholarship to the Grammar School at Lake, but also sang in the choir, looking like a species of angel. Angelic choirboys in private life fall oft from grace, hence Ken's pleasure in the lawless society of Johnny Cossett.

Johnny found him leaning over his front gate with a disgruntled expression on his face. In the middle of the path behind him stood an empty pram. He glanced up on hearing Johnny's footsteps, and his brow cleared.

'Hiya, big boy,' he observed chattily.

'Hiya, kid,' replied Johnny.

Leaning comfortably against the gate, he disposed himself for conversation.

'Coming out?'

'Can't,' said Ken, gloomily. 'Got to see to our babe.'

'Where is she?'

'Indoors. Having a bath. Then I'm supposed to push her out.'

'What? In holiday time?'

'There you are. That's what I told her. As if I hadn't – oh, a hundred better things to do with my time. All she says is, five weeks is too long.'

'My gosh!' said Johnny fervently. 'Is all the cock-eyed world saying that? We only got five weeks, and I already heard it from my old woman, Jimmy Fairfax, and old Mother Hale.'

'Makes you sick,' said Ken.

'You said a mouthful,' agreed Johnny.

For a space they brooded silently over their wrongs. Inside, a baby's voice was heard upraised in passionate indignation.

'There you are,' said Ken, with a wan smile. 'Hollers when she's put in her bath, and hollers when she's taken out of it. What people have babies for I don't know.'

'Ken,' said Johnny, following his own line of thought, 'what be a quadrant?'

'Something to do with a ship, far as I know. Why?'

'Jimmy Fairfax said he'd be in one if his housekeeper didn't come back. Or summat like that.'

'That old goat 'ud say anything.'

'Offered me to come and help lift his early taters. Said I mid earn a copper. Farthen, I 'low.'

Ken laughed heartily, but sobered as his mother came from the house bearing a plump and pleasing baby.

'Mum,' he said earnestly, 'Johnny wants me to go out. Do I have to push that?'

'Now, Ken,' his mother reproved him, 'you've got five weeks' holiday ...'

The eyes of the two boys met.

'... and I should think you could give up a few minutes to your little sister,' she added fondly.

A look of martyrdom crept over the face of her son.

'Oh, all right then. I dunno why babies were invented,' he said bitterly.

His mother relented. It was his holiday, after all.

'She'll be off to sleep in no time. Once she's sound, you can bring her back and have your walk with Johnny. No getting into mischief, mind.'

'You bet your life,' said Ken, instantly restored to cheerfulness.

He gave his mother a smile so angelic that her heart melted within her. Such a contrast to that loutish Johnny Cossett, who was always scowling and making horrible faces. She wished he would leave Ken alone. Look at him now, in that turtle-necked bottle green sweater, riddled with holes, and with the seat of his trousers half out. Ken looks such a little gentleman up against him, thought Mrs Marsh, as the pram and its attendant cavaliers disappeared from sight.

The baby, true daughter of Eve, was charmed to have two swains instead of one. Johnny's saturnine countenance captivated her, and she cooed and gurgled at him without shame.

'Go to sleep, can't you?' muttered her brother.

The baby crowed delightedly, kicked off her coverings, and waved two fat legs in the air.

'You better go on, Johnny,' said Ken, with manly resignation. 'The young toad isn't going to sleep. Keep awake all day she will, just to spite me.'

'I'll hang around,' said the magnanimous Johnny, adding amazingly, 'she's kinda cute when she smiles.'

Ken looked up in surprise to see Master Cossett, his scowl forgotten, leering at the lady in an imbecile manner, to which she responded by again brandishing her legs in the air.

'Don't make her worse than what she is,' said the shocked brother reprovingly.

Johnny, realizing to what depths of weakness he had been betrayed by feminine wiles, scowled again. The baby cooed drowsily, and her lids gradually hid her blue eyes.

'Shsh!' breathed Ken, walking delicately like Agag.

'She's off,' said Johnny.

Five minutes later, Miss Angela Marsh, still peacefully slumbering, was installed on the patch of lawn, whilst the two boys, free of their shameful burden, lounged away.

'Where we going?' asked Ken.

'Where is there to go in this lousy hole?' asked Johnny, gazing at the smiling countryside around them.

'What about the green? We might get a game of cricket.'

'Naw. Kid's stuff,' said Johnny with disdain. The memory of his overthrow at the fête rankled in his manly breast, and he had no desire to be reminded of it by a meeting with his fellows. Ken had not attended the fête. 'I know,' he said suddenly. 'Corpse Path copse. I got a cattypult.'

'Attaboy!' said the policeman's son. He added, struck by a sudden thought, 'Be pretty muddy, won't it, after last night?'

'Mud? Who cares for mud? Course, if you're afraid o' spoiling your sissy clothes ...'

'Who's got sissy clothes?' demanded Ken, flushing.

Johnny observed that his fist was clenching, and thought discretion the better part of valour.

'I never said you had sissy clothes.'

'Yes, you did.'

'You got me wrong. I never meant you. What I meant was if anyone had sissy clothes, then they mid be afraid of a bit of dirt. If. That's what I meant. See?'

'That's OK then,' said Ken loftily. 'But no-one calls me a sissy without getting a dot on the nose.'

'Sure, sure,' said Johnny hastily. 'Anyway, I got to be on the corner by eleven.'

'What's on?'

'Ice cream. Shows what sort o' hole this is that you can only get ice cream once a wick.'

'I can't do that,' said Ken cheerfully, 'not this week, anyway. Spent all my pocket money.'

'My wold 'ooman coughs up,' said Johnny with a diabolical leer. 'She knows she better. Well, where are we going, anyway?'

'Corpse Path copse, of course. I thought we'd settled that.'

They went on fairly amicably through the village and along the lane. The field track was a quagmire, but Ken, with whom Johnny's remark still rankled, took no heed, and they squelched along, both becoming equally coated with mud.

'Wonder if that crazy guy be in?' said Johnny, pausing to look down on Corpse Path Cottage.

'He is. Can't you hear?' asked Ken.

The rattle of a typewriter was borne clearly to their ears. They listened earnestly.

'What is it?' asked Johnny.

'Typewriter. He's an author, isn't he?'

'Not he,' said Johnny, with conviction. 'He's a tough guy come there to hide. Or else he's bughouse, one or t'other.' he added, fingering his catapult. 'I could put a stone through that winder easy as kiss me hand. Bet that 'ud make un hop.'

Ken was somewhat enamoured of the notion, but recollections of the weight of his father's hand spelt prudence.

'Better not,' he said 'We'd have a job to get out of sight before he copped us.'

'I don't care for he, nor for a dozen like un,' said Johnny loftily. But he put his catapult away.

They were turning towards the wood when a black spaniel shot up the slope from the cottage, barking excitedly.

'Look out,' cried Johnny, turning to run. 'That be his dog.'

'It's all right – he only wants to play,' said Ken, who was fond of dogs. 'Hi, good boy, come here. All right, old man. You don't mind me, do you?'

The spaniel approached warily, sniffed him, approved, and courteously saluted him. The typewriter still sounded from the cottage below.

'Look, he likes me,' said Ken, delightedly fondling the silky head, while Johnny, still at a respectful distance, looked on. 'He can come with us, can't you, old man?'

The spaniel wagged his agreement. Johnny looked doubtful.

'S'pose wold feller comes to look for un?'

'We aren't doing any harm, if he does. This is a right of way, and 'tisn't as if we had bunged a stone through his window. We shall bring the dog back, anyway. I didn't mean to pinch him, did I?'

'OK, OK,' said Johnny resignedly, 'you win. Anyway, he can bring in the game.'

'Rabbits aren't game.'

'Who said anythin' about rabbits?' Johnny patted the pebbles in his pocket. He lowered his voice. 'There mid be a cock pheasant in wood. I've 'eared un.'

'Oh, boy!' said Ken, with shining eyes. He felt himself one with the old time desperadoes of the highway as they squelched on towards the woods. The thought of his father, and his father's hand, he pushed into the background. Policeman's son or no policeman's son, the thrill of the forbidden lured him on.

He said suddenly, 'Look at the dog! He's found something already.'

The spaniel, bounding ahead, had pulled up sharply. He was uttering queer little sounds, half yelp, half whine. The fur on the back of his neck had risen slightly.

'Don't make a noise,' whispered Johnny, excitedly taking the lead. 'He got summat there, no doubt o' that. You'd say he were scared to look at un. He be all of a shake.'

He crept forward with the stealth of a red Indian, Ken following him with his heart thumping. This was something like. Whatever it was had not moved for the dog was still rigid, still making those strange sounds.

'Stay where you be,' whispered Johnny, drawing the lethal weapon from his pocket. 'I can see over un. A-ah!'

Ken was electrified to see his friend spring backwards, turning on

127

him a face from which the healthy colour had been wiped. From the dirty mottled pallor, Johnny's eyes gazed at him with an expression of utter terror which would have made their owner's fortune on the screen.

'What is it?' he asked, with a shiver of apprehension.

The wood was no longer a place for gay adventure. The look on Johnny's face had made him feel small, and suddenly afraid. He wanted to step forward and see for himself, but a strange fascination held him rigid, as the dog was rigid, and as Johnny stood rigidly gazing at him with his back turned to whatever he had seen. So they stood in a strange tableau, until a woodpecker laughed crazily from the wood, and seemed to break the spell.

Ken stepped forward and clutched Johnny's arm. He could feel that it was trembling.

He said, speaking angrily, because of his fear, 'What's the matter with you? Why can't you tell me what you saw?'

Johnny shivered violently, and rubbed the sleeve of the bottle green sweater across his eyes. He swallowed rapidly, in an obvious effort for speech. He said in a small voice, quite unlike his own, "Tis a woman lying in there. I think she be dead.'

CHAPTER XV

JUST BEFORE THE MOMENT when Ken and Johnny had moved forward to stare down at the still figure amongst the crushed bracken, Ralph Grey stopped his car at the field gate, stepped out hastily and limped with all the speed he could muster towards Corpse Path Cottage. He was unshaven and his clothing soiled and crumpled. His eyes were red-rimmed and burning with anger. He looked as if he had not slept that night. Mark, strolling thoughtfully up the path, met him with surprise.

'Morning. Looking for me?' he asked, as Ralph halted.

The other man swallowed. He said thickly, 'Where is she?'

Mark blinked. 'She?'

'Yes, blast you!' Ralph pushed a distorted face close to his. 'Don't stand there and pretend you don't know what I mean. My wife. Where is she?'

'How the devil should I know?'

He stared at the older man, saw his trembling hands and the sweat standing out on his forehead, and felt an unwilling twinge of pity mingling with his anger and surprise. The poor fool was suffering torment, there could be no doubt of that. So Laura was at her tricks again, was she? Lovely Laura, who could so lightly take a man's life and tear it into shreds.

'She has been here before,' said Ralph. 'I know that, and I know there's something between you, so you needn't trouble to deny it.'

'I didn't intend to,' said Mark shortly.

He saw the swift movement, and involuntarily braced himself. His anger was now almost swamped by a kind of sick pity. Ralph had asked for trouble when he married Laura – had acted like a fool, and was now paying for it. But he was not the only one.

He said, not unkindly, 'Hold on to yourself, you fool. Believe it or not, I've no idea what all this is about. Surely …'

A sudden pounding of feet made both men turn. Across the field, splashing through puddles and slipping on patches of mud, tore two boys, a black spaniel racing ahead. The dog came panting to his master's side.

'And what the deuce is wrong with you? Is everyone mad this morning?' demanded Mark, looking from the cringing dog to the distraught faces of the two lads with pardonable exasperation.

The boys, who had pulled up and now stood trying to regain their breath, broke into simultaneous and gasping speech.

'There's a woman—' said Ken.

'By the gate —' said Johnny.

'Dead,' they said together.

There was a pause of stunned incredulity. The two men stood silent and motionless, as if the utterance of that one word had taken from them the power of speech and movement. It was Ralph who broke the silence.

'No,' he said loudly. 'Oh God. No.'

Mark disregarded him. Turning on the two boys, he urgently gripped an arm of each.

'I don't know if this is your idea of a joke—'

'It's true,' said Ken.

Johnny nodded dumbly.

'All the same,' said Mark, still holding them, 'I think we had better see for ourselves.'

'You take your hands off me, then,' said Johnny, in a queer high pitched voice. 'Whadda you want to touch me for? I ain't done nothen. And I aint goin' back there neither, not if you was to pay me for it. Lemme go home. I want my mum.'

With these surprising words, a loud sniffle escaped him and tears gathered in his eyes.

'That's all right – you'll be able to go home,' said Mark. 'Just show us the spot first.'

'It's over here,' said Ken, his own voice shaking slightly. 'By the gate.'

They followed him in a silence broken only by Johnny's rending sniffs.

'The dog found her,' said Ken, in a hushed voice. 'It's in here.'

He moved aside, and the two men who had loved her looked on

what had been Laura Grey.

She lay face downwards with her fair hair darkened by the rain, and by something which matted it above the left ear. One arm was flung clear of the body with fingers outstretched, and a great diamond winking on the third above the platinum wedding ring. She wore gumboots caked with mud, but beneath her transparent mackintosh showed the turquoise dress in which, the previous afternoon, she had drifted across the vicarage lawn.

Mark bent forward, and was pushed aside by a blow so heavy that he staggered and almost fell.

'You damned murderer,' whispered Ralph Grey. 'You killed her. I knew it all the time. Keep away from her. Don't dare to touch her. Laura – Laura ...'

He fell on his knees beside the body, clutching at the limp hand. Holding it, he looked up at Mark and said, quite calmly, 'She's dead. You killed her. I tell you, I knew it all the time.'

'I didn't kill her,' said Mark dully.

Ralph disregarded him. He laid the hand he held gently on the ground, and staggered to his feet.

'I feel so damned ill,' he said. Turning away, he collapsed in a huddled heap on the ground, burying his face in his hands. A shudder shook his body, and another.

With an effort Mark pulled himself together, and spoke to the two staring boys.

'Get the policeman, and tell him to bring a doctor,' he said. 'And hurry.'

'Dad ought to be back from Grange by now,' said Ken. 'I'll get him.'

The two flying figures were out of sight almost before he had finished the sentence. Mark looked at Ralph to see that he was still huddled on the ground, still shivering. He gently touched the hand which Ralph had held. There was no life in it.

He went over to the other man and touched him on the shoulder. Ralph lifted a ravaged face.

'Come to the cottage instead of sitting there. I'll get you a drink. You need one.'

Ralph shook his head. He said in a flat voice, with no sign of anger or emotion, 'She always hated to get wet.'

'She wouldn't know,' said Mark gently.

He understood perfectly the feeling which had prompted the words. To him, also, out of all the pattern of violent death, the shocking thing seemed that one so pampered and luxurious should have been the target of the rain. In a little while the thought of murder and all its surrounding and sordid accompaniments would take its rightful place. For the moment, that one pathetic detail swayed the imagination of both men. Little cause as she had given Mark to pity her, his heart was wrung for Laura Grey, who had hated to get wet.

'Why did you do it?' asked Ralph suddenly. There was still no anger in his voice. It remained flat and dead, as if after that initial outburst, with the realization of his wife's death, all power for emotion had left him. He did not look at Mark as he spoke, but gazed away towards the wood and the thick tracery of green above the fronds of bracken.

'I told you before, I didn't kill her,' said Mark. 'I had no idea that she was here, and I don't know why she came. Why should you think I did it?'

He spoke as one curious for an answer, but the accusation had brought him neither fear nor anger. Ralph's frozen calm might have communicated itself to him, for he spoke as if their conversation were the merest stuff of everyday. Afterwards he was to remember this, and wonder at himself.

'Well, of course, she wouldn't be here,' said Ralph reasonably, 'unless it were to see you. And she would never have slipped away on such a night if you had not some hold over her. I don't know what it was yet, but I shall find out.'

For the first time, and with a definite shock, Mark became conscious of his own position. The quiet voice, so calmly denouncing him, was no longer a mere background to his thoughts, but the shape of things to come. All his reactions had been numbed by the impact of the discovery, but now they rang a warning bell. Innocent men had found themselves suspected before now – for all he knew had paid on the gallows a debt they did not owe. Laura was dead, and Corpse Path Cottage was all too near at hand. Fate had brought him here, innocent as a lamb to the slaughter, and fate, apparently, had not finished with him yet.

'Look here,' he said, speaking urgently. 'I tell you once again that I knew nothing of this. Laura—'

As if the sound of the name had stabbed him back to life, Ralph sprang to his feet, his face suddenly congested with dark colour.

'Laura. Yes. The name comes very easily, doesn't it? What was she to you?'

Mark made no reply, and Ralph lost his final shreds of control. His hands shot out and gripped the other man's throat.

'Now, then,' said a surprised but authoritative voice, 'what's going on here?'

At the critical moment the arm of the law had arrived.

Superintendent White was a large man, so massive of build that his actual height of well over six feet was seldom realized. His face was heavy and highly coloured, in keeping with the slow Dorset drawl of his speech. In his youth a fine figure of a man, he was now running to flesh, but his girth did not prevent him from showing a quite surprising turn of speed when the occasion demanded it, just as the heavy features and slow speech served to mask an equally agile brain. The newly appointed Chief Constable, Sir Henry James, now facing him across the desk in his office, was wondering if the brain were agile enough for the investigations which lay ahead.

He said, his clipped speech contrasting strongly with the Super's measured utterance, 'Right. Let me just run over it to see if I've got the details. Matter of fact, murder is a new angle for me.'

'I'm not all that familiar with it myself, sir,' said the Super. 'It's not an everyday occurrence with us, thank God.'

'No. Well, let me see. Deceased Mrs Laura Grey, twenty-eight, wife of Ralph Grey, God's Blessing Manor, was discovered between 9.30 and ten this morning at the entrance to a small copse beside a right of way locally known as Corpse Path. Appropriate name, by the way,' said Sir Henry, with a short laugh.

'Very, sir,' agreed the Super.

'Yes. Shot through the head by a revolver, the bullet entering just above the left ear. Death must have been practically instantaneous, and occurred between nine and midnight the previous night. Can't they get it any nearer than that?'

'Not from the doctor, no. Further questioning as to the lady's movements should help.'

'Quite. And I know you won't let anything slip in that line. To continue, the body was discovered by two lads on their way to the wood. Coming back across the field they ran into a man named' (the Chief Constable consulted his notes) 'Mark Endicott, who lives in a cottage in the field itself, and was then in conversation with the husband of the deceased.'

'The husband of the deceased,' echoed the Superintendent, in a completely expressionless voice.

The two men looked at one another for a moment, sharp grey eyes holding sleepy brown.

'Does Grey happen to own the cottage?' asked Sir Henry.

The Super shook his head.

'No, sir. It belonged to one of the villagers, a man named Fairfax. He put it up for sale in the early spring, and this Endicott bought it. Nothing to do with Mr Grey at all.'

'I wondered. Rather strange,' said the Chief Constable, drumming thoughtfully on the surface of the desk. 'However. The boys told of their discovery, and the two men accompanied them to the spot where the body was lying. On seeing his wife, Grey struck Endicott, remarking, "You damned murderer, you killed her. I knew it all the time." And what, precisely, do you make of that?'

'Well,' said the Super slowly, 'it might mean anything or nothing.'

'A very profound remark,' murmured the Chief Constable, gazing at the ceiling.

The Super's colour deepened slightly. Of course, it had to be this new man when a thing of this kind broke. With old Colonel Lee you knew where you were – he could listen without damn fool interjections which made a man feel he had talked utter rubbish. Too quick, altogether. You didn't get there any faster in the end by being so smart. He looked at the sharp features of his superior with no sign of the dislike he felt showing in his heavy face.

'I mean to say, sir, the lady was rather remarkably attractive. Not the usual type of farmer's wife at all. Or so I am told.'

'Grey is a gentleman farmer, of course. His family has been in the Manor for generations. But I understand you. You mean that he was jealous?'

'I gather from PC Marsh that he was well known in the village to be madly jealous. His wife was a great deal younger than he, and scarcely the type to be buried in the country. Stagey – a real pin-up girl was the expression the PC used.'

'I have heard that the marriage aroused a good deal of comment. Picked her up in London, didn't he?'

'I believe so, sir. We shall have to go into all that, of course.'

'Yes. And there had been local gossip about her and this Endicott?'

'That's the strange part of it,' said the Super, looking rather pleased. 'There wasn't.'

'No?'

'No. There had been scandal, bags of it, in connection with Laura

Grey and a young bank clerk named Brian Marlowe. As far as I can gather, Endicott had never so much as spoken to her.'

'That's queer, as you say. But Grey must have thought he had some reason, to speak as he did. You don't think the affair with Marlowe was merely a cloak?'

'I doubt it, sir. Pretty difficult, you know, in a village like God's Blessing. And another thing, Endicott didn't arrive in the place until the beginning of April, and Mrs Grey was away for a month after that. It didn't leave much time for anything to work up between them.'

'No, there is that.'

'Besides, he seems to be a peculiar character. Some sort of writer, who goes out very little. The entire village has the fixed idea that he's a man with a past. He comes out of the blue, pays a fancy price, even by modern standards, for a tumbledown shack slap in the middle of a field, and has nothing to do with anyone. At least, that isn't entirely correct. There has been some talk about his being friendly with his nearest neighbour, a Miss Faraday.'

'Living alone?'

'Not now, sir. She did for a spell after her mother died last December, but now she has a lodger – a Miss Morris, who teaches at the village school. Miss Faraday teaches music at Lake Girls' School.'

'Is she young?'

'Fortyish. Typical spinster, very nervous and fluttery, PC Marsh says.'

'He seems to be an observant fellow.'

The Super scented sarcasm, and spoke rather quickly.

'You can't live in a place like God's Blessing without hearing all the details of your neighbour's life.'

'Yes. I wasn't thinking of that. I was wondering why you yourself seem to take such an interest in this fluttering spinster.'

The Super, a just man, gave Sir Henry a high mark for observation.

'I'm interested in everything connected with the case, sir. Naturally,' he said gently. 'But when anonymous letters come into it—'

'A middle aged spinster is your first buy?'

'I wouldn't go so far as to say that. They're not invariably written by spinsters, or even by women. Not by any manner of means. But she can't be left out of our calculations.'

'And I understand Ralph Grey had a letter?'

'Yes, sir. That was what sent him straight to Endicott when he discovered that morning that his wife was missing. He had been up all night himself with a sick cow – he's trying to work up a herd of TT tested Jerseys, and she was a valuable animal – and didn't discover her absence until he got home.'

'He took no notice of this letter at the time he received it?'

'So he says, sir. I think myself it worried him a bit. I imagine he's never been too sure of his wife, and anonymous letters are nasty things, you know, very nasty. They lie fallow, as you might say, for months, but you don't forget them.'

'He didn't, evidently.'

The Chief Constable cleared his throat raspingly. 'Well, that's about as much as you actually know. The scene of the crime didn't help you much, I understand?'

'No, sir. The rain had washed away any footprints. The ground where she was lying was practically a bog.'

'And no sign of a weapon?'

'None, sir. We've searched all around, of course. Her handbag was lying near the body, but nothing else.'

There was a pause. The Super looked down at the large fingers resting on his knee, and the Chief Constable looked at him.

'Well,' said Sir Henry at last.

The Super looked up. A slow smile creased his face.

'That's the question, isn't it, sir?'

The Chief Constable gave a short bark of laughter, and looked across the desk with more approval than he had shown hitherto. The fellow was quick enough on the uptake, it seemed, for all his heaviness of feature and slowness of speech. And his record was good, too, of course. The old man, his predecessor, had spoken most highly of him. But then – the Chief Constable began drumming on the desk again – the Colonel had really been past his work. Far too inclined to leave things in the capable hands of the Super, and hope for the best. And that was all very well in minor cases, but there was nothing minor about this. Murder, with a capital M. Murder of a young and beautiful woman. Quite likely to prove a *crime passionnel*. There would be newspaper headlines screaming all around the country, masses of publicity, and himself newly appointed. And there was this fellow on the other side of the desk, like a large dog placidly awaiting the bone which he knew to be his due.

'Of course,' he said irritably, when the pause had lasted for some minutes, 'I, personally, would prefer that we kept it in our own hands. Naturally.'

'Naturally, sir,' murmured the Super.

'At the same time, if – mind, I say if – outside help is to be called in, now is the time. There should be no delay.'

'Most unfair to turn it over to others once the scent is stale,' agreed the Super dreamily.

The Chief Constable suddenly gave vent to his irritation. He banged his fist on the desk.

'Damn it, man, don't sit there cooing at me! Why the devil can't you speak out and say what you think?'

The Super, seeming neither surprised nor perturbed by this outburst, looked at him but did not speak. The Chief Constable glared back at him. Slowly the colour which anger had brought to his face faded. He sat back in his chair, and his lips twitched.

'You win. Have it your own way,' he said, as if the other had spoken.

'Thank you, sir,' said the Super gently.

'And I only trust you won't give me cause to regret it.'

'So do I, sir, I'm sure,' said the Super.

CHAPTER XVI

THE SUPER PAUSED AT the field gate, leaned his arms along the top bar, and gazed thoughtfully at the path leading to the copse. With the brown tweed coat wrinkled across his powerful shoulders and the placid contentment written on his large face, he might have been a farmer surveying his domain, and unusually conscious that all was well with it. The police car modestly parked a little way down the lane appeared to have no connection with him.

Having viewed the landscape to his own satisfaction, the Super opened the gate and strolled meditatively into the field, observing without surprise that many feet had trodden the path since his last visit. God's Blessing was in the news at last, and somewhat stunned by its own importance. On the previous day, Mr Richards had preached, without pleasure, to a gaping and overflowing congregation, the main part of which, he could not but feel, had entered the church moved by curiosity pure and simple. The Ring and Book had sold out before seven o'clock. Young men with notebooks had appeared from nowhere, scribbled strange hieroglyphics, and disappeared again. But the day of rest had passed, and with the dawning of Monday, the full force of the invasion was checked.

The Super paused, much as Mark had done on the morning of his arrival, to gaze down on Corpse Path Cottage. The front door was closed, and no smoke showed at the chimney. The Super strolled meditatively down the path.

'Looking for me?' said a voice behind him.

He turned without haste to see Mark Endicott with James at his heels. In that first sleepy glance, he saw that the man looked desperately ill, was unshaven, and that a little nervous pulse was twitching incessantly in one brown cheek.

'Mr Endicott? My name is White, Superintendent White, of the Downshire Constabulary. I wondered if I might have a word with you.'

'By all means. It will give your watchdog the chance of a rest, won't it?' He laughed unpleasantly. 'You needn't have gone to so much trouble, you know. I hadn't thought of running away.'

'No, sir. We hadn't supposed it.'

'Oh? Then why set a man to watch the cottage?'

'Watching the cottage was incidental. He was actually keeping an eye on the scene of the crime.'

'Waiting for the criminal to revisit it?' Mark laughed again. 'If so, he got his money's worth. Hundreds to choose from. The whole damned hedge was lined with staring faces yesterday, from morning till night. Cars, cyclists, hikers, all day long they were streaming in. God …'

He put a hand to his face, as if conscious of the twitching there. The hand was shaking.

'They will do it, you know,' said the Super indulgently. 'It's nothing but human nature, after all. Why, I've known a crowd to gather at the spot where a horse had fallen even after it had been taken away. Funny things, crowds. And you see, murder is always a draw.'

He saw Mark flinch at the quietly spoken word, and noted the movement in his patient and retentive mind.

'Yes,' said Mark, in a queer voice. 'I hadn't thought of it like that, but as you say, murder is undoubtedly a draw. Do you know yet who did it?'

'Well, sir,' said the Super placidly. 'Things are falling into place.'

'How nice. And the police are, undoubtedly, working on a clue. Thank you so much for telling me. And now, to end this pleasing conversation and get down to business if you want to question me, hadn't you better come in? And shouldn't there be someone to take notes? Correct me if I'm wrong.'

'Not at the moment, sir. We have your signed statement at the station. I only want information on one or two additional points.'

'No handcuffs?'

'Not as yet, sir,' said the Super, laughing.

'That's a relief. Well, come in, anyway, and get it over. I'm afraid the place is in rather a mess. The woman who cleans it for me has been called away.'

'You're lucky to have anyone these days,' said the Super, stooping his head to follow Mark into the house.

'The gentleman who sold me this palatial residence farms out his housekeeper to me from time to time. Suits me very well.'

'Yes, no doubt.' The Super lowered his bulk to the chair which Mark pushed forward, and looked mildly around him. 'A nice little place you have here, Mr Endicott.'

'And a nice little price I paid for it. Nine hundred, if it interests you.'

'As a matter of fact, it does. I should very much like to know why you were prepared to pay such a high price to come here, if you don't mind telling me. What brought you here, in the first place?'

'A desire for solitude in which to write.'

'Ah! An author,' said the Super, with respect. 'Now that's a thing I could never do, sit down to write a book.'

'No?'

'No. Not that I've ever tried. However. You answered that very clearly, Mr Endicott, if I may say so. How did you hear of the place?'

'I saw an advertisement and got a local solicitor to act for me.'

'I see. And this desire for solitude in which to write was the sole reason for your coming here?'

Mark stiffened. 'That's what I said.'

The Super nodded like a benevolent Buddha.

'That is so. Yes. Now, with regard to the murdered lady, Mrs Laura Grey, on what terms were you with her?'

Mark's face did not change, but the sleepy brown eyes saw that the little pulse was beating violently.

'I had scarcely spoken to her since I came here.'

'On what occasions did you meet?'

Mark hesitated. He said carefully, 'I saw her once at a meeting of the village Literary Society.'

'Yes?'

'We did not speak then. And once we had a short conversation here.'

'Here. The lady came here to see you?'

Mark rubbed his forehead irritably. He felt dizzy and confused. The slow and kindly voice of the Super seemed to have sounded in his ears for hours. You're in a spot, my lad, he told himself, and looked up to meet the Super's speculative gaze.

'She was walking. We happened to meet.'

'Yes.' The Super took a sheaf of typewritten notes from his pocket and consulted them. 'Would it surprise you to know, Mr Endicott, that there was a witness to that meeting?'

'Well, I'm damned,' said Mark helplessly.

For a moment the room faded. With the utmost clarity he saw Laura's face, white against the drooping lilac as he returned from a fruitless search that sun drenched afternoon. He had told her not to worry – that there was no-one there, and all the time he had been wrong. Or was he so wrong, after all? It was, indeed, not Laura's worry, since once again she had gone out of reach of it all, leaving others to pay the piper. He began to laugh.

'Pull yourself together, Mr Endicott.' The voice of the Super was sleepy no longer.

'Sorry,' gasped Mark, regaining control. He said in his normal voice, 'Was it the husband?'

'Who saw you? Oh, no. Mr Grey received an anonymous letter telling him his wife had been here.'

'Another!' said Mark involuntarily.

'What do you mean by that, Mr Endicott?'

'Exactly what you are thinking. That I received one also – or rather, two.'

'You kept them?'

'The second one. The first I burnt.'

'I should like to see it, if I may.'

Mark frowned. 'Why? I don't think it has any bearing on the matter.'

'I'll be the judge of that, Mr Endicott, if you don't mind.'

'Oh, very well,' said Mark.

As he pulled the flimsy sheet from his notecase and handed it over, he was conscious of nothing more than an engulfing weariness. The letter, with what the Super was bound to read into it, could only land him deeper in the mire, but what did it matter, after all? Innocent men, it was to be hoped, were seldom hanged, though it certainly seemed that a malicious fate was heavily weighting the dice against him.

The Super had unfolded the letter and was deliberately reading it, his face expressionless. After what seemed a long time, he looked up.

'Have you any idea who wrote this?'

'None.'

'You see, of course, what it implies?'

Mark's grey face twisted in the ghost of a smile.

'Give me credit for at least sufficient intelligence for that, Superintendent. I realize that you have now been told that I knew Laura before.'

'I had already gathered that,' said the Super surprisingly. 'No – what I mean is that someone who had known you previously also knew that you had come here.'

He looked again at the letter in his hand, and slowly read sentences aloud.

'*Why the hell did you come here if you haven't the guts to get cracking?* ... um, um, more mere abuse ... *like to see her with him under your very nose* ... um, um ... *call yourself a man.*'

He looked up, the brown eyes suddenly keen. 'What was in the one you burnt?'

'Apart from the frills, something like this: *So you've come sniffing after her again, have you? Think she is as lovely as ever? Others do, if you don't. Better get going, hadn't you?*'

The Super slapped his thigh. 'Don't you see how that narrows the field? Can't you get the writer now?'

Mark shook his head. 'Don't get so excited, you needn't think I haven't tried. None of the villagers knew me before, none of my old crowd knew I was coming here. I wanted to cut myself off. I assure you, Superintendent, it's no good. And I can't see why you're fussing over it. After all, you're supposed to be investigating a murder.'

'I am, indeed, Mr Endicott. So you can't understand? Oh well, never mind. We'll leave it for the moment. You have admitted that you knew Mrs Grey before coming here. How long before?'

'We met in the summer of 1940,' said Mark carefully 'I was on leave. Then I was sent overseas, and later taken prisoner in Malaya. That disposed of me for quite a while. When I returned home she had disappeared.'

'And you heard nothing of her?'

'She had left a letter with a friend of mine.' Mark stared out of the window. 'She said her ... feelings for me had changed. It was over.'

'I see. But you had other ideas. You traced her and came here—'

Mark sprang to his feet, pushing back his chair with a crash. Resting his hands on the table, he pushed his face close to the unmoved countenance of the other man.

'Yes, you were bound to think that, weren't you? It makes it all so simple – so neatly rounded off. I've seen it coming all the time. If I weren't a damned fool I should have burnt that letter too. Because it isn't true. Whatever it looks like, it isn't true. It's been the most damnable filthy trick that fate could play on a man.' His voice rose. 'I follow Laura – I come here in search of her? I tell you, it was the last thing on earth I wanted. If I had known she was here, I would have cut my hand off before I signed the cheque for the place. But of course you won't believe me – no-one would believe such a tale—'

He broke off suddenly, and groped behind him for his chair. Sinking into it, he said indistinctly, 'Sorry. Made a bawling fool of myself. Of course I can't make you understand.'

'You needn't be too sure of that, Mr Endicott,' said the Super gravely.

He rose slowly, and walked to the window, his broad figure almost blotting out the light. In all his efficient painstaking days as a policeman, he had never been able to remain entirely untroubled by compassion. Not that he ever allowed it to affect his work. From farm worker to constable, constable to sergeant – sergeant, inspector, superintendent, he had travelled the hard way. He might, and did feel pity for the tormented creature he was questioning, but he was after the truth, and the truth he would have, since to discover it was his job. It was just as simple as that.

'Do you mean to say,' said Mark's voice from behind him, 'that you're prepared to take my word for it that I didn't know Laura had come here?'

'I have no reason to doubt your word, Mr Endicott,' said the Super gravely, 'as yet!'

He turned as he spoke and looked directly at the other man. Mark stared back, at first with resentment, then with a faint smile.

'All things considered, fair enough,' he said.

The Super smiled solemnly back. He returned to his chair and sat down, crossing one large leg over the other.

'Well, now, let's have a recap, as they say. You met Mrs Grey in 1940, you fell in love, you returned at the end of the war to find that she had left you. I take it you made some effort to find her?'

'Only once. I ... couldn't believe the letter, at first. I went to a theatrical agent we'd both known. He said Laura had left the Repertory Company, and as far as he knew given up the stage for good. There was a rumour, he said, that she had married, but where she was he had no idea. There had been a spot of trouble.'

'What sort of trouble?' asked the Super, rather quickly.

'Need we go into that? I don't know the rights of it, or even if it was true.'

'I should like to hear it, all the same, Mr Endicott.'

Mark frowned. He said reluctantly, 'According to him there was some scandal about Laura and the leading man. Laura was enough to turn any man's head – if you'd ever seen her as she was, you'd know that – and he said she drove this bloke Arbuthnot completely crackers. He had a wife, too, in the company – quiet little woman who played minor parts – but she hadn't a look-in once Laura came along. Anyhow, it seems that Arbuthnot took an overdose of sleeping tablets one night, and was found dead.'

The Super looked up.

'Accidental death. No blame to anyone. But there was, it seemed, a good deal of feeling against Laura in theatrical circles. People thought that she had led the poor devil on and let him down with a pretty considerable bump. It was rather a habit of hers. Once she'd got a thing, she didn't care about it anymore. Anyway, she left, as I told you, presumably already having this Grey on a string, and that was the end of that. And what the devil it all has to do with this business—'

'You never can tell,' said the Super thoughtfully. 'I find it interesting. Very. What became of the widow?'

'God knows. I imagine she stayed with the company, but I certainly didn't ask about her.'

'No. Of course not,' said the Super absently. In his mind he was building a picture, with the figure of Laura Grey for centrepiece. Laura Grey's husband, the man now facing him, the unhappy Arbuthnot, and, if local gossip were to be trusted, Brian Marlowe, all caught in the net of the blonde beauty. Femme fatale, said the Super to himself, and felt a certain pride at his own turn of phrase.

'You're a peculiar fellow,' observed Mark, looking at him with curiosity.

'In what way, Mr Endicott?'

'You go delving into the murky past, and leave the present to take care of itself. What about my movements at the time of the crime?'

'All in due course, sir. We have your statement, you know. And the past has a good deal of bearing on the present, one way and another. Shall we go on?'

'By all means,' said Mark wearily.

'After this meeting with the theatrical agent (I'd like his name and address later, by the way, and the name of the Repertory Company you mentioned) you made no further attempt to trace the lady?'

'None. I've already told you that. Strange though it may seem, I didn't want my nose rubbed in it again. She made it abundantly clear that she wanted none of me, and that, as far as I was concerned, was that.'

'Very wise. You simply put her out of your mind.'

Mark scowled. 'I don't know what you're getting at ...'

'The truth, I hope, Mr Endicott. Nothing but the truth.'

'Well, if you had known her you'd realize it wasn't so simple as that. I thought coming here would help.'

'And you discovered her here. How soon would that be?'

Mark considered. His head was aching violently, and the father confessor opposite him seemed bent on drawing every detail into the light of day. All the same, the discovery of the compact might surely be omitted.

He said, choosing his words with care, 'I came here at the beginning of April. I didn't know – that is, I wasn't certain – until the end of May.'

'But you suspected her identity before that? Why?'

'The first evening I was here a woman passed me, coming from the wood. Her perfume – something about her – reminded me of Laura, but I wasn't sure. I couldn't see her face.'

'And how did you feel about it?'

'How do you think?' snarled Mark.

'I'm asking you, Mr Endicott.'

'Naturally a trifle annoyed. Furious in fact. Not murderous, if that's what you're getting at.'

'And you became certain of her identity …?'

'At a meeting of the Literary Society. She was there with her … husband,' said Mark, with a queer hesitation before the final word.

'Did you have any conversation?'

'No. Soon after I arrived they left. It seemed the lady felt unwell.'

'I see. And then you met here. As friends?'

'Not precisely. We didn't come to blows.'

'What was her motive in coming to you?'

'She wanted to make sure that I had no intention of spilling the beans. I told her my opinion of her behaviour and general character, but I gave her the promise she wanted. I told you, she got what she wanted, as a rule.'

The Super, remembering the figure he had seen at the entrance to the wood, thought this remark in doubtful taste. His voice held a hint of reproach, like a father with an erring son, as he continued.

'In what state of mind did she seem to be?'

'I thought her unusually nervous. But that was to be expected.'

'Nervous? Of you, or of her husband?'

'She certainly wasn't afraid of me,' said Mark, with a short laugh.

'No. I understand. Well, Mr Endicott, you have been very patient – very. I'm afraid the next question is a personal one.'

'Don't mind me,' said Mark resignedly.

'You have spoken of your relations with the lady. What, precisely, were they?'

Mark conquered a wild desire to reply, in the accents of Mr Claude Dampier, 'You'll never guess!' Though he said in a completely expressionless voice, 'Do I have to answer that?'

'Not unless you wish, sir. But—'

'But if I don't, you'll find out? I believe you!' He drew a deep breath and sat back in his chair. 'She was my wife.'

CHAPTER XVII

THE INQUEST ON LAURA Grey was held in blazing heat in the village hall, where she had once turned in her seat to see Mark Endicott's gaze upon her. Today it was packed to suffocation point and the coroner, a solicitor named Thomson, from Lake, looked at the massed avid faces with no friendly eye. Fresh air was a fetish of his, and though every window that could be opened stood wide, even at the beginning of the proceedings, the atmosphere was stifling. The roof of corrugated iron seemed to attract the sun's rays like a burning glass. Mr Cossett, amongst his fellow jurymen, sweated unhappily in a tight collar, and the patriarchal countenance of Mr Fairfax was bedewed with drops. In the heavy air, excited anticipation hung like a tangible thing.

The Super recognized it, and knew, with some satisfaction, that it was doomed to be unsatisfied. Mr Thomson was a trustworthy coroner, who would make no trouble, and cared for ghouls and sensation-mongers no more than the Super himself; a good thing for them to be sent empty away. And as for the reporters, their day would come. This was merely a necessary evil – a stepping stone on the road to the real business. Make haste slowly was a good enough proverb, always providing that one got there in the end. The Super thought that he would.

He sat with his heavy lids deceptively downcast, very observant of every participant in this little drama. He saw the three men who had been connected with Laura Grey, and thought that the woman who, in life, had been able to make them suffer, was still not powerless to afflict. Ralph Grey looked an old man, bowed down by grief; across the room. Endicott's face was grimly set as if he, like the Super, was fully conscious of the glances, all curious, many hostile, sent in his direction.

A little behind him the fair head of Brian Marlowe showed above its fellows. A good looking boy, if you liked the pansy type, but his looks just now were marred by lines of incredulous pain, as if he could not believe it possible that life should use him so ill. A dark haired girl at the end of the row was watching him; once Marlowe turned, caught her eye, and smiled. There was a slight pause before the girl smiled briefly back.

Queer, thought the Super. Most girls would be glad enough to receive a smile from Master Marlowe, even if he had been philandering with pretty ladies. And the girl looked almost as worn and haggard as the young man himself.

That was Miss Faraday sitting next to her. On information given him by Endicott, the Super had interviewed her on the matter of anonymous letters. She had let him see them without hesitation – had, indeed, seemed anxious only to help. Same type of printing, same green ink, same rubbishy paper. The letters intrigued the Super, not that, as anonymous communications, there was anything remarkable about them. He had seen many such in his time. The point was that by the pricking of his thumbs, he was convinced that the letters had some connection with his investigations. This conviction he had imparted to none as yet. He had no intention of doing so until he had something tangible to offer.

He looked across at Miss Faraday again, somewhat puzzled. Since his interview with her, the little woman had changed. He recalled a colourless, shrinking creature, all nerves and flutter, and here she was sitting as upright as a grenadier, and with a brilliant colour in her cheeks. Make up? No, natural, he would swear; and as he watched, he saw her lean forward in her chair and flash Endicott a smile so vivid that it transfigured her. Endicott nodded, not smiling, but with a definite softening of his grim face. The nudges of those around made a visible stir in the body of the hall.

Oho, thought the Super, considerably surprised, so that's it. Some doubt as to Endicott's feelings, none at all as to the lady's. And that would account for the letter she received – that brought another piece of the puzzle sliding neatly into place. The Super's brain worked furiously, and the opening proceedings passed merely as a background to his thoughts.

When he came back to the surface, PC Marsh was on his feet. The Super looked at his straight back with approval. The country Bobby, target for comedians, writers, humourists, there he stood in person, giving his evidence nervously, but clearly and well, speaking like a

148

Dorset man (and why shouldn't he?) but showing that he had done his job to the best of his ability.

The coroner, an experienced skater, moved swiftly over thin ice. The presence of Mark and Ralph beside the body was mentioned but without detail, to the obvious disgust of many listeners, Mrs Cossett in particular. That was to be expected; it was bound to get around. Marsh, presumably, had sense enough to hold his tongue and to make his son do the same; the other boy was a different matter. The Super recalled an interview with Johnny, in the course of which the youth had alternately whined, boasted, and attempted to wisecrack. The brooding maternal presence at his side had restricted the Super; nowadays, he reflected sadly, you daren't so much as look at the young varmints, when a clip over the ear would do untold good, and cost nothing. And how much the better were they for all the coddling? Even now the palm of the Super's hand itched at the recollection of Johnny's sneer.

The Police Doctor followed Marsh. He was a tall sandy Scot, with a disillusioned eye, and he rattled off his information amidst rolling Rs as if he were anxious to be done with it. The bullet, from a Smith and Wesson revolver, had entered just above the left ear – powder marks showed that it had been fired at extremely close quarters – death would be instantaneous. The doctor, with a glint in his eye, here broke into a spate of technicalities which left the main part of his audience mentally gaping.

'Yes,' said the coroner meekly, as he paused. 'I'm sure that is very clear to us all.'

The doctor gave an incredulous smile.

The coroner consulted his notes.

'Were there any other marks on the body, Doctor?'

'A certain bruising of the wrists, especially the right.'

'Have you any theory as to the cause of these?'

'I should say a struggle. In one place there was slight laceration of the skin, as if by fingernails.'

A ripple of satisfaction stirred the hall. This, the faces seemed to imply, was something like. The reporters scribbled busily. The coroner made a note.

'What do you estimate to be the time of death?'

The doctor drew a deep breath and again became technical. Having spoken for some time he paused, and said abruptly, 'Between nine and twelve that night.'

The coroner thanked him and he stepped solemnly down, giving the

Super the ghost of a wink as he passed. The coroner cleared his throat, shuffled his papers rather nervously, and called Ralph Grey.

As Ralph limped up, a buzz of comment began. Mr Thomson leaned foward, flushing with anger.

'If there is any noise whatsoever,' he said, 'I shall clear the hall. This is not a place of entertainment. I shall give you no further warning.'

The hush was instantaneous and complete. Ralph stood with the light of the window full on his ravaged face. Poor devil, thought the Super, recalling his reception of the news that Laura had never been his legal wife. He had taken it calmly enough; one shock, the Super supposed, had served to cancel the other. He had shown no further animosity towards Endicott, and very little emotion of any kind. Laura, who had done this to him, was dead; it seemed that his own feelings were dead also. He had appeared faintly relieved when told that the fact of the previous marriage need not be brought out at the inquest, otherwise it was as if nothing could touch him deeply any more.

The coroner handled him very gently and, having given evidence of identification, Ralph continued in a low voice, but without faltering. He had received word while at the Garden Fête of the illness of a pedigree cow – he had sat up with it through the night, discovering his wife's absence on returning home in the morning. He had then gone in search of her—

'You went to a Mr Endicott, living at Corpse Path Cottage?'

'Yes.'

'He was a friend of your wife's?'

'To my knowledge they had never met.'

Mr Thomson cleared his throat. 'In that case, Mr Grey, perhaps you would tell us why you went to him?'

Ralph hesitated. The coroner waited patiently. The silence which he had demanded was still complete.

'I had received a letter,' said Ralph at last, 'coupling the name of Mr Endicott with that of my wife.'

There was no sound or movement, yet the Super received the distinct impression that a collective sigh of satisfaction had been heaved. Something for them to chew on at last. The dark haired girl beside Miss Faraday was frowning; young Marlowe had coloured darkly. The Super stored it up for future reference.

'I see. The letter was unsigned?'

'Yes. At the time I ignored it,' said Ralph. 'When I found my wife was missing I recalled it.' He added, half apologetically, 'I was extremely tired and anxious at the time – scarcely myself, in fact.'

'That is very understandable. And Mr Endicott was unable to help you?'

'He was unable to help me,' Ralph agreed.

The faintest buzz, instantly checked, rose from the body of the hall. The coroner, with a momentary glance at the Super's watchful face, left Endicott, and took Ralph through the discovery of the body swiftly enough before asking a different question.

'Have you in your possession a Smith and Wesson revolver?'

'I had,' said Ralph.

'It has gone?'

'I kept it in a drawer of my desk. On the day when my wife's body was found I went to the drawer. The revolver was not there.'

'Oh. Was it kept loaded?'

'Yes.'

'The desk was locked?'

'Not that particular drawer.'

'Would your wife know of the presence of a revolver?'

'Yes. She often teased me about it, saying that it was time I realized the war was over. She knew that I originally kept it loaded in the days of the invasion scare.'

Here there was a movement amongst the jurymen. The coroner turned to them enquiringly. Mr Cossett rose.

'We should like to ask what people was able to go to that there desk?'

Ralph considered. 'Theoretically, anyone who went into the room. Actually, being a kind of office, it was scarcely entered except for myself, and for the maid who cleaned it.'

Mr Cossett grunted, and sat down. Ralph was dismissed, and Mark Endicott called. Amy clasped her hands in her lap so tightly that the knuckles shone white.

Mark admitted his identity and his ownership of Corpse Path Cottage. His tone was curt and his attitude rather defiant. The reporters began to scribble furiously again, and every eye was fixed on his untidy figure. Mr Thomson took him with the utmost delicacy through the events of the morning of the discovery, handling him with care and respect, like an unexploded bomb. No mention was made of Ralph's accusation. Mrs Cossett nudged her neighbour fiercely, and swelled with wrath.

'This letter received by Mr Grey – was there any justification for it?'

'Since my arrival at God's Blessing,' said Mark, in a measured tone, 'I had spoken to Mrs Grey on one occasion only, outside my cottage.'

Mr Thomson nodded, and passed hastily on. A reporter glanced at one of his fellows with raised brows.

'What were your movements on the evening of 26th July?'

'I returned from the fête at about seven. I worked for a couple of hours and took my dog for a run. There was a heavy storm, and as I was passing the house of Miss Faraday, my neighbour, I called. She very kindly allowed us to shelter in her porch.'

Every eye turned to Miss Faraday, who sat with burning cheeks but with her head held high.

'What time did you leave?'

'Somewhere about ten. There was a slight lull, I ran back to my cottage, worked for another hour or so, and went to bed.'

'Thank you. Your cottage is the nearest dwelling, is it not, to the spot where the body was found?'

Mark agreed curtly.

'Did you, at any time that night, hear the sound of a shot?'

'I did not. But that is easily accounted for.'

'You mean by the thunderstorm?'

'Ah! A real twister. Wust we've aknowed in God's Blessing since 1903,' observed a juryman, for the moment forgetting himself.

There was a faint titter, instantly quelled by Mr Thomson's icy stare. Mark was dismissed, and Amy Dora Faraday took his place. The Super again took note of the change in her, and thought what strange creatures women were.

Amy gave her evidence in a voice which shook slightly, but which was clearly heard at the back of the hall. She had returned from the Garden Fête in company with Mr Endicott, reaching home just after seven. They had parted at her gate, Mr Endicott remarking that he had work to do, after which his dog, which had been shut in, would need a run. She herself had sat down to read but had been troubled by the approaching storm. It was very close indoors, and she had stood for a while in the porch. When the rain began and she saw Mr Endicott passing with his dog, she had called to offer him shelter.

'I see. And he remained with you, how long?'

'I looked at the clock when he had gone. It was then a quarter past ten.'

'Thank you, Miss Faraday. And you, like Mr Endicott, heard no sound of a shot?'

'I heard nothing but the thunder and the rain,' said Amy. She stepped down, her colour still vivid, and took her seat beside Dinah, who squeezed her hand. Amy looked at her with surprise and gratitude. She prayed that she had said nothing wrong – she would do anything, anything, she thought incoherently. Her first sight of Endicott's face that day had rent her bosom with an almost maternal pang. He must have been hurt most cruelly to look like that.

Brian Marlowe, in a subdued voice, said that he had found Mrs Grey resting inside the vicarage when he arrived at the fête. That was just before seven o'clock. She told him that her husband had been called away. He – Brian – offered to drive her home, and she accepted.

'Did she appear to be in her usual spirits?'

'I thought her a little nervous. She said the thunder had made her head ache, and that she intended to take some aspirins and lie down.'

'Did you go into the Manor with her?'

'No. I went home, and soon after ten, hearing the rain, I drove back to the vicarage and picked up Miss Morris, who was playing for the dancing. I drove her home, went back myself, and to bed.'

'I see. In her conversation with you, did Mrs Grey give you any idea that she might be going out again that night?'

'No, sir. She said that she was going to lie down. And it was not a night to tempt anyone out.'

'Thank you, Mr Marlowe. I think that will be all.'

There was no further food for the sensation hunters. The maid was called, and said that she had been given the evening off to go to the fête and went straight to bed when she returned. Expert evidence was given as to the type of bullet which had ended Laura Grey's life. The coroner, still treading decorously along the straight and narrow path outlined for him, addressed the jury. The proceedings closed with a verdict of murder by some person or persons unknown. Disgust and dissatisfaction was writ large on many faces. The Superintendent smiled.

CHAPTER XVIII

ENDICOTT, TURNING TO FOLLOW the muttering crowd making its slow way towards the door, felt a hand on his shoulder and turned, with a violent start. The Super looked at him mildly.

'Did I give you a start, Mr Endicott? I'm sorry.'

'What do you want now?' asked Mark rudely.

'Come over here for a moment, sir, if you don't mind. I should be glad of a word with you, once I've got rid of these reporters. I'm not too good at dealing with them, not being used to more than the local men, in general.'

Mark followed the broad figure unwillingly enough. He had reached the stage when he looked on his fellowmen with a deep loathing, and longed only for solitude. This fellow, now, burbling away with his bedside manner turned full on – what was at the back of his desire for yet another word with himself? Surely not a euphemism for an imminent arrest? Mark believed that he would take out his handcuffs without any alteration in the placidity of his manner. He rubbed his nose irritably. Since the discovery of Laura's death, he had scarcely slept, and such food as he had taken had done him little good. Mrs Shergold was still away, or, at least had not condescended to put in an appearance, and he was in no mood to fuss over preparing meals for himself. An acute dyspepsia, relic of those days in a Japanese prison camp, added to the blackness of his mood. He was a suspected man, was he? Let them suspect, and be damned to them. It was all part and parcel of the way life had dealt with him since the moment he opened Laura's letter; or before that, dating back to the day he first set eyes on her, and was completely lost. Laura; the pain swept him yet again, so that he forgot

154

his own position, his fruitless resentment against fate, and knew only the poignant sense of loss. Those long days and nights in Changi gaol he had lived only for the time when they could meet again had, in fact, refused to die as so many had around him, slipping almost thankfully from a life which held no savour any more. It might have been better for him had he joined their company; only, with memories of those hours after the rushed and secret marriage he had not. And he had returned to England to find awaiting him those few lines, with empty phrases of regret to show him the magnitude of his folly.

And, after all, once the first shock had passed, he had not behaved too badly. He could look back on his behaviour, even now, with a faint satisfaction. The stinging humiliation of his betrayal had, at least, helped to bring pride to his aid. He had been fooled, like many a better man, most grievously used, but he would not sit down to whine over his folly. Neither would he go in search of a woman who did not want him. He was not completely penniless, though Laura had done well enough out of him in the course of their time together, and there was always work. Work, and new surroundings. Corpse Path Cottage had seemed the answer to all his problems. And the road to Corpse Path Cottage had brought him back to Laura, and to this.

He looked around him to see that the hall was now practically cleared. The little Faraday had gone, of course, with the rest, probably cursing the limelight which her association with himself had brought upon her. Though she had spoken up well, and had given him a pretty enough smile for all the staring eyes to see. The rabbit could show spirit at times, and it was something to know that even one person was on your side.

PC Marsh was standing by the door, looking younger and less important with his helmet in his hand. Queer that his boy should have been one of the two to discover Laura – and to hear Ralph Grey's immediate reaction. Straight from the horse's mouth – queer, too, that it had not been brought out at the inquest. A good sign, or not? Only the Super knew. A decent enough fellow he seemed, painstaking and fair, but you never could tell. He was out to get a conviction, naturally. Mark looked across to the spot where the Super was patiently dealing with a group of reporters, his monumental calm unshaken.

'This anonymous letter business, Super – poison pen in a peaceful village – any lead there?'

'We're working on it, naturally. I'd be grateful if you didn't headline it too much as yet.'

'Making bricks without straw to write up anything after an inquest like this,' said a gentleman in a very dirty raincoat, closing his notebook with a snap. 'I'm sure I don't know why I left my little home for Fleet Street. Had the coroner well and truly in his place, didn't you, Super? All most remarkable for what was left unsaid.'

'That's as may be,' replied the Super, unruffled. 'And as to making bricks without straw, as soon as I'm in the position to give you any straw, I promise I'll do so. Fair enough?'

'Fair enough,' they admitted sadly, and drifted away. The Super turned to Endicott.

'Sorry to keep you, sir, but they're very persistent.'

'What are you going to do – arrest me?'

'Not at the moment, sir.' The Super chuckled indulgently, as if to say that Mark would have his little joke. 'I only wondered if you would care for a lift back to the cottage.'

Mark gave him a hard stare.

'Very nicely put, I'm sure. I take it that what you actually mean is that you're keeping me under observation.'

The Super gave him a look of dignified reproof.

'I wish you wouldn't put words into my mouth, Mr Endicott. That wasn't my meaning. Naturally we shall keep in touch with you until this affair is cleared up.'

'You think it will be cleared up?'

'Oh, yes,' said the Super gently. 'I think so. In time. But I assure you that the lift was offered for your sake, and not for that of my investigations.'

Mark flushed darkly. 'You mean …?'

'I mean that there's a certain amount of local feeling against you, Mr Endicott. It's to be expected, really, and you needn't take it too hard. You see, they're what they are, and you're what they call a foreigner. Added to that, it seems you made some rather foolish remarks on the bus, which have been remembered, and probably magnified to use against you, and now this murder happens almost on your doorstep, so to speak …'

'Very unfortunate, wasn't it? I should have planned it better. All the same,' said Endicott savagely, 'I don't fancy I stand in need of police protection just yet.'

'I wasn't suggesting that you did. This isn't a mob, you know – only a crowd of villagers, very excited by recent events, who may have taken a notion against you. There might be a few remarks and unfriendly looks which I thought you might prefer to avoid. That's all.'

Mark smiled suddenly. 'Thank you. Super, I don't know what this touching care for my well being implies, but it's very good of you. Sorry I was terse.'

'That's all right. Quite understandable, I'm sure. Are we ready, then? The car's outside.'

'As I said, it's very good of you,' repeated Mark. 'All the same, if you don't mind, I think I'll walk.'

The Super looked at him steadily, without sign of anger or reproof.

'It's up to you, sir,' he said.

When Amy, with Dinah, left the hall, her colour was still burning brightly. Looking at her, and in the midst of her own preoccupations, Dinah was as conscious of the change in her as the Super had been. Why, despite an, as always, deplorable hat, the little creature was almost pretty. Strange that it should have taken a murder to shake her from the drab anonymity which had enfolded her for so long. Though that, reflected Dinah, was hardly fair, it was not the fact of the murder which had changed Amy, but that all her loyalty had been roused in defence of the grim faced Endicott. Rather pathetic, really – the first man to take notice of her, and he could bring to life all this. And he would need all the loyalty he could get, too.

She looked at the waiting, whispering groups outside the doorway with a little chill at her heart. Endicott, whatever he might mean to her surprising housemate, was little more than a name to herself, but from childhood she had known a horror of crowds. A book containing a mob chase, a film with a lynching sequence even now had power to trouble her through sleepless hours of the night. This was no mob, she told herself, unconsciously echoing the Super's words; only a group of country folk, quiet, decent, but just now shaken from the even tenor of their way, waiting for the 'furriner' – the stranger within their gates. One would think that his name, and no other, had been coupled with that of the dead woman. After all, she felt the chill, the sensation of coming evil again, but this time it was not due to the crowd.

She had asked herself the question so many times since the moment when the news had first reached her. Once again it beat its way through her weary brain. Why, why, why, had Brian, who had wanted none of her for so long, Brian, who had loved Laura Grey, or had been bewitched by her – why must he needs choose that evening, of all others, to come in search of herself? And what had made him look so strangely stricken, so utterly unlike himself?

She hated herself, but this insidious thought had made a home with her, and once there could not be dislodged. Could it be possible that she herself had been used as a covering for Brian's movements? If Laura had been killed, as seemed possible, before ten, suspicion would surely be diverted from the man who had come to drive another girl home just after the hour. It was not possible, it would be too horrible, she told herself, almost more horrible than the murder itself. She hated herself for thinking of it, but it all came back to the same weary question: why had Brian looked as he had that night?

A hand touched her arm. With a violent start she looked up into the face of the man who was troubling her thoughts.

'I wanted to see you,' said Brian.

Dinah found that her mouth was dry. As always, whatever reason she had to mistrust him, his nearness had power to affect her, however she might despise herself for the weakness.

She said, rather coldly, 'Well, here I am.'

He glanced around him, his lip curling with disgust.

'Do you suggest a conversation here, amidst this pleasing crowd of harpies, with their ears flapping in the breeze? Thank you so much.'

This sounded so like the old superior Brian that she was vaguely comforted.

'Why don't you walk on together?' suggested Miss Faraday.

Dinah, who had entirely forgotten her, turned in surprise.

'What are you doing?'

'I'm waiting,' said Amy briefly, with the light of battle in her eye.

'Oh, I see,' said Dinah doubtfully. 'Then I think I had better wait with you. I can see Brian later.'

She had suddenly become uncomfortably conscious of the glances cast at the small champion of the oppressed, and could guess the subject matter of the muttered remarks. Alone with the feller until after ten at night – ought to be ashamed of herself, no fool like an old fool, more in it than met the eye …

'You go on. You needn't worry about me,' said Amy.

Dinah marvelled yet again. She said reluctantly, 'Very well. We'll go as far as the corner, and wait for you there.'

'Yes, do,' agreed Amy absently, her eyes fixed on the door through which Mark Endicott must emerge.

'I feel I ought to stay with her,' repeated Dinah as she and her companion moved away.

'Why? She told you to go, and surely she's old enough to take care of herself.'

'That's a pretty foul tone to take,' said Dinah crossly.

'Sorry. As I may have mentioned before, I quite realize that you don't like anything about me. Entirely my own fault, of course. Only that doesn't stop it from hurting.'

His voice broke suddenly. He turned away from her, laying his arms along the top of the gate, as if his interest was in the sleek brown cows contentedly going about the business of their day. The sun made a dappled pattern through the leaves of a solitary oak just inside the gate. Away from the buzz outside the hall, it was very still.

'What did you want to say to me, Brian?' asked Dinah. Her voice sounded coldly repressive in her own ears. She was torn between pity and fear – pity for Brian who, whatever he had or had not done was certainly suffering now, and fear lest that monstrous suspicion of hers should prove to be founded in fact. Oh God, prayed Dinah, don't let it be that. Not that. I couldn't bear it.

Brian had turned as she spoke, looking down at her as she stood with the sunlight on her dark head. He looked rather puzzled.

He said gently, 'What's wrong, Dinah?'

The note of sympathy was her undoing. Her face twisted suddenly, like that of an angry baby. Enormous tears welled into her eyes.

'Oh, I say,' said Brian, who had never seen her cry.

Dinah found, quite naturally, that her face was pressed against his coat, and his arms around her. For a luxurious moment she sobbed whole-heartedly, finding an actual pleasure in giving way at last.

'Is it because of me?' asked Brian above her tumbled head. 'Don't cry, Dinah. I'm no good ...'

She lifted her head, and pulled herself away, mopping fiercely at her disfigured face. She said bitterly, 'Here we go again.'

'What do you mean?'

'I mean I'm sick of hearing you pity yourself. All that's done – let it go. You make me tired, Brian.'

There was a pause. Dinah, who knew well enough what grief could do to her countenance, kept it steadily averted. Brian was probably now too furious with her for words; after all, it was rather much to howl all over a person and then accuse him of self pity. Oh dear, she thought, I'm all muddled up.

She said, apprehensively, 'You still haven't told me what you wanted me for.'

'I'm half afraid to say anything, after those few kind words,' said Brian. He sounded faintly amused. 'Oh, don't apologize – quite justified, no doubt. I only wanted to tell you I was sorry.'

'Sorry?' echoed Dinah, catching her breath on the ghost of a sob.

'For the way I behaved to you. It was unforgivable. I knew it all along, I suppose, but I only realized it fully the other night.'

Dinah forgot that her face would be best hidden. She looked straight at him, her swollen eyes burning.

'Which night?' she whispered.

Brian started. He looked at her in surprise.

She said, still in a whisper, 'Would it be the night that Laura Grey ... died?'

At once she knew with a cold certainty that she had voiced her dread as clearly as if she had put it into words. She saw Brian stiffen, and his blue eyes grew dark. He looked as if he had never seen her before. She tried to speak, to break the silence which was dragging on and on, but for the life of her could not find words.

'I suppose I deserved that,' said Brian at last, in a completely expressionless voice. 'All the same, I didn't expect it. I would never have believed that you could think that of me, Dinah.'

He turned, and walked slowly away. She did not follow him, or try to call him back.

Mark stood in the doorway of the hall and deliberately filled his pipe. His hard gaze took in the waiting groups and the many eyes turned towards him, and did not waver.

'He be coming out by hisself,' said a disappointed voice, clearly audible above the prevailing buzz. 'What did I tell 'ee?'

So that was it, thought Mark. Obviously they had seen the Super call him back, and hoped to see him reappear under arrest – a Eugene Aram walking for their pleasure, with gyves upon his wrists. Too bad to disillusion them.

He came slowly down the three steps which led from the hall, his face utterly unmoved but with his heart beginning to beat in quick, sickening throbs. Not a mob, indeed; he did not know that a mob would not have been easier to face. A man assaulted by blows might at least go down fighting – a warm blooded affair, with the satisfaction of crashing your fist into a face or two before the end came. To this coldly inimical stare from a now completely silent crowd there could be no retaliation. A poor devil in the pillory must have felt something like this, thought

Mark, stepping on with his head held high.

He recognized a face here and there. Two men with whom he had played a friendly game of darts at the Ring and Book; their faces were not friendly now. There stood Mrs Hale and Mrs Cossett, side by side, their eyes fixed unblinkingly upon him with a certain satisfaction, as if they were two soothsayers who had seen their words proved true. There was the benevolent face of Jimmy Fairfax; Mark slowed up suddenly. That old twister at least should speak to him. But Mr Fairfax had other ideas; his face, like a conjuring trick, flickered, and was not. Mark walked on.

A small figure crowned by a shapeless hat emerged from the crowd and confronted him. In the utter silence her voice rose clearly.

'As we are going the same way, Mr Endicott, I thought we might walk along together.' She drew a gasping breath. 'It's – it's pleasanter, don't you think, to have company than to go alone.'

Mark halted. Amy looked up at his forbidding countenance, quivering but undaunted. For a long moment they stood silent, as if they were alone together, and the people of God's Blessing had melted into space. Then Mark smiled, half quizzically, but with a certain tenderness, such as one might show to a child. Amy heaved a sigh of relief. She had thought it quite possible that he might turn and rend her. It had not been a mistake, after all.

'Thank you, Miss Faraday,' he said gravely. 'It's very good of you to have waited. I shall be glad of your company.'

They moved away, hearing a buzz of indistinguishable comment. Above the sound a voice cried tauntingly, 'Why don't she go arm in crook wit un, the dirty murderer!'

Mark swung round. His face was white, but a fierce joy moved him. Something definite at last – something he could answer.

He said clearly, 'If the gentleman who made that remark cares to come forward, I shall be most happy to give him what he deserves.'

There was a kind of swirling movement in the crowd, but of a backward rather than a forward nature.

'I see,' said Mark, with a short laugh. 'You haven't even the courage of your convictions. In future, if any of you wish to speak to me, I should be obliged if you would do so to my face, and not behind my back.'

He paused hopefully, but the silence was complete. With Amy at his side, he walked slowly away. God's Blessing broke into speech again.

CHAPTER XIX

'OF COURSE,' SAID THE Chief Constable bitterly, 'it had to happen now.'

'Very bad luck at any time, sir. Particularly now, as you say,' the Superintendent agreed in a soothing rumble.

The two men were in session not in the familiar surroundings of police officialdom, but in a private ward of Lake hospital. Sir Henry's face, for an invalid, was surprisingly red and angry against the white pillows; under the coverlet a long hillock told of the cage surrounding his leg. The Chief Constable, who fancied himself as a horseman, had bought and attempted to ride an animal which fancied him as a rider not at all. A fall and a fractured leg had followed swiftly, and Sir Henry was out of action at the moment when he least desired it.

'Those miserable fellers and their women who must go picnicking all over the country as soon as the sun shines,' he grumbled obscurely. 'A curse, they are.'

'Picnickers, sir?'

'Littering the whole place with their filthy bits and pieces, when they aren't lighting fires for other folk to put out. I had the brute well under control, and mind you, he took some handling, when a damned great paper bag blew under his nose. Naturally, that, was that.'

Mr White, cleverly hiding a certain gratification, felt by himself for reasons of his own, murmured sympathetically.

'Well, don't waste time,' snapped his superior, 'let's get down to it for God's sake. Now, touching this alibi business—'

'Alibi? Neither of them have one. On the other hand, there's no proof that they are not speaking the truth. But of course, watertight alibis are not necessarily a sign of innocence.'

'Don't quite follow you there,' objected Sir Henry, moving slightly and muttering under his breath.

The Super leaned forward, and pointed a finger at him. 'It's like this, sir. Take it, for the sake of argument, that you planned a murder, what would your first thought be? To protect yourself from the consequences of the crime which is to say, have an alibi well and truly prepared.'

'That's all very fine. You're talking about a premeditated crime. You don't know that this one was planned.'

'I don't think it was, sir,' said the Super.

'Then why the devil are you bringing in all this stuff about prearranged alibis?'

'I must have expressed myself badly, sir,' said the Super sadly. 'I only meant that the lack of a suitable alibi is not in itself a sign of guilt.'

Sir Henry snorted loudly, and regarded him without pleasure. 'You're talking a lot of poppycock. All that you say may be true, but when you have lack of an alibi plus motive plus opportunity, surely that adds up to something. Even you must see that.'

The Super stiffened slightly. 'Even you' struck him as being unnecessarily rude. That's what you get with these trumpery puffed up jacks in office, he thought bitterly.

'Yes, sir,' he said in a subdued voice.

'There you are then,' said Sir Henry triumphantly. He warmed to his theme. 'Let's run through that, and clear our minds.'

'Sure it won't be too much for you, sir?'

The Chief Constable looked at him sharply, but was reassured by the stolid countenance. No hint of a hidden insult there. Probably the feller hadn't the brains for it. He had made a mistake in the first place, and now this had to happen. With himself laid by the heels and Old Slow and Sure taking his imperturbable way, the affair might drag on and on.

'I've hurt my leg, Superintendent,' he said coldly. 'My brain, such as it is, remains undamaged. Perhaps we could go on. Take Ralph Grey first. Motive?'

'Jealousy,' said the Super, like an obedient schoolboy.

'Opportunity?'

'Ownership of a weapon, probably the one used for the crime.'

'Alibi?'

'Shaky. He was called from the vicarage to look at this sick cow. At 9.30, or thereabouts, he says, he sent his man home for supper and a rest. When he returned an hour later, Grey was still there, but it would have taken him not ten minutes to drive himself to Corpse Path – say five to walk along, meet his wife and kill her, ten minutes back again. Oh, it could have been done in half an hour, and no-one the wiser. But ...'

'But?'

'I don't believe it happened that way. In the first place the animal was really in a bad way. She's extremely valuable, and he's putting everything he has into working up this herd. I've seen the vet and cowman, and they both say that Grey, who is a marvel with animals, did a fine job in pulling her round. I don't believe, under the circumstances, he'd have left her between life and death.'

'Men have left more than a sick cow to pay a debt of jealousy. Still, I suppose it's a point. Go on.'

'He was jealous of his wife, certainly, but we know of nothing which should have led him to believe he would have found her near Corpse Path Cottage that night.'

'We know of nothing, as you say. But then, there's still a hell of a lot we don't know. It's possible that he had a message. And anyhow, it's a fact that his investigation the next day led him straight to Endicott.'

'That's the point,' said the Super, 'straight to the cottage. If Grey suspected his wife of visiting Endicott, and went that night in search of her, why by-pass the cottage? The body was a couple of hundred yards beyond the dip, you know.'

'All that's easily overcome. Grey might have gone to the cottage first – who's to say he didn't? Endicott was supposed to be out at the only time when Grey could have managed it. And again, he might have seen his wife as he approached.'

'I doubt it. She wouldn't have shown herself too clearly. If he had to wait for whoever she was meeting, the obvious thing would be for her to hide herself just inside the copse.'

'In that weather?'

'She went out in it. And probably she couldn't have got any wetter. I never saw such a storm.'

'Well, she might have been intending to hide, and been overtaken by her husband on the way.'

'I don't think so. I think she came the other way, by the path through the copse.'

'Why?'

'Otherwise she must have taken the road through the village. We've made very close enquiries, and she wasn't seen. I think she would have been noticed. People did notice her, you know.'

'Oh, well, have it your own way.' Sir Henry sounded and was unconvinced. 'I gather that you don't think Grey did it.'

'At present, sir, I don't. He had provocation, undoubtedly, but I don't think he did.'

'Well, for the moment, pass Grey. What about Brian Marlowe?'

'Motive,' said the Super, looking down at his hands, 'a violent infatuation for the lady, who may have grown tired of him. She had been away for a month, and might have made fresh contacts. We're looking into that. Opportunity – of getting Grey's revolver? None. His meetings with the lady didn't take place in her home. But there's this – if she brought the revolver with her for reasons of her own, he might have struggled with her for possession of it, as the marks on her wrist show, and accidentally shot her, afterwards losing his head. That sort of thing does happen. Time – he drove her home from the fête just after seven o'clock, her husband having then been called to the farm. They sat in the car outside the Manor until 7.30, when the maid saw him drive away. Mrs Grey came in, saying that she had a headache and intended to lie down. The maid, who was going to the dance, then went out, returning at 10.15. She went straight to her own room and to bed.'

'Yes, yes, but get back to young Marlowe.'

'I'm coming to that, sir. He reached his own home at 7.45, having garaged his car. This his mother corroborates. She looked at the clock when he came in. The thunder had upset her, too, and she went to bed at nine, took some aspirins, and slept through the worst of the storm. She woke at eleven, and feeling hungry, went to find something to eat. Brian was in, and told her that he had been to the vicarage to give Miss Morris a lift home on account of the rain. She was playing the piano for the dancing. The affair finished early owing to the storm, at ten minutes past ten. Marlowe arrived during the last dance.'

'Ah! Then between nine, when his mother went to bed, and say five to ten when he set off for the hall, we have only his word that he remained at home.'

'That's it, sir.'

'But you don't think he did it, either. You're remarkably full of objections, I must say.'

'I only want the truth, sir. It won't do us any good to be in a hurry and get things wrong.'

'I know that as well as you do. But we haven't all the time in the world.'

'I realize that, sir,' said the Super gently.

Sir Henry smiled suddenly. He looked at his officer rather apologetically.

'Afraid my temper is none too sweet. You must put up with me – I know you're doing your best. But why this affection for young Marlowe?'

'No affection, sir. It's just that if Mrs Grey went to meet him, I don't think she'd need a revolver.' There was a faint note of contempt in the slow voice. 'He is not that sort. Weak type, too good looking. Needs a decent girl to take him in hand and make a man of him.'

'You're quite a psychologist, Super.'

'Oh, no, sir.' He sounded shocked. 'Nothing like that. But I don't think Marlowe is our man.'

'Very well,' said Sir Henry resignedly. 'Dump Marlowe in the ashcan with Grey. There remains this Endicott.'

'Yes,' said the Super thoughtfully.

'Motive, opportunity, lack of alibi. All there, aren't they? Added to which, he's the man on the spot.'

'Yes, sir. Endicott had good reason to hate Laura Grey. Their wedding in 1940 was a rushed affair, which she insisted on keeping secret. During the time of his captivity, I imagine he thought of little else than coming back to her. And he came home to find that she had left him flat.'

'And he says he had no idea she was here. D'you think that holds water?'

'I think he was speaking the truth. You get to know ... but of course, finding her here and calmly masquerading as the wife of another man would be enough to make him feel murderous. He could have arranged a meeting under the threat of exposing her, and she might well feel desperate enough to bring the revolver – a struggle, and that would be that.'

'And it sounds pretty good justification for a warrant, if you ask me,' said Sir Henry emphatically.

'I know, sir.' The Super gave him a deprecating glance like a child expecting to be convicted of an act of folly. 'But there are flaws in it, all the same. If Endicott killed his wife, why do it practically on his own doorstep, knowing that suspicion would inevitably fall on him?'

'If it was, as it seems, unpremeditated, he wouldn't stop to think of that.'

'At the time, no, but afterwards he would. He's a queer kind of fellow, but no fool. He would be bound to realize his position. It would have been easy to have moved the body, say into the copse. Or he could have left God's Blessing the following morning. It would take a pretty good nerve to stop calmly in the cottage that night, waiting for her to be found a few yards away.'

'That's no argument. He's a hardboiled type, and murderers have done worse than that. Look at the feller who took a girl to his bungalow for the night with the body of the woman he'd killed in the next room. I still think he's suspect number one, and so do the villagers, judging from the letters you're receiving.'

'Shoals of 'em,' said the Super gloomily. 'All shapes and sizes. But not one of 'em in green ink.'

The Chief Constable frowned. He looked across at White with doubt and misgiving. A good man, solid, conscientious, hard working, but once again he wondered if he could cope – especially now – with such a task as this. No use to be precipitate, of course, but someone had murdered the wretched woman. If White were to make his slow obstinate findings in favour of every suspect, where the devil would they be? If only he had called in Scotland Yard at the time – if only he had never set eyes on that accursed horse. He pulled his moustache irritably, recalling the Super's last words.

'Green ink? You're making a devil of a fuss about those anonymous letters. Don't you think your preoccupation with them is holding you up?'

'Why, no, sir,' said the Super gently, 'I can't say that I do.'

He put a hand in his pocket and brought out a bulky wallet. From this he extracted a small envelope, neatly labelled and dated. He laid it, with the pleased air of a good retriever, on the bed before the other man.

'What's this? Something up your sleeve, eh?' asked Sir Henry.

'It's a fragment of paper, evidently part of a torn-up letter,' said the Super. 'It was found in Laura Grey's handbag.'

'Wait a minute,' objected Sir Henry. 'I read the list of articles found in the bag. Powderbox, purse, handkerchief, rouge, lipstick – no mention of a scrap of paper there.'

'No, sir. We sent the bag and its contents off for fingerprint tests, and this scrap of paper was found caught in the fastening of the gold powder compact. Take a look at it, sir.'

The Chief Constable opened the envelope, and gingerly drew out a scrap of flimsy pink paper. The edges were jagged. On it, in block capitals with the top of the 'M' torn away was what had obviously spelt 'MRS' and a curve which might have been part of a 'G.' The letters showed brightly green.

*

The night following the inquest, strangely enough, Mark slept like a baby. He awoke feeling improved in mind and body, investigated the contents of his larder, and cooked a weary rasher and a couple of eggs. The condemned man made a hearty breakfast, he thought, with a somewhat twisted grin.

He knew well enough that he was not by any means out of the wood, but the first bitterness was past. He did not feel love towards the good folk of God's Blessing, but he admitted in all fairness that there was some ground for their suspicion shown so clearly towards himself. Ralph Grey's instant reaction had doubtless gone the rounds. Poor devil; he, like Mark, had suffered at the hands of Laura, through no fault of his own. Had he followed her that night, crazy with jealousy, and fired the shot? That, of course, would be the obvious solution – the betrayed husband, as he believed himself, taking the law into his own hands – only it had not happened like that. Mark was coldly certain of that much. Ralph had not been acting when he turned on the man he thought to be the murderer of his wife.

But someone had shot her, thought Mark, his mind following the same track as that of the Chief Constable. She had come there to meet someone, and someone had killed her. You couldn't get away from that. Brian Marlowe, who had been enslaved by Laura, and who was, at times, capable of losing his temper? Mark fingered his nose reminiscently, and wondered. Yet the police, who, presumably, knew what they were doing, seemed to have dismissed Marlowe from their calculations. Marlowe had looked ghastly that day at the inquest, but it might not necessarily be due to guilt; and perhaps the police were actually watching him all the time, patiently waiting for proof. And if Brian, like Ralph and himself were innocent, then in God's name, who? It was the old weary question, to which he could find no answer.

He got up to clear the table. Looking around his kitchen, it struck him as wearing a neglected air. He wondered if Mrs Shergold had returned. A strange woman; when she was with you it was quite easy to forget her presence, but for compensation you missed her when she did not appear.

His train of thought moved to Mr Fairfax, who was also (presumably) progressing without the aid of his good working 'ooman. Dear Mr Fairfax, with his benevolent smile and his flow of conversation – until public opinion had turned against one. Rather clever the way he had shimmered into the crowd and disappeared from view. The rabbit had not done that.

He smiled suddenly. Bless her funny little heart, it had taken nerve to come forward and range herself at his side, so obviously his champion. Who would have thought it that first morning in the bus, when she shrunk from his merest glance, obviously regarding him as a kind of unlovely Byron, mad, bad, and dangerous to know. Their acquaintanceship had moved along strange paths, with the ludicrous never far round the corner, until now. Amy emerging from the ditch, Amy weeping on a stranger's shoulder, Amy slinking across the field to hide with him the evidence of her guilt – all food for mirth. But Amy, small and undaunted, resolutely offering herself as a buffer between himself and an unfriendly world – something to smile at perhaps, but there was nothing ludicrous. He wondered suddenly what she would think when she heard of his marriage, and felt surprisingly uneasy. It was, he discovered, of some importance that Miss Faraday should continue to believe in him.

He said aloud, 'When I get the chance I'll tell her myself,' and was vaguely comforted.

A scratching on the door and a sharp bark told of the arrival of James. Endicott let him in and fed him, noticing that the supply of dog biscuits was running low. That meant a visit to the post office cum general stores, which he did not anticipate with enthusiasm. All the same ...

'I'm damned if I'll hide away from them,' said Mark, and put on some water to shave.

Twenty minutes later, he emerged from the hollow to observe a tall figure in a sports coat and flannels, negligently strolling along the lane. Mark grinned, and went deliberately on his way. James bounded ahead and greeted the stranger like an old friend.

'Morning,' said Mark.

'Morning,' replied the stranger cautiously.

'I'm obliged to go to the post office,' said Mark kindly. 'Perhaps you would care to join me?'

'As a matter of fact I did want some cigarettes,' said the other, looking up from the wagging James with a faint smile.

'Come along, then. Never let it be said that I was uncooperative.'

'It's very good of you, I'm sure, sir,' said the plain-clothed man imperturbably.

'Not at all,' said Mark graciously. 'I shall be glad of your company.'

He glanced at the white house which they were passing at that moment, but there was no sign of its occupant. Have to see her, he thought, before someone gets in first.

'What's your name?' he asked suddenly, turning to his silent companion.

'Pulleyblank,' replied the plain-clothed man.

'Good Lord,' said Mark. 'I only heard that name once before in my life.'

The fair skinned face of Mr Pulleyblank flushed. 'It's fairly common around here,' he remarked coldly.

'The fellow I knew, a Peter Pulleyblank, was in Changi Gaol with me. We were in the hospital for a good spell together. Nice chap.'

'Why,' said Mr Pulleyblank, becoming entirely human, 'that's my brother. I've heard him speak of you.'

'No, is that a fact? What's he doing now?'

'He's in a garage at Southampton – they kept his job open. Pretty well, considering a spot of tummy trouble now and then. His wife had a baby last year.'

'Good for him. I must look him up – that is,' said Mark, 'if I have the opportunity to look anyone up in the future.'

Pulleyblank looked uncomfortable, as if the other had committed an error of taste.

'The Super's a good man,' he said awkwardly. 'Old Slow and Sure, we call him, but if he is slow, he generally gets there in the end.'

'Brother,' said Mark warmly, 'I only hope you may be right.'

Miss Margetson served them both with a haughty reserve masking her blazing curiosity, and eyes strained to observe every detail. Most unusually the shop was empty, so that their business was conducted with dispatch, but as they went out they saw Mrs Richards hurrying up the path. She caught sight of Endicott, and gave a quite perceptible start.

'Here we go again,' said Mark, moving to one side that the lady might pass.

To his surprise, Mrs Richards, her colour rather high, paused.

'Good morning, Mr Endicott,' she said pleasantly. 'I trust you are better? My husband tells me you were far from well when he called.'

'Thank you,' said Endicott gravely, 'I am quite well now.'

He smiled at her and walked on. Mrs Richards entered the post office, feeling shaken but rather uplifted. He looked quite nice, after all, when he smiled. Her judgement had been too hasty. Her husband, moved by the behaviour of his flock to unusual indignation, had spoken strongly the night before on the subject of charity, also on the British rule of a man being innocent until he was proved guilty. Mrs Richards felt that he would be pleased with her now.

The two men strolled back to the field gate without further encounters, chatting amiably enough of this and that. In deference to his companion's apparent feelings, Mark did not refer to the murder again. It was James who brought them back to the affairs of the day. He had been missing for some time when Endicott, about to return to his abode, looked round for him.

'Where the devil's that dog?'

'Not so far away,' said Pulleyblank, grinning. 'Using up a trifle of superfluous energy.'

The two men strolled across to a spot in the bank, not far from the gate, where the hind quarters of the dog and a quivering stump of tail were dimly visible through a flying cloud of dust.

'Hope springs eternal,' said Mark. 'He always fancies he's going to dig out a rabbit. Good Lord!'

Something unearthed by the violently digging James had fallen with a thud at his feet. He bent to investigate.

'Don't touch that,' said Pulleyblank sharply. Mark lifted his head. He was rather pale.

In a curious voice he said, 'I wasn't going to.'

Pulleyblank pulled out his handkerchief and bent forward.

The shape of the revolver showed plainly through the encrusting earth as he carefully picked it up.

CHAPTER XX

'YES, MY LAD,' SAID the Super. 'You did very well. And it was very good of Mr Endicott to come in with you.'

'Say a kind word for the dog while you're at it,' said Mark, glancing at the black figure sleeping as peacefully under the table as if a visit to Lake police headquarters was all in the day's work. 'He did the difficult part.'

The tone was light, but his brain was working furiously. This discovery of the weapon – was it another pointer against himself, or not? Pulleyblank, justifiably pleased at his success, could vouch for it that Mark had shown no sign of excitement or distress when he found what the dog was about. Queer, out of the innumerable burrows which pocked the bank, that James should have chosen the one into which the murderer had pushed his weapon. Once again, too near Corpse Path Cottage for comfort. But then, the cottage, so rightly named, had been the focal point of all the trouble from the very beginning. Far from the madding crowd – a place of seclusion in which to write! Oh, a hell of a joke.

'Yes,' said White thoughtfully. His eyes were on the three objects ranged before him – the revolver, rusty, caked with earth, and looking surprisingly innocent – the handkerchief of the resourceful Pulleyblank, and another square of linen, the colour of the mud in which it had lain. It was at this that the Super was looking.

'You say this was dug out by the dog with the revolver?'

'Yes, sir,' answered Pulleyblank. 'Actually it flew out just before. I didn't pay it any heed until I bent to pick up the revolver, and thought it might belong.'

'I fancy it belongs all right,' said White. He added dreamily, 'My men searched the field and the banks. I suppose I could hardly expect them to be like Alice in the book, and go down a rabbit hole.'

Pulleyblank smiled dutifully.

'It was pretty well in, sir,' he pointed out. 'The dog was practically out of sight.'

'Oh, I'm not blaming anyone. It's a great relief to have the thing at last. We have sent for Mr Grey, and I don't doubt he will identify the weapon. No chance of finger prints, naturally, even if that hadn't been seen to in the first place. Too many books written nowadays.'

He broke off as a constable opened the door to admit Ralph Grey.

'Good morning, Superintendent,' he said, coming straight to the desk. 'You wanted me?'

Glancing round for the first time, he saw Endicott. There was a momentary pause. From behind his desk, White watched the two men, noting every detail of bearing and expression. Then Ralph said, quite calmly, 'I see I'm not the only victim.'

Mark, who had involuntarily braced himself, relaxed.

'Not victims, I hope, sir,' said the Super smoothly. 'Merely the matter of the discovery of a weapon.'

'I see,' said Ralph, showing as little emotion as if they were discussing a change in the weather. 'Where was it found, or shouldn't I ask?'

'It's no secret, sir. Mr Endicott's dog unearthed it when he was digging in a rabbit burrow near the cottage.'

'Near the cottage,' said Ralph thoughtfully.

Mark stiffened again, but Ralph did not pursue the subject. He was looking at the revolver.

'You want me to identify this?'

'If you would, sir. It's rather dirty, but perhaps you could tell if you have seen it before.'

Ralph bent over the table, the light showing up the patches of white at his temples. The Super saw that his hands were trembling slightly.

'It's the same type as mine. As far as I can see it is mine,' he said slowly.

'Is there any mark of identification?'

'No, but under the circumstances I think there can be very little doubt. And you'll be able to tell ...'

For all his self-control, he could not finish the sentence.

Quietly, the Super did so for him.

'If it is the weapon from which the fatal shot was fired? Oh, yes, sir, we can do that. And I'm much obliged to you for your assistance. How is the cow?'

Ralph looked faintly surprised. 'Doing very well, thank you. I'm rather busy, so if that's all …?'

'Certainly, sir.'

'You'll keep me in touch with any developments?' said Ralph, glancing at Mark as he moved towards the door.

'I'll do that, sir. Good morning.'

With a murmured farewell Ralph went out. The Super stood up briskly.

That's that. You can take this along, my lad, and ask them to get out a report on it right away. Get yourself some food and be back here at two. Now, Mr Endicott, will you have a bite with me? We could give you a lift back to the cottage afterwards if that suited you.'

'Oh,' said Mark thoughtfully. 'You're coming there?'

'Yes, I want to take a look around, and pay a few visits.'

'Social calls?' asked Mark, grinning.

'Not precisely, sir,' said the Super, and smiled solemnly back.

He took Mark to a queer little eating house tucked modestly away in a back street belonging to the older part of Lake. Here they were served with a surprisingly good meal, without frills but well cooked and piping hot.

'Make a good meal, Mr Endicott,' said White benevolently, adding roast potatoes to the runnerbeans and roast beef on his companion's plate. 'If you don't mind my saying so, you look as if you could do with it.'

'I haven't had much appetite lately,' said Mark, picking up his knife and fork, 'but this certainly smells good.'

'Best meal you can get in Lake,' said the Super, setting happily to work. 'You might pay three times as much in one of those posh hotels on the front, but you wouldn't do half as well. And as for those shiny restaurants – blow you up for five minutes and then you want another meal. No good to me.'

He attacked his food with a vigour which, for some time, did away with speech. Little more was said until they had each finished a mountainous helping of apple tart, and a pot of tea had arrived.

'Better than the coffee,' said White, 'I'm a real old woman for my cup of tea.'

He helped himself to two spoonfuls of sugar and poured out the tea.

'None for you? I wish I could give it up, but the flesh is weak, and

I've all too much of it these days. I tell you another person with plenty of weight to carry, Mr Endicott – that mother of young Marlowe. Do you know her?'

'I met her once,' said Mark, rather surprised.

'Queer woman,' said the Super, stirring his tea. 'Nothing seems to move her, yet she knows all that goes on. And I suppose she thinks the world of that boy of hers.'

Mark sat up suddenly. A monstrous suspicion came into his mind. He looked at the Super, calmly drinking his tea with a wild surmise.

'Why are you interested in her?'

'Interested? I'm interested in anyone connected with this case. That's my job, Mr Endicott.'

'But Mrs Marlowe never went out.'

'So I understand, sir,' said the Super. He added without changing his tone, 'No more anonymous letters?'

Mark shook his head impatiently.

'I think you're barking up the wrong tree,' he said.

For the first time he heard the Super laugh – a chuckle of genuine amusement.

'Maybe I am,' he said, 'Maybe you don't know what tree I'm barking up. Let's change the subject.'

'Just as you like. I don't want to pry.'

'I'm sure,' said the Super soothingly, and chuckled again. He pulled out a pipe almost as disreputable as Mark's own, and pushed his pouch across the table.

'So you haven't had a decent meal lately,' he observed between puffs. 'Is Mrs Shergold still away?'

'I suppose so. At all events, she hasn't condescended to come to me. But of course, that may be merely to show that she shares the general view.'

'I should go and find out.'

'What? Her opinion of me?'

'Now, now, Mr Endicott, don't you be so quick. I meant find out if she's back. No reason for you to be left in the lurch like this. My wife always says a man on his own is the most helpless creature on the face of the earth.'

Mark looked across the table curiously. The wide face, wreathed in smoke, was calm and placid; it seemed that the one thing on Mr White's mind was the utmost enjoyment of his pipe. Old Slow and Sure – not as slow as he looks, thought Mark.

He said, frowning, 'To tell the truth, I'm not too keen on visiting our friend Fairfax. He took the utmost care not to speak to me after the inquest. Slimy old devil – after what I paid for the cottage you wouldn't think he'd have the nerve.'

'There are not so many people who can fly in the face of public opinion,' pointed out the Super. 'Very much like sheep the general run of folk, I always say. Follow the crowd – but I understand you had company home all the same, Mr Endicott.'

A faint twinkle lit the sleepy brown eyes. For a moment he looked a roguish Cupid, grown stout and middle-aged.

'If you ask me,' said Mark slowly, 'there's precious little that you don't understand. I suppose you wouldn't care to tell me if you have made any steps forward in your investigations? I don't wish to speak out of turn, but this affair touches me rather closely. Too closely for comfort, in fact.'

'Yes. Circumstances have placed you in a very ugly spot. And in answer to your question, I may say that today I have made a very definite step forward.'

'Because of the gun?'

'That and other things,' said the Super.

He knocked out his pipe and, heaving himself to one side, began investigating his pocket.

'My party. We'd best be moving now,' he said.

At the station they picked up James, who had been fed and cared for in his master's absence. Pulleyblank was dutifully waiting with a note which he handed to White, who read it without comment before they all piled into the waiting car and drove out of the town.

Pulleyblank sat in front with the driver; Mark, James, and the Super were installed in state in the back.

'I've had the report on the weapon,' observed the Super at length.

'Oh. Was it…?'

'Yes. Definitely. One shot had been fired, and that the fatal one.'

He gazed contentedly out of the window, as if all his mind was on the fleeting landscape, adding, in precisely the same tone, 'A week's rain is wanted now. Not a crazy storm, like that affair last week, but steady stuff. Badly dried up everywhere.'

Mark agreed.

'Very poor potato crop, I'm afraid. Very poor.'

Mark found himself unable to continue the theme. Yet again he was wondering what might be passing behind the other man's baffling facade. For all his pleasant ways he gave nothing away. Lately a companion at lunch, he might even now be coldly convinced that he sat beside a murderer. And if so, he would go about his business of tightening the noose as calmly as he had just uttered his remark about the weather. Slow spoken, kindly, looking anything rather than a keen-witted policeman, but definitely not to be underrated. Rather to be feared.

He said suddenly, speaking out of his thoughts, 'I had every reason to hate Laura. I came to the village where she was living, she was killed close to my cottage, and now you have found the gun, also close to my cottage.'

White turned his slow gaze on his companion. He looked mildly interested.

'All very true, Mr Endicott. What about it?'

'Only that, in spite of it all, I didn't do it,' said Mark.

'Then you've nothing to worry about, sir. Nothing. It's the guilty party I'm after. You ought to know that.'

For some reason a wave of relief swept Mark. It was as if, for the days since the murder, he had been a child screwing up its eyes in the dark, afraid to open them for fear of what might be there to see. And there was nothing, after all. What had he to fear? Old Slow and Sure would get there in the end.

'Just you leave it to me,' said the Super indulgently. 'You've been worrying too much, and not looking after yourself properly. Do as I said, and get that Mrs What's-her-name back.' He turned to the window again. 'That corn looks pretty well, doesn't it?' he said.

'You see, Miss Faraday,' said the Super, 'I'm very interested in these letters, and any help you could give me would be much appreciated.'

He sat back in his chair, feeling that he had turned his sentence rather well. Unobtrusively he looked around him. A woman's room, definitely, but not too finicky. This chair was comfortable, even for a man of his weight; the furniture was old but solid. Plenty of books, with historical and period fiction holding a place of honour – a whole row with the name of Annabel Lee on the back. And very nice too, thought White, who in his rare moments of relaxation had a weakness for tales of damsels in distress. A nice piano across the corner of the room. Of course, Miss Faraday taught music. A handsome woman in the large photograph over the fireplace; rather a dominating face, but a humorous curve to the mouth. Not much likeness to Miss Faraday there.

177

That lady sat primly on the edge of her chair like a good child, her feet tucked under it, her hands folded in her lap. She was sick with apprehension, not for herself, but for what she might be about to hear. Mark she had not seen since their walk from the hall, and as the glow of excitement had faded, the usual pitiful uncertainty had taken its place. At the time the gesture had seemed not only a far, far better thing than she had ever done, but also the one thing for her to do; ever since she had drearily wondered if she had only succeeded in being foolish yet again. He had scarcely spoken all the way back; if, by her well meant championship she had made him feel ridiculous, Amy wished that she were dead.

'The road to hell,' she said suddenly, as if coining a phrase, 'is paved with good intentions.'

The Super, taken by surprise, actually jumped. Miss Faraday blushed hotly, and smiled a sickly smile.

'I was thinking,' she explained lamely.

'It often clears the mind to speak one's thought aloud,' said the Super, recovering himself. 'I hope your own good intentions haven't got you into trouble?'

'Not into trouble. Only it's so hard to know if what one has done was really for the best.'

She ceased to fear her visitor, and sat back more comfortably in her chair. Pretty legs, thought the Super, his fatherly smile unchanged.

'When a thing is done it's done. The moving finger,' said Mr White, rather surprisingly, 'writes, and having writ moves on. Etcetera.'

'That's all very well,' said Amy earnestly, 'but it doesn't prevent you from wondering if you've made a fool of yourself.'

'That's something we all do from time to time. But if you're thinking of what I'm thinking, Miss Faraday, I'm sure you're worrying yourself without cause. I think when referring to your conduct, folly is the last word Mr Endicott would use.'

Amy suddenly liked her companion very much.

'You see, I know he didn't do it,' she said, as if the statement explained all things.

'That's very interesting. How do you know?'

'He wouldn't, that's all. And if he did,' added Amy triumphantly, 'he would have more sense than to do it on his own doorstep.'

'There is something in what you say. All the same, murder has been done, and it's my job to find the murderer.'

Amy shivered. Murder – murderer. Such ugly words; words that screamed at you from headlines, words to touch the lives of unknown people, never of yourself – or so one had thought until now, wrapped in a false security.

She said in a low voice, 'If I can help ...'

'Thank you, Miss Faraday. I am, as you might say, a seeker after truth. And it isn't the innocent who need fear the truth. I wanted to go back to that anonymous letter of yours.'

'Oh, that,' said Amy. She felt vaguely disappointed.

'Yes. It seems a long way from the crime, I know, but things often link up,' He took out his wallet and extracted the familiar sheet, printed in straggling green capitals. He read, in an expressionless voice, '*Keep away from him you* (we'll pass that bit) *if you know what's good for you. Creeping round him like a ... um um ... Mad for him, you crazy old maid, but he has other fish to fry. Can't you keep off a man who belongs to someone else?'*

He folded the letter carefully and put it away.

'Very pretty. What did you think when you received it?'

'I thought Jimmy Fairfax had been talking.' She met the Super's gaze and continued reluctantly, 'Mr Endicott had promised to store something for me. I went round one morning and found he was ill. I put him to bed, and Mr Fairfax arrived as I was coming downstairs.'

She paused to think how utterly unconvincing a truthful story could sound.

'I see,' said White thoughtfully. 'Mr Fairfax.'

'I never thought he wrote the letter, though. Gossip and scandal-mongering is more his style.'

'And gossip spreads in a village, which makes it all the more difficult to find the writer. Do you suspect anyone?'

Amy shook her head.

'There's one thing I can't understand, Miss Faraday. You have a nice place here, and Mr Endicott that tiny cottage. Why ask him to store anything for you?'

'It was books. I didn't want them here.'

'Why not, Miss Faraday?'

Amy took a deep breath and told him.

'Thank you,' said White. 'That's all very clear. I think your secret is safe with me.'

'If it would help at all,' said Amy confusedly, 'I wouldn't mind the whole village knowing.'

The Superintendent rose, picking up his hat. He seemed very large as he smiled down at her.

'Don't you worry,' he said. 'Everything will be all right.' And I only hope that's true, he added to his immortal soul.

He was smiling to himself as he took his leave, but before he reached the gate, was looking thoughtful again. A few steps on he met PC Marsh, on his bicycle. The constable dismounted and straightened his tall figure.

'Waiting for me?' asked the Super.

'Yes, sir. Phone message from Lake.'

'Well?'

'They cleaned up the handkerchief found with the revolver and found initials in the corner.'

'What were they?' asked White quickly.

Marsh told him.

'That convey anything to you?'

Marsh told him again.

'Well, well,' said the Super.

'Yes, sir,' said PC Marsh.

CHAPTER XXI

'STILL THEY COME,' SAID Mark. 'Bobbies, bobbies all the way, and ne'er a criminal in sight. Unless, of course, you count me.'

Mr Pulleyblank grinned, but his eyes were speculative.

'Old man's excited about something,' he said softly.

'Looks much as usual to me,' said Mark.

'Don't you believe it. See the way he is tapping his thigh with his fingers? It's a sure sign. And Marsh was after him just now, hell for leather, and he looks like the cat that swallowed the canary. Something's up.'

'I hope to God it is,' muttered Mark. Personally, he was doubtful. White was certainly making that movement with his right hand, but it looked far more like absence of mind than excitement, and as for PC Marsh, his rosy countenance generally did show a mild contentment with life.

'One more call to make,' announced the Super as he reached the car. 'You can wait here.'

'Yes, sir,' said the driver, his eyes on the gently drumming hand.

'I saw old Fairfax,' said Mark conversationally.

The Super looked round as if he had never seen him before. The large eyes of the constable also became fixed in an interested stare.

'You saw him?' queried White.

'Why, yes. You told me to. About Mrs Shergold. Don't you remember?'

'Oh, that. It had slipped my memory for the moment. And is the lady back?'

'No. He's pretty sick about it. She isn't coming back at all, it seems.'

'Poor Mr Fairfax. Dear, dear.' The fingers were tapping again.

'Poor me, too. I shall have trouble enough to find anyone else,' said Mark.

'You'll have to find yourself a wife, Mr Endicott.'

PC Marsh uttered a short laugh, coloured, and gazed into the distance.

'Very funny,' said Mark, scowling.

'I didn't intend to be humorous,' said the Super, giving his perspiring underling a dignified glance of reproof. 'However, we mustn't stay chatting here.'

Pulleyblank swung around and watched the two stately figures disappear.

'Oh, yes,' he said with deep conviction. 'No doubt about it, there's something up.'

If Mr Fairfax had overheard the Super describe him as 'poor', he would have been in the most complete agreement. He felt that he had, like another gentleman, been most despitefully used. Left in the lurch with scarcely a word of apology, his good working 'ooman gone like a beautiful dream; he looked around the increasing disorder of his home and mourned. And it was not only in cleanliness that Mrs Shergold had shown her worth; her cooking, too, had been an inspiration and a joy. No extravagance, either, reflected Mr Fairfax, sadly shaking his patriarchal head. Well, it was over now. The lean days had returned, and for good. Working housekeepers in these degenerate days were like snow in harvest. Never, he felt, would he look upon her like again.

He had lunched without zest on liver belonging to some animal unknown, which the butcher had handed to him as a pearl of great price. In the skilled hands of Mrs Shergold, it would have become a meal fit for a prince; under his own ministrations it had formed a knife-blunting crust on the outside whilst remaining revoltingly raw and red inside. Mr Fairfax possessed three teeth. He had bolted what he could not chew, and Nemesis, in the shape of internal pangs of anguish, was upon him. He looked like a Father Christmas who had lost his sleigh.

He heard a tap on his door without enthusiasm. Not that feller Endicott again, he hoped. A nasty look he had given him; did he expect all the world to fall on his neck that day after the inquest? If Amy Faraday was fool enough to do it, that was up to her. Old maids would do anything that put them in the way of a man.

The knock at the door was repeated, this time more forcibly.

'All right, all right,' said Mr Fairfax, wincing as the liver had its way with him, 'bain't I coming so fast as I can?'

He opened the door upon the massive form of the Super, and his greenish pallor made him look a guilty man.

'Mr Fairfax? I'm Superintendent White. I'd like a word with you, if I may.'

'Step inside,' said Mr Fairfax in a hollow voice.

The Super followed him across a stone paved passage and into a stone paved room which, even on that blazing day, struck cold. Above the fire place hung an enlargement of the nuptials of Mr Fairfax, in which the gentleman himself looked cowed, his bride frightened, and the mother of the bride sternly triumphant. The room was sparsely furnished, and though clean wore a faint air of neglect. There was dust on the chair which Mr Fairfax pulled forward for his visitor, and the plush table cover had crumbs caught in its surface, and hung askew.

'What can I do for you, sir?' asked Mr Fairfax, seating himself and speaking in a subdued voice.

'As you know, I am investigating the murder of Mrs Laura Grey.'

'I don't know nothing about that,' said Mr Fairfax, moving uneasily in his chair.

'So we had imagined,' said the Super, fixing him with a cold eye, 'until this morning.'

Mr Fairfax gaped, looking foolish and immensely surprised.

He said breathlessly, 'Here! What do 'ee mean by that?'

'Just this, Mr Fairfax. The weapon from which the fatal shot was fired has now been discovered. Have you any idea where?'

Mr Fairfax recovered his breath. A sly and unpleasing smile creased his pallid cheeks.

'That's easy. Some place nigh Corpse Path Cottage,' he said.

'How do you know that, Mr Fairfax?'

'Stands to reason,' said Mr Fairfax simply. 'He – Endicott – shot her, didn't he? Everybody knows that – 'cept, seemingly, the police.'

He spoke recklessly. His pains were worse, and he hated all the world.

'The police,' said White slowly, 'know something else. They know what was wrapped round the revolver when it was hidden.'

Mr Fairfax, past caring, uttered a dolorous groan.

'I want you to answer this carefully. Do you own a large white linen handkerchief with the initials J. F. hand-embroidered in the corner?'

'Six,' replied Mr Fairfax briefly.

'Six?'

'That's what I said. My dear wife gave them to me for a Christmas box the year afore she died. Waste o' good money, but she liked such foolishness.' He broke off, laid a hand on his stomach and rumbled loudly. 'Pardon. This here indigestion,' he said.

'Have a couple of these?' said White, taking a small bottle from his pocket. 'I use 'em myself.'

Like a drowning man clutching a straw, Mr Fairfax took the proffered tablets. White saw the colour creep back to his cheeks. The old boy hadn't been sprucing, then.

'Better?' he asked.

Mr Fairfax nodded. 'I was a bit short with you, sir, I'm afraid, but I was in mortal pain. I be no cook at the best of times, and when a man's worried into the bargain—'

'Worried?'

'Wouldn't you be worried if your housekeeper as you depended on had gone and left you?'

'I should, indeed. But going back to these initialled handkerchiefs – could I see them?'

Mr Fairfax stared. 'If you don't mind my asking, whatever for?'

'A handkerchief was found with the revolver, and had evidently been wrapped round it. Those initials are in the corner.'

The eyes and mouth of Mr Fairfax became three perfect Os. He breathed, 'No!'

'I assure you it is a fact.'

'Well, then,' said Mr Fairfax, coming to himself and turning purple with anger, 'it can't be one o' mine. My six be upstairs in a box in the right hand top drawer o' the chest o' drawers my wife's mother give us for a wedding present. And that,' he added, drawing breath and triumphantly clinching the matter, 'were in February, 1901.'

'Yes. But a handkerchief bearing your initials was found.'

'And what if 'twere? I suppose there be other folk whose names begin wi' J. F. in the world. Circumstanttle evidence, that's what it be. Trying to pin a thing on a feller—'

'You just show me your six handkerchiefs,' said White sternly, 'instead of wasting your breath like this.'

Mr Fairfax closed his lips and shot him a malevolent glance. He got up hastily.

'Better come with me, hadn't 'ee?' he said bitterly. 'When you've counted six good handkerchiefs for yourself, you mid stop doubting an honest man's word.'

'Thank you,' said White gently. 'Perhaps that would be best.'

'Circumstanttle evidence!' muttered Mr Fairfax, and led the way up the stairs.

The bedroom was dominated by a majestic double bed, with head and foot crowned by large balls of brass. The coverings had been pulled over it by an unskilled hand, and the brass was filmed with dust. Mr Fairfax, still bursting with indignation, stumped across the room to the mahogany chest, large and solid like the bed. He pulled open the top right hand drawer. Good workmanship there, reflected the Super parenthetically – they don't run so smoothly these days. A piercing odour of mothballs filled the room.

'Come and see for yourself,' invited Mr Fairfax.

White crossed the room and looked over his shoulder. Two black ties, some rolled up woollen socks, a few khaki handkerchiefs, an enormous cashbox, a pair of black gloves and a mourning band – Mr Fairfax took out these articles one by one and laid them on the bed. There remained in the drawer a flat blue cardboard box.

'Now,' said Mr Fairfax, in a voice quivering with conscious righteousness, 'you see for yourself. Six handkerchiefs, as she give them to me. See for yourself.'

The Super raised the lid to see a neatly folded handkerchief, the topmost of a small pile kept in place by narrow strands of blue ribbon running from corner to corner of the box. In the corner the initials had been worked with painstaking care. The handkerchief had never been used.

'Take 'em out,' urged Mr Fairfax. 'Take all six of 'em out and count 'em.'

Mr White did as he was told. He said soberly, 'There are five handkerchiefs here, Mr Fairfax.'

There was a pause. Mr Fairfax, one hand clutching a brass knob, stood as if frozen. A clock on the mantlepiece made the agitated sound of its ticking fill the room.

'Here,' he said, coming suddenly to life. 'Let me count. One mid be folded in 'tother.'

Squares of linen flapped like flags. Convinced at last, he sat heavily on the bed, dropping his hands on his knees. His face expressed a childlike bewilderment.

'Five in the box, right enough,' he said, 'but there had ought to be six.'

'Have you never used one?' suggested the Super, watching him.

'Never. That I do know. She give them to me that Christmas morning. "Here James," she said, "good linen, and hand-embroidered wi' my own hands. Fit for a lord," she said, and I said, "naught but foolish waste o' money for a working chap." So 'twere, but I never should ha' said it. I never would have if I'd aknown. A wick later she were gone, and I never had the heart to touch 'em. Never opened the box from that day to this.'

He wagged his head with a kind of brooding melancholy, looking down at the varied articles on the bed. Suddenly he turned to the Super, and his face was changed and afraid.

'Here,' he said, 'one o' my handkerchiefs be gone.'

The Super agreed.

'And you found one like 'em wi' the weapon.'

'As far as we can say, identical with them.' He was adding some remarks about checking up and identifying, but he saw that Mr Fairfax was working things out for himself.

'The murderer had my handkerchief. Then you think,' his voice cracked suddenly, 'as I be the murderer?'

'No,' said the Super gravely. 'I don't think that at all.'

'Don't 'ee?' said Mr Fairfax. He added surprisingly, 'Put a power o' work into those handkerchiefs she did, poor maid.' Without the slightest warning, he put his hands to his face and began to cry.

Mr White brewed the tea himself, and according to his own standards. If his host was shocked to see the number of spoonfuls ladled into the pot he made no protest, and sipped the resulting dark and sugary fluid with the best possible grace. Two large cupfuls were disposed of by each man before the Super settled down to business once more.

'Feel better for that, don't you?' he remarked jovially. 'I do, I know. My wife says I'm a terror on the ration.'

'Mrs Shergold, she made ours go round wonderful well,' said Mr Fairfax sadly. 'There, I mid ha' knowed she were too good to last.'

'How long had she been with you?'

'Middle of March she came. Morning after the affair at Corpse Path,' said Mr Fairfax delicately, 'she went. And by this morning's post I get a card – no more.'

He reached for a postcard which was pushed behind a leering china dog on the mantelpiece. White took it and gazed at it casually.

There was no address or date. The few lines scrawled across it in an undistinguished hand said baldly enough:*Sorry unable to return. Will send for things later.* It was signed M. Shergold.

'Yes, it's pretty cool,' said the Super looking up, 'I should write and tell her so if I were you.'

'How can I do that?' asked Mr Fairfax reasonably. 'I don't know her address.'

'I saw there was none on the card, but surely she gave you an address when she went?'

'She did not. It came all of a rush, as you mid say. The letter come by the first post to say her sister needed her and by the next bus she were gone, for the few days, as I thought. Never dreamed I should need to use paper and ink on her for so short a time as that.'

'I suppose not. Still, she hasn't treated you well. How did you get her in the first place?'

'Advertised for a working housekeeper in the *Lake and District Courier*. An expense, but someone I had to have. She answered, and I met her in town for an interview. All done proper and as it should be.'

'Yes. Did you put your address on the advertisement or a box number?'

'My address, of course. Didn't want to make out I lived in town, did I?'

The Super agreed. His right hand had begun a rhythmic tapping on his knee.

'Right. So you interviewed her and engaged her. References?'

'Three, and good ones too. From a vicar, a doctor, and a schoolmistress. All spoke most highly of her.'

'Did you take up any of them?'

'I gave them back to her, of course.' Mr Fairfax looked somewhat offended.

'I mean, did you write to any of the people to check up on the statements?'

Mr Fairfax smiled pityingly. 'Lord bless you, why should I want to do that? She was prepared to come and to take what I was minded to give. No need to waste stamps on that.'

No, you miserly old buzzard, thought the Super.

'It's always as well,' he pointed out. 'References have been faked before now.'

'Well, I never thought to do it. You had only to look at her to know as there were nothing wrong.'

'And yet, see how she is treating you now. Can you remember any names from the references?'

'No, that I can't. I didn't clutter up my head wi' none of it. They were all Londoners, and that's the most I can tell 'ee.'

'Londoners, were they? She came from London here? Why?'

'She said as she had been born and bred in the country and since her husband died she'd been wishful to get back.'

'When did he die?'

'She said two years ago.'

'Yes. And she wrote to you before the interview. From what address?'

Mr Fairfax looked blank. 'That I can't say.'

'Can't you remember? Didn't you keep the letter?'

'I did have it,' said the badgered Fairfax defensively, 'but she spring cleaned 'tother day, and got rid o' piles o' stuff. How was I to know 'twould be wanted?'

'Never mind. Can you remember what part of London?'

'Putney, I can't remember no more than that, and 'tis no manner o' use for 'ee to ask me. Why be you keeping on about her, anyway? 'Tis the murderer as you should be after.'

'You leave me to do my job in my own way,' said the Super with perfect good humour. 'I might be able to find this vanishing lady for you. She mentioned on her card 'things' left here. What are they?'

'Best come up again,' said Mr Fairfax resignedly.

The room which had been Mrs Shergold's was neat, bare and unwelcoming. In the built-in wall cupboard hung a solitary dress of cheap woollen material. A grey flannel dressing-gown drooped from a peg on the door.

'She took a case with her, I suppose?'

'Yes, and wore her coat over a jacket and skirt. I told her she'd be hot enough before the day was done.'

White turned his attention to the dressing chest which stood before the window. The bottom drawer yielded a selection of unseductive underclothes, the second a grey jumper and two blouses. The top drawer was empty, but the Super remained gazing into its depths as if it were a crystal in which he might read the answer to all his problems. He stood silent for so long that the pink face of Mr Fairfax came over his shoulder to be reflected, puzzled and inquisitive, in the glass.

CHAPTER XXII

THE LONDON TRAIN WAS not crowded, and they obtained a compartment to themselves. White settled himself in a corner seat, stretched his mighty legs, and smiled across at his companion.

'Just the two of us, Mr Endicott. And very nice too.'

'Very nice indeed,' agreed Mark. 'Especially as you will now be able to tell me what it's all about.'

'Ah,' said the Super, taking his disreputable pipe from his pocket and proceeding to fill it, 'I suppose you are feeling rather in the dark.'

'You put it mildly. Here am I, reft from home, whirled off to London on the pretext that you wish me to take you to a theatrical agent whom, on reflection, I realize that you are well able to discover without my help. You haven't brought me merely for love of my blue eyes, so what is the idea?'

The Super's pipe made a horrible gurgling sound. He said, 'You can be of the greatest help to me, Mr Endicott. I told you that when I asked you to come with me, and I meant it.'

'I'd like to know a little more about it, all the same.'

White regarded him indulgently. The Chief Constable's number one suspect, he felt, was behaving very well. No ifs or buts about setting off at the shortest possible notice; he merely changed his trousers, put on a clean shirt, made arrangements for the welfare of his dog, and there he was. Make a good policeman, thought the Super, mentally conferring high praise.

He said, 'Tell you what, you ask me some questions, and if I can answer them I will. And you needn't start with the reason for this trip. Begin at the beginning—'

'Go on till I come to the end, and then stop?'

'It's a very good rule, you know,' said White seriously.

'And would that more writers of modern fiction were of your opinion! Well, to go to the beginning – why didn't you arrest me right away?'

'Because I wasn't sure that you had done it.'

'Why not?'

'Because you showed me an anonymous letter.'

'I don't see—'

'Oh, there were other reasons as well. We won't go into details now, Mr Endicott, if you don't mind.'

'A fat lot of use for me to mind,' grumbled Mark, staring discontentedly at the bland smoke-wreathed face. 'I know you'll tell me precisely what you think fit.'

'Well, naturally. But you can always ask me some more.'

'Thank's very much, I'm sure. I suppose you dismissed Grey and Marlowe for equally good reasons?'

White nodded.

'Then throwing out the three of us, where the dickens do you find your murderer? Other people in the village were nothing to Laura.'

'I'll ask you a question now,' said the Super, removing his pipe and pointing a large finger at Mark. 'How do you know that?'

'Good Lord, man, that's easy. The whole of God's Blessing, if you remove Brian Marlowe, held no-one who would interest her in the slightest degree. Laura's preoccupations weren't with women, you know. And strangers in the place would scarcely pass unnoticed.'

'Especially,' said the Super with severity, 'if they make foolish jokes on their arrival about forgers and murderers and wanted men. Very ill judged of you, those words, Mr Endicott.'

'I know that now,' said Mark meekly. 'At the time it seemed a good idea. I only wanted to shut the mouths of the two females sitting in front of me – and to take a rise out of Miss Faraday, who was convinced that I was either mad or drunk.'

'Nice little woman, that. More to her than meets the eye,' said the Super warmly. He chuckled suddenly. 'She and her book,' he said.

Mark stared. 'She told you about it? That is a queer thing! The other day she would have gone through fire and water rather than let that out.'

'I fancy she would go through fire and water now,' said the Super, 'though not for quite the same reason.'

'Having trailed your red herring sufficiently across the path,' said Mark, with his colour somewhat heightened, 'suppose we get back to the subject? Not that my questions seem to be getting me very far up to now.'

'They don't, do they?' The Super, who seldom laughed, chuckled again. 'Perhaps you don't ask the right ones.'

'Probably not. At any rate, I've finished asking, and my lesson is learnt. I'll wait until you're prepared to spill the beans.'

He pulled a newspaper from his pocket and disappeared behind it. White smoked placidly until his pipe was done, then leaned forward.

'You see, Mr Endicott, it's like this,' he said.

'I'm going for a stroll,' said Dinah, putting her head in at the sitting-room door. 'Shan't be long.'

'It's a lovely evening,' said Amy, looking up. 'I'd come with you only I must wash my hair.'

'What a pity,' said Dinah, rather too heartily. She added in haste, lest the older woman should change her mind, 'If you like I'll set it for you when I come in. I have some really good setting lotion.'

'It's very good of you,' said Amy, with a deprecating smile, 'but I don't think anyone can do much for hair like mine. It never would stay tidy.'

'You wait until I get going. You won't know yourself when I've finished with you,' said Dinah.

The encouraging smile faded from her face as she went out, and the dark shadows under her eyes emphasized the look of strain which had been noticeable of late. It was an evening of breathless heat, but the weather was not responsible for her lack of energy. Her feet moved as reluctantly as if she were one of her own pupils, creeping like a snail unwillingly to school.

She passed through the village, turned the corner and came, as Endicott had once done, to the gate of Killarney. Pausing there a moment before entering, she found her breath coming unevenly and her heart beating so fast that when she glanced down, she actually imagined that the bodice of her thin dress was visibly stirred by its violence. Hold on to yourself … don't be a complete fool, she thought, and opened the gate.

'Well, Dinah,' greeted Mrs Marlowe from the deckchair set in a shady patch on the lawn, 'come and get cool.'

No word of surprise at seeing her after her long absence, reflected

Dinah, as she crossed the lawn, but you could trust Mrs Marlowe for that. Not a hearty welcome, either, but nothing to make you uncomfortable for your past neglect. It must be very pleasant never to be troubled by emotion – to take life as it came, and be ever placidly content. But one must be old to embrace that Nirvana, so perhaps it wasn't so enviable after all.

'There's another deckchair over by the wall,' said Mrs Marlowe looking incuriously at her visitor. 'It's cooler here than indoors.'

'It's all right, thanks,' answered Dinah. 'I'll sit on the grass.'

She did so, tucking her brown legs under her and making an attractive enough picture in her pale cotton dress against the green background. Mrs Marlowe's calm gaze saw beyond this, noting the nervous movement of the hands in the girl's lap, and the lines of strain about the sensitive mouth.

'You've been worrying your head about that boy of mine,' she said. 'You shouldn't, you know.'

Dinah flushed unhappily but did not speak.

'He's got himself into a spot of trouble, I know that well enough, but it won't last. He'll find his feet again.'

Just as simple as that, thought Dinah, and wondered. Once again she saw Brian's face as she had seen it that night in the hall while the thunder rolled overhead. A spot of trouble …

'I was pleased when he drove off that night to fetch you from the dance,' said Mrs Marlowe, settling back more comfortably in her chair. 'I knew that silliness with Laura Grey wouldn't last.'

Dinah found her voice at last. 'You knew about that?'

'There's not much,' said Mrs Marlowe simply, 'that goes on in God's Blessing that I don't hear of sooner or later.'

'But – but didn't you mind?'

Mrs Marlowe looked down at her shocked face with an indulgent smile.

'My dear, men have to make fools of themselves over women like that sooner or later. Like puppies and distemper. His father had it late in life, and it's worse then. Besides, I hadn't learnt how to take it. I know better now.'

'But it was wrong! And it didn't even make him happy.'

'Unhappiness like that doesn't last,' said Mrs Marlowe placidly. 'Any more than growing pains. But he wasn't the only one who suffered.'

For a moment her plump hand touched the girl's downcast head. The gesture was a tender one, though the placid face was unchanged.

'You don't have to tell me,' said Mrs Marlowe. 'I know.'

Dinah glanced up quickly and began to understand. The protective covering, after all, was something achieved, not granted easily by a benevolent Providence. It was as if she saw, beneath the comfortable exterior, a girl who had once been hurt, humiliated and afraid.

She said in a choked voice, 'I think life is horrible.'

'You won't go on thinking that.'

With the desolate certainty of youth, Dinah knew that she was wrong. Whatever might happen in days to come, life was horrible. It took you just when happiness, that shining thing, seemed well within your grasp, and behold, the shining thing was a bubble which you had never really held at all. The brief moment of understanding for Brian's mother had gone. She meant to be kind, but there was nothing more.

'You're vexed with him, and of course you've reason to be,' said Mrs Marlowe drowsily. 'He's weak, like his father and always has been, but he'll come back to you.'

'Like a dog crawling back to be forgiven,' said Dinah under her breath.

'What did you say, dear?' There was an enormous yawn. 'So sorry – I'm half asleep.'

'It was nothing.' There was a pause. Mrs Marlowe closed her eyes.

A shadow fell across Dinah, and she looked up with a start.

'Brian! I didn't hear you come.'

'I thought you didn't.' He sat down beside her on the grass. 'The car's at the garage. I've walked up.'

'Your mother's asleep.'

'Yes. She feels the heat. Did you come to see Mother, or me?'

'You. Brian, the Superintendent has been to see Miss Faraday again.' He looked up quickly. 'Any news?'

'Not about – that.' The word 'murder' she found herself reluctant to use. 'He was talking about the anonymous letters.'

'Good Lord,' said Brian disgustedly, 'do you mean he's still wasting time nosing after that? I can't imagine why. They put such an old apple-woman in charge of the case. Good enough for motoring offences or petty thieving, but out of his depth in an affair like this.'

'I wouldn't be so sure. He's nobody's fool,' said Dinah.

Her heart was uplifted. For the moment she forgot what Laura had meant in her life. Brian wished the criminal to be found; she had been utterly, gloriously wrong in her suspicions.

'What are you looking so pleased about all of a sudden?' asked Brian.

'Nothing. Just that it's a lovely day.'

'Yes. It has been all along. Could you break away from your preoccupation with the weather sufficiently to go on with your tale?'

The tone took them easily back to their old relationship. It seemed that Brian was himself again. Wicked to rejoice in the death of another, but it was as if with the passing of Laura Grey the shadows had been swept away.

'I remembered that anonymous letter you had the evening when you and Endicott went to fight.'

'Oh yes. Have you told him?'

'What do you think? But it would be a good idea if you told him yourself.'

'It would, indeed. Only there's no need, you see. He got it out of me when we first met. Though what the devil it has to do with his investigations—'

'Apparently he thinks it all links up.'

'I'm dashed if I can see it. However, I was a good boy, and made my life an open book to the great detective.' He dropped a hand lightly over hers as it lay on the grass. 'May I take it that you've ceased from casting me as the first murderer?'

'I didn't,' said Dinah in a choked voice.

'Oh, my pet. You know that you thought I came to you with gore on my hands, to make you a cover for my activities. I was very hurt until I got things straight and realized how feasible it must have seemed to you.'

'I hated myself for thinking it – I never really believed it. Only it was the way you looked that night, as if the world had come to an end.'

'That's how I felt.' He hesitated, and his face was shadowed again. 'It's hard to explain but you see, Dinah, it's one thing to think that you and another person are both victims of a grand passion – quite another to know that you've been a conceited, misguided fool.'

The hand beneath his quivered slightly.

'I don't want to hear about you – and her,' said Dinah.

'Let me tell you. I ought to have known in the first place – but she made me believe it was real.'

'And wasn't it?'

'That evening when I drove her home, she made it clear enough. I had been good enough to pass the time for her, but she was utterly sick of me – bored to tears. I'd had it, in fact. She wanted no part in me then or ever.'

Dinah snatched her hand away. She turned on him, flaming with anger.

'So you came to me!'

He said in a low voice, 'You were all I wanted.'

'Thank you so much.' She sprang to her feet, her cheeks blazing. 'How simple. She didn't want you anymore, so you came to me. Am I supposed to be grateful?'

He had risen when she did. Now he laid his hands on her shoulders, compelling her to look up at him.

'Like a dog crawling back for forgiveness,' he said.

'You heard? Well, it's true! Don't think I'm sorry that I said it!'

'You're perfectly right, yet you've got it all wrong. I know I behaved abominably to you – my God, I don't need to be told that! But what I felt for you was utterly different.'

'I don't doubt it,' snapped Dinah.

He gave her shoulders a little shake. 'Shut up, will you, and listen. I didn't turn to you as second best. Can't you realize that a man can be mad and suddenly come to his senses? I swear to you my misery that night wasn't because she'd turned me down. It wasn't that at all.'

'How can I believe that? You looked as if you'd been through hell.'

'I felt it.'

'At losing her!'

'Can't you understand it wasn't that? It wasn't, I tell you! I was miserable, utterly humiliated, yes, but it was because in that instant I realized what a fool I'd been. I had lost her, but that was nothing. I'd never really had her to lose. The thing was that through my own damned folly I'd lost you.'

He released her and turned away, pushing his hands into his pockets. Forgotten in her deckchair, Mrs Marlowe cautiously opened her eyes.

'So now you know. You won't believe, of course, but there it is. The dog came crawling back all right, didn't he?'

There was a pause before Dinah said, in a queer voice, 'Yes, he did.'

Brian swung round, saw her face, and pulled her into his arms. Smiling, Mrs Marlowe closed her eyes again, and the ghost of Laura Grey went sighing down the breeze.

'It's a queer thing,' said Mr Julian Ross, leaning back in his chair and examining his shining nails with critical approval. 'I hadn't set eyes on the woman for a couple of years until three days ago, and now you come in making enquiries about her. I call it very queer.'

The Super, sitting very foursquare, nodded. He looked as out of place in the glossy surroundings of the theatrical agent's office as Laura had looked in God's Blessing. Mark, on the contrary, appeared quite at home.

'Poor Kathryn,' continued Mr Ross, tapping his teeth reflectively with a silver paperknife. 'Very dependable actress, and extremely good in her line. But her husband's death broke her all to pieces. When she walked out of the company no-one saw or heard of her again. Until now.'

'The husband was an actor too?'

'That's right. Gerald Arbuthnot. Real matinee idol – bundle of conceit until our Laura got her claws into him. Then, they say, he went completely dippy. Mad about her. The company thought the balloon would go up at any moment. Then Laura turned him down—'

'Why?'

'Lord knows. She tired easily. Probably for a better proposition. Anyhow, Arbuthnot's nerves go all to pieces, he becomes a wreck, takes an overdose of sleeping tablets and makes his final exit. Laura disappears and, it is rumoured, meets one of the landed gentry and becomes a pillar of county society. Kathryn goes no-one knows whither. And that's the end of that.'

'Until Kathryn reappeared,' said Mark.

'Yes, that's right. And Laura, too, makes her final exit.'

He looked at them intelligently. 'You aren't hinting that Kathryn is mixed up with the murder?'

'We have no evidence,' said the Super heavily, 'that she was implicated in any way. But the past life of the murdered lady might shed a light for us.'

'A pretty lurid light if you ask me,' said Mr Ross candidly. 'However, I sent Kathryn off to the Bunthorne Rep Company. They had a couple of actresses down with food poisoning, and were in a bad way.'

'Where are they now?'

'Sandbourne Bijou Theatre. Month's run. Second week,' said Mr Ross succinctly. 'That be all?'

'You haven't a photograph of the lady, I suppose?' asked White, glancing round at the lavishly endowed walls.

'Well, it's some time ago, and Kathryn was never a star. Just character parts. But I tell you what, if you'd like to call back in an hour, I'll have my secretary look through some old stuff. Might be lucky, might be not. You never can tell.'

'We can do that,' said the Super, looking at his watch.

Mr Ross nodded. 'Give you time to catch your train – for Sandbourne?'

'Thank you, sir. Plenty of time,' said the Super noncommittally.

When his two visitors had gone, Mr Ross sat for a few minutes before calling in his secretary. His fleshy face was furrowed with thought. He drummed impatiently on the shining surface of the desk.

'Don't like it. Don't like it a bit,' he said.

'Well, sir?' asked White. 'Any luck?'

'We've found them for you,' replied Mr Ross, indicating some papers on his desk with a wave of a beringed hand. 'Got out for a season in Bournemouth. Help yourselves.'

The two men leaned over the selection of dazzling smiles and thoughtful profiles presented to them. Mr Ross leaned over his desk, uttering helpful comments.

'There's Kathryn – Nannie, in *Dear Octopus*. Here again – Mrs Hackett in *The Ringer*.'

'Never know it was the same woman,' said White.

'No – she was good that way. Got right into the skin of her part. Seemed to change her entire personality.' He flipped over the pages. 'Look at this one. Gild blood and thunder – *The Grey Shadow*. Bigger part there – the murderess. Hallo. Found something?'

Mark had stiffened and exclaimed. From the shiny paper beneath his hand, a face he knew looked coldly up at him.

CHAPTER XXIII

THE SUPERINTENDENT AND MARK reached Sandbourne at 8.30 that evening, and drove straight to the Bijou Theatre. Mark sat back in his corner of the taxi, scowling upon the crowds of holiday makers who made a coloured pattern in the streets, enjoying to the utmost the sunshine which the season had so lavished upon them. He was very silent, as he had been during the journey from town. White leaned across and touched him on the arm.

'What's up, Mr Endicott?'

'If you must know,' said Mark, coming to life and looking at his companion with distaste, 'I loathe all this. Laura is dead, and you can't bring her back. Why hound down a woman who has had a raw enough deal already?'

'Why, indeed?' asked the Super, using sarcasm for the first time in Mark's memory of him. 'I'll tell you why, and I may have mentioned it before. I want the truth.'

'That sounds fine. All the same—'

'Look here, my lad,' interrupted the Super, speaking as if Mark were an erring constable, and with his voice surprisingly changed from its normal drawl, 'this won't wash, you know. I seem to remember that you were pretty glad I was out for the truth when you thought you were in danger. Now you're more or less clear, you start all this namby-pamby stuff. Do you want an innocent person to be pointed at as a murderer for the rest of his or her life? Whether you like it or not, I've got a job to do, and I mean to do it.'

'All right. Sorry. Get on with your job.'

'Don't worry, I'm going to. But if you feel so bad about it—'

'I said I was sorry. I'll go through with it.'

'Good. I know it's not pleasant, and if it weren't for the matter of identification, I wouldn't bother you.'

The taxi drew up. Surprisingly Pulleyblank advanced from a doorway and fell into conversation with his superior. Mark waited with a creeping sickness at the pit of his stomach. Closing in, the woman was nothing to him, and the curtain lecture in the taxi had been undeniably true, but it could not alter his feelings. And he thought again with a bitter mirth into what strange paths a desire for a cottage in the country had led him.

Pulleyblank, giving Mark a nod, returned to his doorway. Mark and the Super moved to the stage door. The doorkeeper looked up from a pessimistic study of the evening paper and viewed them without pleasure.

'Whaddya want?' he asked inhospitably.

'Not you, my lad. We want to see Miss Kathryn Arbuthnot.'

'Then you're unlucky. She ain't here.'

'What!' The Super's tone made the man look up with faint curiosity. 'You mean she's left?'

'I don't mean no such thing. How could she ha' left when she ain't been? No person of that name in the company.'

'All right. Then I'll see the stage manager, or someone in charge.'

'Oh, you will. And who do you think you are, Lord God Almighty?'

'No. I'm Superintendent White, of the Downshire County Constabulary. Will that make you move yourself?'

'Gaw!' said the doorkeeper, his jaw dropping. 'What the 'ell's up now?'

'You'll soon know,' said White ominously, 'if you keep me dangling here.'

The man laid down his paper and shambled ahead of them along a stone paved passage between rough cast walls. Turning a corner, they came to a row of cell-like dressing rooms, the first ornamented by a modestly tarnished star. This door opened as they approached, and a very blonde and voluptuous lady in a pink chiffon negligee emerged hastily.

'My God,' she observed, catching sight of the three men, 'what's this, the watch committee?'

'No, miss,' said the doorkeeper with relish, 'it's the police come to see Mr Marjoram or Mr Peters.'

'White slave traffic, or drug smuggling? My dear, how devastating! I only wish I could hear the fun, but I haven't a moment.' She gave White a dazzling smile, clutched the folds of pink around her admirable form, and moved off. Over her shoulder she said, 'If I meet them I'll send them back.'

'Darling, curse you, for God's sake! You're on!'

An excited gentleman had appeared from nowhere and was dancing in the passage like David before the Ark.

'All right, pet,' said the blonde soothingly. 'I'm OK. It's you they want.'

She was gone. The gentleman mopped his brow and spoke blasphemously of actresses in general and his leading lady in particular.

'Mr Marjoram, sir,' said the doorkeeper, advancing.

Mr Marjoram jumped. 'Well, Jones, what the devil is it now?'

'Police, sir,' said Jones with gloomy relish.

Mr Marjoram turned, caught his first glimpse of the visitors, and gave a very guilty start. He came forward uneasily.

'So sorry. I didn't see you before. A trifle preoccupied. What can I do for you?'

'We wish to see a member of your company. Miss Kathryn Arbuthnot.'

Mr Marjoram's brow cleared. He shook his head.

'Some mistake, old boy. The lady's not for burning – that's to say, she's not with us.'

'Do I understand that you know she is elsewhere?'

'I don't know a sausage, old boy. Never heard of her.'

'I was given to understand,' said White heavily, 'that an actress was sent to you at the beginning of the week by Mr Julian Ross.'

'Oh yes, certainly, but not the one you said. He sent us an Isobel Martin. She's on now.'

'Isobel Martin?'

'Yes, I didn't know her, but she's good. Playing the maid. This is her last performance.'

'How's that?'

'Something personal. Said she had an upsetting phone call. Fortunately Mary Garland, whose place she took, will be well enough to go on tomorrow.'

'Could we see the lady? Now, if possible.'

Mr Marjoram looked worried. 'I told you she's on. This is her big scene.'

'Surely we could stand somewhere without interrupting your play?

You see, sir, it's a matter of identification. If she turns out to be not the person I'm looking for, that will be that.'

'Well ...' Mr Marjoram fingered his chin doubtfully. He met the Super's eye and capitulated. 'Oh, all right. Can do. Only be quiet, if you will. This is a very tense scene, and we've got a full house.'

'We'll take care, sir,' said White soothingly.

Mark, walking in a dream between dangling ropes and dusty flats, found himself at length looking into a warmly lit oasis of colour – the stage. It was set for a woman's bedroom, all pink hangings, with shining glass on an elaborate dressing table where, before the triple mirror, sat the rose clad leading lady. Bending over the bed, her back turned to the watching men, was a maid in grey, a coquettish bow in her hair and with organdie strings hanging crisply from her waist. The full house of which Mr Marjoram had boasted was hushed and intent. In their dusty corner the watching men listened too. The blonde, nervously turning a hairbrush in her hands, haggard eyes gazing into the mirror, was speaking.

'Why I go on – why I bother myself to go on living at all when it's such a mess. Oh God – such an utter vile mess ...'

The maid said smoothly, 'You are tired, madam. You will feel better when you have rested.'

As she spoke she moved from the bed to stand beside the woman at the dressing table, so that she faced the audience with her profile to the two men. Mark felt an urgent hand on his arm and screwed up his eyes. Black hair instead of grey, colour on lips and cheeks – it was too much to ask.

'I can't be sure yet,' he whispered.

The hand gripped his arm and was withdrawn. White nodded.

Turning to Marjoram, he breathed, 'Which side does she come off?'

'Here,' mouthed Marjoram.

The maid had begun to move about the stage, picking up a dress and some underwear which lay strewn around. When her face was turned from the other woman, a smile touched her lips, faint but wickedly triumphant. Like a living thing, the sense of tension in the audience grew.

'Rested!' said the woman in pink. 'That's funny. That's damned funny. You know I can't sleep anymore.'

The maid said, 'But you will tonight, madam. I have some of the tablets which helped you before. I thought you might need them.'

'It won't be any good. Nothing is any good. What's that ham line?

Something about "I heard a voice cry, sleep no more."'

"'Macbeth hath murdered sleep, the innocent sleep."'

The woman on the stool swung around.

'How strangely you said that! As if – as if you were gloating over me. As if you were glad that I'm suffering like hell.'

'I, madam? Surely not. Your nerves must be playing you tricks.'

'I suppose so. I'm all broken up since Gerald died. Oh God, if only I could sleep! Sleep and forget.'

The golden head went down admist the appointments of the dressing table. A low and desolate sobbing moved tender hearts in the packed house. Marjoram, mindful only of the play, nodded his appreciation. He whispered to White, 'Look at the maid now.'

The woman in grey had not moved to look at the weeping figure, and offered no touch or word of comfort. Instead she gazed over the bowed head into the darkness of the theatre, and on her face the smile grew and grew – a Medusa smile, changing her to something with power to hurt, exultant in that power. She held the pose for a long moment, and when at last she moved a faint ripple stirred the audience, as if it had been unable to breathe until then. Mark wiped his forehead, amazed at his own reaction. The play was poor stuff enough, the dialogue mediocre, the situation threadbare with usage, but something in this woman had lifted it from the depths, to make it, for that instant, living and authentic. He had even forgotten the reason for his presence, forgotten the Super silent and watchful at his side.

The smile faded slowly, leaving the maid's face respectful and unremarkable as before. She said, laying a hand on the pink-clad shoulder, 'Come to bed, madam, I will get the tablets, and you will sleep tonight.'

The woman raised her head to gaze once more into the mirror. Pushing back her hair with a shaking hand, she said, 'Very well, Foster. No doubt you're right. You are always right. How long have you been with me?'

'Six months, madam,' said the maid smoothly. 'Since the New Year.'

'The New Year!' echoed the other. 'Since Mr Gerald died.'

'Yes, madam. Since Mr Sumner … died.'

The pause before the final word was very marked. A faint but perceptible ripple moved the audience again.

Her mistress rose wearily but with conscious grace, and drifted towards the bed.

'Turn the lights low,' she said, 'my head aches.'

'I'll get the tablets for you, madam,' said the maid.

The lights dimmed as she moved to a door on the right. White turned enquiringly to Marjoram, who whispered, 'OK. No exit. Glass of water and the tablets. Watch.'

On the stage the woman removed her wrap, revealing a clinging nightgown, also pearly pink. She posed for a moment seductively, then climbed into the bed. The maid came back.

She moved towards the dressing table, and the spotlight found her. Mark caught his breath. If he had not been sure before, there was now no shadow of a doubt. Some trick of the lighting had wiped colour from face, lips, and hair. Grey, absorbed and passionless, for that moment he saw her as he had seen her moving about her work in the cottage. His heart gave a sickening lurch, and his mouth was dry. He saw not the composed figure on the stage, not Mrs Shergold amazingly transformed, but a hunted creature on whom the jaws of the trap were slowly and remorselessly closing. It was a physical effort to nod to the Super; horrible to see the quick flash of satisfaction in the other man's eyes before he turned his attention to the stage again.

The maid put down the tumbler of water she was carrying, and came centre stage. With her back to the bed she lifted a small white box, and shook some tablets into her hand.

'Be careful with those things. They're dangerous,' warned the exhausted voice from the bed.

'I'll be careful, madam.' The maid was smiling again.

She moved deliberately to the dressing table. Her hand, caught in the light, seemed to float above the tumbler. There was a menace about the drooping fingers which made even the Super hold his breath. The hand swooped suddenly, and lifted the tumbler. The maid turned to the bed.

The light moved to the golden head, now raised from the pillows. Another hand took the tumbler and tilted it.

'Ugh! If taste counts for anything this should be good.'

'It is good, madam,' said the maid.

The woman handed back the tumbler and lay back. She said drowsily, 'Strangely enough, I believe that you are right. I feel that I shall sleep tonight.'

The maid said, in a soft voice which could be heard in the farthest corner of the theatre, 'I know that you will.'

'You … know?' Drowsiness faded; the voice was puzzled, with an underlying note of fear. 'You sound very sure about it, I must say.'

'I am sure, madam.'

'What the hell do you mean by that?'

The maid smiled. 'Only what I say.'

The woman in the bed pulled herself up, the quilt falling back and the light shining on her shoulders. Her wide eyes were fixed on the insignificant figure at her side. She said, in a suffocated voice, 'You haven't – you can't have been fooling with those damned tablets.'

The maid did not speak.

'I told you! I told you they were dangerous. You didn't – you can't have given me more than two?'

There was a pause, in which the only sound was the hurried breathing of the woman on the bed.

'Oh yes,' said the maid at last. 'Quite a number more.'

The woman in the bed screamed suddenly. She leaned out, reaching for the telephone which stood beside the bed. The maid gripped her shoulders and threw her back.

'Better save your strength, hadn't you?' she mocked. She bent over the other woman, her face transfigured by triumphant hate. Mark forgot where he stood, forgot the stage trappings, forgot Mrs Shergold. If this were acting it was beyond anything he had ever seen. He felt that he looked on reality – on a woman who watched another woman die by her hand and gloried in the act. At his side he heard the Super draw a deep breath. Mr Marjoram had ceased to admire, and was looking puzzled and slightly apprehensive.

The woman on the bed sank back amongst her pillows as if all strength had gone from her. She said in a breathless voice, 'You can't do this to me. My God! It's murder!'

'It is indeed, Dawn,' sneered the maid. 'How clever of you to discover it.' Her voice hardened, became edged with fury. She pushed her face close to the other woman, glaring down at her.

'You always were clever, weren't you, Dawn Allinghan? Clever Dawn, who could always get what she wanted, especially if it belonged to someone else. And yet not clever enough to know why I've done this to you.'

Only a muffled moaning answered her. She leaned over to slap the prostrate woman's face. It was an honest slap which sounded through the theatre. Mark saw the victim jump and her lips move in soundless remonstrance. Mr Marjoram ran a finger under his collar and looked as if he, too, suffered pain.

'Don't think you're going yet, damn you! I've things to say to you first. Wake up and listen to me.'

'Why must you torture me? If you've killed me, at least let me die in peace.'

'You'll die, Dawn, never doubt that. But in peace? Why should you expect that? Did Gerald die in peace? Yes – it makes you start, even now, to hear me speak his name – as if I hadn't a better right to it than you! He was mine, do you hear, mine – until you had to come along and steal him from me.' The voice broke on a sudden dry sob. She pressed the palms of her hands to her eyes, and when she removed them tears shone on her cheeks. 'I wasn't beautiful, or clever, or anything like you, and yet he loved me. We loved one another, and we were happy. Until you came along.' The dreaming voice hardened again. She fairly spat the next words. 'Then you saw him, didn't you, and wanted him, and couldn't bear to think that he had strength to resist you. So you went on until he hadn't the strength to fight any more. It was horrible the power that you had – like the sorceress who turned men into swine. It is right that I should send you where you can't use it any more.'

'Could I help it if he loved me?'

'Oh, yes. You could have helped it.'

'You're mad, mad! I'm dying, through you. Isn't that enough for you?'

The other woman said softly, 'Gerald died, too.'

'I didn't kill him! You can't blame me for that!'

'No? When you had bewitched him until he had thrown aside everything for you, and then learned that you had no further use for him? Can't you understand that's the one thing unforgivable? Your taking him I could have borne but when you had him, you didn't want him any more. How do you think he felt then? You'd sucked him dry of everything, Dawn – he had nothing left. Not even self-respect. So he died. As you are dying now.'

'No!' She pulled herself up again, leaning out, clutching at the other woman's unresponsive arms. 'I won't die, I tell you. My God, I can't die – I'm not ready. I'm afraid to die. Can't you do something – get me something, anything! You must, you must, you must! Can't you see what you're doing? Help me now – only help me. I swear I'll make it worth your while—'

'You couldn't do that, Dawn,' said the maid.

She pushed the other woman back and stood watching her, all trace of passion fading from her face. Mrs Shergold again, cold, grey, lifeless. The sobbing from the bed changed to heavy breathing; the golden head seemed to settle into the pillows. One arm fell heavily over the side of the bed. The maid bent forward and gazed for a long moment before she spoke.

'Yes,' she said, 'you – and I – will sleep tonight.'

It was her exit line, spoken as it had been written. But immediately after, she broke with precedent by leaving the stage on the opposite side to the group of men waiting in the wings.

CHAPTER XXIV

THE CURTAIN FELL TO a thunder of applause. Under cover of the sound, the Super barked a word not used in polite society, and turned menacingly on Marjoram, who was fairly gibbering with surprise.

'You told me she would come out here!'

'So she should, but she's been altering her lines and now she's altered her exit. My God,' wailed Mr Marjoram, wringing his hands, 'will someone tell me what the hell is going on here?'

His plaint fell on the empty air. White, with Mark at his heels, was already pounding across the stage. The leading lady, rising briskly from her deathbed, fell back with a shriek of mingled mirth and surprise. White tugged viciously at the door through which his quarry had disappeared. The canvas quivered, but the door gave and he shot through, with clamour growing in his wake. A scene shifter appeared in his path and was swept aside by a hamlike hand. Blasphemously enquiring what went on, he regained his balance, to be pushed out of the way yet again by Mark. Blinking, he stood back wondering what might follow, and was therefore no impediment to the progress of Mr Marjoram, the leading lady, a fireman and various bewildered members of the stage staff who had joined in the chase.

'The crazy gang come to brighten us up a bit. I don't think,' said the stage hand, and himself joined the throng.

The pounding feet of the Super had carried him at a surprising speed along the passage to the stage door. The doorkeeper once more lowered his paper and viewed him with displeasure and surprise.

'You again?' he said wearily.

'Which way did she go?' barked White.

'She? 'Oo?'

'Isobel Martin,' volunteered Mark.

'Oh, 'er. No ways that I know of.'

'You mean she hasn't come out?'

'Course she hasn't. She won't have had time yet to get dressed, will she?'

White stepped into the doorway and beckoned Pulleyblank, who was leaning in a Formbyesque manner on a lamppost on the opposite side of the street. He came to life on seeing the Super and stepped briskly over to him.

'Anyone come out?'

'Not a soul,' said Pulleyblank.

'And for why?' demanded the doorkeeper. 'Because no-one ain't ready yet to come out. Don't I keep telling you?'

Like Mr Marjoram, he discovered that his audience was not.

'Flatfooted potbellied slops,' he said, and returned to his studies.

'What is up?' muttered Pulleyblank to Mark as they raced after his superior. 'Never saw the old man in such a flap.'

Mark explained hastily. Pulleyblank looked worried.

'Bit of bad if she's slipped him. One thing's dead certain, she didn't come out of that door. I've had my eyes glued to it till they fairly popped.'

Mark did not answer. He was listening to White, who had now made contact with Mr Marjoram, still surrounded by staring and whispering satellites, and was snapping questions at the flustered gentleman.

'No other way out? You're sure?'

'Of course I am. Unless ...'

'Unless what?'

'My dear chap, don't bellow at me!' Mr Marjoram uttered a distraught bleat. 'I was only going to say unless she went through the pass door at the side of the stage into the auditorium. But she'd still be in her maid's dress and makeup, and someone would be bound to notice her. And I personally—'

'What?'

Mr Marjoram winced. 'I should think, if you don't mind my saying so, that you're making a devil of a stink over nothing. Isobel is probably in her dressing room peacefully taking off her makeup at this moment.'

'I doubt it,' said the Super grimly. 'All the same, we'll go and see.'

The procession surged forward. Mr Marjoram indicated a door.

'Thanks,' said White, raking the gathering with a cold eye. 'I'll deal with this.'

He glanced round to see that Mark and Pulleyblank were close behind him, turned the handle gently and opened the door.

They looked into a tiny room, brightly lit and unbearably stuffy. The figure of the maid, still in her stage uniform, was seated at the littered dressing table, her back to the door. She did not move as the three men entered the room. That much was seen by the watching group before the little scene was shut away from them.

Inside the room for one second, the eyes of the two policemen met. Mark, standing a little to one side and with the old distaste for this business swamping him, saw that he was forgotten. This was a police matter, in which he had no part.

The Super cleared his throat loudly and stepped towards the still figure. Unobtrusively Pulleyblank moved in on the other side. Mark tried to look away, and could not. His heart was beating unevenly, and his throat was dry. He felt as if he himself were a fugitive, with no space left him in which to turn.

The Super said interrogatively, 'Isobel Martin? I have some questions to ask you.'

The woman at the table moved for the first time. Turning on her stool she faced them, so that the back of her head, flanked by the watchful faces of the two men, was reflected in the light-framed mirror. She had taken off her dark wig, and her hair was grey and dishevelled. The makeup, too, had been wiped from her face, and it showed under the cruel light plain, faded, and unutterably weary. She looked not at the Superintendent but across the room at Mark, and her eyes seemed faintly amused. He swallowed, and looked away.

'I am sorry to seem rude,' said the woman who had been Mrs Shergold, 'but I have had an exhausting day, and am very tired. Could your business wait until tomorrow?'

'I'm afraid not,' said the Super gravely. 'I am a police officer, and my questions must be put to you now.'

'Very well,' she said wearily. 'If you must.'

White cleared his throat again. 'You have been known as Kathryn Arbuthnot?'

'That was my stage name. I have also, as Mr Endicott will have informed you, used another.'

Her voice was low and expressionless, completely without fear. She rested an elbow on the table, and laid her cheek on her hand. The pose was that of a tired child, totally uninterested in what was going on around it, wishing only to be left alone. Her fatigue was obvious in every line of her thin body. Mark hated himself again.

'I have to ask you to tell me your movements on the night of 20th July last. The night of the murder of Laura Grey.'

'It wasn't murder,' said Kathryn Arbuthnot gently.

Mark caught his breath. He saw the Super stiffen, and one hand begin a soundless drumming on his thigh.

'If you wish to make a statement, I will have it taken down and read over to you so that you may sign it. I have—'

The tired voice broke in upon his measured utterance.

'There is no need. I have been very good.' She actually gave the ghost of a laugh.

'I don't understand,' said White, rather uneasily.

'I mean that I've saved you the trouble. It's all written down, here, in my bag. I never meant an innocent person to suffer – there has been suffering enough already. I killed her, but it wasn't murder. I'm glad she is dead – very glad but I didn't mean to kill her. I wanted her to live and be hurt much longer.'

There was still no expression in the whispering voice. It was as if a ghost were speaking, looking back on life from a great distance. In that lifetime there had been pain and passion. There was no feeling any more.

'Hurt,' said White quickly. Pulleyblank had his notebook out and was writing busily.

'I wanted to hurt her.'

'So you had been blackmailing her? Why?'

'It wasn't blackmail. I didn't want money. I didn't want anything of her except to know that she was suffering, as she had made others suffer. You needn't bother me any more. I told you, it's all written down.'

'That's all very well—'

She said, 'I'm too tired. It's no use. She's gone, and there's nothing left for me to do. I've told you, I killed her. It's all over. I didn't think you'd find me, but you did. I still can't think why. But you won't get me, all the same.'

'What do you mean?'

The Super leapt into action. He gripped her thin shoulders, forcing her to lift her head. She looked up at him, and there was faint triumph in her shadowed eyes. He stared into her face, and saw that her lids were closing.

'Wake up. My God—'

'It's no use,' she whispered, her voice the merest thread of sound,

'I took them when I went off stage to get the water. I knew you were coming – anyhow – don't want to go on ...'

The whispering voice faded and died. She seemed to settle herself against the broad shoulder of the Superintendent as if too comfortably drowsy for further speech. Across her head, the eyes of the two policemen met again.

'Get a doctor – call an ambulance,' said White hoarsely. 'And hurry, for God's sake. You – Endicott – come and help me.'

But even as he worked and sweated, he knew that nothing would bring her back again.

It was written down, as she had said. The Super showed Mark the statement the next day, and as he read it he was glad to know that Kathryn Arbuthnot would never stand her trial. And as the story unfolded itself, he heard most clearly the voice of the stage maid who had spoken words of her own as she played her final part. 'He was mine – you took him away from me and when you had him you didn't want him any more.' Yes, there it was. That said everything. And it spoke no more than the truth of Laura, too – Laura, who would never grasp, and grow weary, and make others suffer again.

The statement began abruptly.

As soon as I discovered where Laura Grey had gone I followed her to God's Blessing. It had taken me a long time to trace her, but I managed it in the end. Of course I had to wait my chance of getting into the village, but the advertisement for a working housekeeper was just what I needed. I had played that sort of part often enough, and though old Fairfax was a slavedriver I had never been afraid of work. I was brought up on a farm, and life wasn't easy there. I hadn't thought I should go back to scrubbing and washing again, but I would have done harder things than that to work out my plans. I did not mean to kill her. Living can be so much harder than death. I wanted her to live and suffer and be afraid. My husband, who had loved me, killed himself because of her. I thought it only fair that she should suffer too.

When I saw Mr Endicott on the bus I thought that he had followed her, like me. At one time he was mad about her, I know. He didn't recognize me, and of course it was years since we met, and then we hardly knew one another. I had a part in a play of his, which didn't run very long. I was a charwoman in that; I often thought of it when I was cleaning his cottage for him.

211

I thought, by taking the job when the old man suggested it, I might discover Endicott's game. I thought he might cause a good deal of trouble between Laura and her husband, but nothing happened. Young Marlowe was no good, either, though the village talked enough. I suppose the husband was like all the other fools, and would believe black was white if she told him so. Anyhow, nothing happened. So I had to do it all myself.

When I saw her that afternoon floating across the lawn and looking as innocent as an angel, I found it hard not to shriek out what she was then and there. But I managed to wait. She couldn't have been feeling as calm as she looked, because she had read my last letter by then. I told her to meet me by Corpse Path copse that evening. She wouldn't know who had written, of course, but I thought she would be frightened enough to come, and I was right. Old Fairfax and I went back to the house for tea – it would have hurt him to pay for a cup out, of course. When I had cleared away I said I had a headache, so I put his supper ready and went to my room. Getting out was easy enough; I had cleaned the windows that morning, and left the ladder outside. The thunder was so loud as I climbed down that once I missed a rung, and nearly fell. I was more careful after that. I wondered if the weather would keep her from coming, but when I crossed the field she was there, waiting.

She looked at me as if she was surprised, and moved back to see if I should go by. I said, 'I think you are waiting for me.'

She said, 'Is it you who wrote to me?'

I said, 'Yes, Laura. I wrote the letters.'

She said, 'But, for God's sake, why? I don't even know you.'

I said, 'It doesn't matter now who I am. Once I was Gerald Arbuthnot's wife.'

She said, 'Kathryn!'

If I had been a ghost she couldn't have sounded more afraid. I was glad to hear her like that.

She said, 'You followed me here.'

I said, 'You thought you were safely hidden. You could never hide from me.'

She said, 'What do you mean to do?'

I said, 'One day I am going to tell your husband what kind of woman you are. It may be tomorrow, it may not be for months. But one day I shall tell him.'

I saw her face clearly, in a flash of lightning. She didn't look pretty then. It was worth the waiting, to see her so brought down. She gasped out that her husband would not believe me, but I only laughed. Then she began to plead, and to offer me money – as if that was what I wanted. The thunder crashed and the rain poured down. I remember it now. At the time I scarcely noticed it.

I leaned forward and shouted in her ear, 'Now you know, you can go home. I shall be watching and waiting ...'

It was then that she brought the pistol from her bag. I hadn't expected that. I remember it struck me that there must be more than I knew for her to be so desperate. I gripped her wrist and tried to get it away, but she was very strong, and she wouldn't let go. I saw her face, with the hood fallen back. It was streaming with rain. I don't know who touched the trigger, and I scarcely heard the report because just then the thunder crashed again. She went limp, and fell. The revolver was in my hand. I didn't touch her, but I knew that she was dead.

I left her there, and ran towards the gate. The rain seemed to beat me down, and the lightning frightened me. All the same, I was glad of the storm, because I knew it would keep sane people indoors. I was almost at the gate when I remembered the revolver.

There was a handkerchief in my pocket. I had taken it from a box in the old man's bedroom the week before when I had a cold. I knew he wouldn't miss it because he always used khaki ones, and anyway I meant to wash it and put it back. Now I wiped the revolver and wrapped the handkerchief round it. I knew the bank was full of rabbit holes. I found one and pushed the thing in as far as I could reach.

I didn't see a soul on my way back. I slipped in through the back door with my shoes in my hand. I rolled them up inside my mackintosh and pushed it into the copper. I crept up to my room and got there just in time. A few minutes after, the old man came to the door to ask if I was all right.

I didn't sleep much, and I was up before six the next morning. There were things for me to do. I wrapped up the mackintosh and my muddy shoes and put them into my case. I remembered to put the ladder back in the woodshed, and I scrabbled over a footprint on the path. Then I wrote myself a letter, went round to the front of the house and when I saw the mail van go by, I pushed it through the letterbox.

When I took Mr Fairfax up his tea, I showed him the letter. He was sorry I was called away, but he took it all in. I left a few things in my room to look as if I was coming back. When I caught the bus I couldn't think of one thing I had left undone. I did wish that I had not taken the revolver, because if I had pushed it into Laura's hand it might have looked like suicide, and saved a lot of bother. And, of course, I could have

stayed. I just didn't want to. I didn't run away because I was afraid,
because I didn't see how the police could possibly pin anything on me.
But I've just had a phone call, and it seems they have.

   I'm not going on. I don't suppose they would bring it in as anything
but manslaughter, but I shan't wait to see. I don't want to go on at all.
There's nothing left without him, and it's time for me to go. I have what
I need. I should have used it when Gerald died, but I wanted to find
her first. At least, I've done that. I should like to know how the police
tumbled to me, but it doesn't matter. I'm going to die, so nothing matters
any more. And she has gone first!

Mark folded the paper and handed it back to the Super. He said, with an
effort, 'You did a smart job of work. Congratulations.'

White shook his head. 'I slipped up. Badly.'

'In not realizing she'd taken that stuff?'

'Of course. It's my job to see things like that. I thought she looked
ghastly, but put some of it down to her having just removed her make
up. But I should have realized. Bring 'em back alive White – that's me.'

He shrugged his great shoulders as if throwing off a burden. 'What's
done is done. No use chewing the fat now.'

'At least,' said Mark, 'you didn't arrest the wrong person, which I
imagine many people in your shoes would have done.'

'There is that,' agreed White, his thoughts winging to the Chief
Constable.

'And I think it's rather a good solution.' The Super looked at him
with faint contempt.

'Yes, indeed. Very nice and tidy, isn't it? Like the ending to one of
those damn fool detective novels, when the author doesn't want the
trouble of writing up a trial. The little woman has gone to her Maker –
all debts paid. Very touching. She had reason to hate Laura, no doubt,
but have you forgotten that she went calmly off, leaving you in the front
line of suspects?'

'I haven't forgotten that I owe my life to you.'

'Oh come, now,' said the Super, looking coy, 'that's going a bit too far.'

'I don't think so. As I said before, a smart piece of work. Now that the
tumult and the shouting have died, would you mind telling me what
put you on the right track in the first place?'

'The anonymous letters,' replied White briefly.

Mark frowned. 'I don't see—'

'You could if you stopped to think. They were all sent to people having some connection with Laura Grey. Young Marlowe, yourself, Ralph Grey.'

'That won't do. What about Miss Faraday?'

The Super's eyes twinkled. 'Oh, she comes into it all right.'

'I don't see where.'

'At the door of your cottage. Being a ministering angel. Her letter was warning her to keep off the grass.'

'Good God,' said Mark.

'Mind you, I didn't get that clear for some time. The thing is, the writer was out for Laura's blood. You might compromise her, therefore you were not to be distracted from the good work by the wiles of Miss Faraday. Young Marlowe, too, might be hoped to do his stuff, but neither of you did what she wanted, so she took action herself.'

'You mean she hoped an open scandal would be made, so that Ralph would give Laura what she deserved?'

'That's it. She told Marlowe where the powder compact was (by the way, you didn't mention that to me, Mr Endicott. You should have, you know) thinking that you and he might start something. You did have a slight scuffle, I believe.'

'Lord save us,' said Mark helplessly, 'the man knows everything.'

'Just as well for you that I do,' said the Super, with some severity. 'But as I say, matters didn't move quickly enough for her. And you know the rest.'

'I'm damned if I do. Anonymous letters, well and good. That doesn't explain how you knew that the innocent Mrs Shergold wrote the things.'

A slow smile lightened the Super's face. He looked like a contented Buddha. He said ruminatively, 'You know, it is true what they say.'

'What who say?'

'All of them,' said the Super dreamily. 'It's a saying.'

'If you don't want to tell me,' said Mark frigidly, 'say so, and I'll break up the party.'

The Super started. 'Eh? Sorry, Mr Endicott, I was just thinking. They say that every criminal makes one slip.'

'And had she?'

'She had. As she said, she was very careful. She packed everything incriminating. But in the top drawer of her dressing chest was something that gave me a clue. A real clue, like the detectives in books find. On the newspaper lining was a smear of ink.'

'Ink?'

'Green ink,' said the Superintendent. And he smiled again.

CHAPTER XXV

THE NEWSPAPERS, AS THE Superintendent had promised, received their straw, made their bricks, and erected therefrom a pleasing edifice. The stage parts played by Kathryn Arbuthnot had been minor ones, but now, for a brief moment, her name shrieked from the headlines before the world forgot her. Mr White tied up loose threads and went happily back to his normal round. God's Blessing exclaimed, discussed, marvelled, and slowly sank to the even tenor of its days.

Mr Fairfax, a sadder and a wiser man, advertised no more, but the village with nods and becks and wreathed smiles hinted that his lonely state would not be a lasting one. Mrs Hale was on the track, half a bed and a piller to let, said God's Blessing, and awaited the outcome with interest.

'... and say what you like,' said Mrs Cossett to one and all, 'house-keeper or no housekeeper, he at Corpse Path Cottage were in it more than meets the eye. Nothing happened here afore he come ...'

Miss Faraday arrived early for the meeting of the Literary Society. She looked pale but determined, and, amazingly, almost pretty. Dinah, overflowing with happiness and with a laudable desire to pass some of her superfluity to others, had taken her in hand. Her hair was cut short without straggling ends, and softly waved; for probably the first time in her life she wore a hat which looked as if it belonged to her. Dinah had said, marvelling, that ten years had been shorn from her apparent age, and in this she spoke no more than the truth. Warming to her work, she added a faint touch of rouge, the correct shade of powder and a trace of lipstick, and eyed her creation like Pygmalion.

Amy submitted amiably, but with so little real interest in the proceedings that Dinah felt it probable that she would, left to her own devices, swiftly backslide into the mire of utter dowdiness. When taxed with this, Amy merely smiled vaguely, murmuring that she had always known her taste was poor. Her tone added so clearly that she added small importance to this defect that Dinah, exasperated, said no more. Nonetheless, she felt a justifiable pride as she glanced from her seat into the body of the hall and saw her handiwork. But when Brian came in with the old look of sulky boredom gone, and a quick glance at herself, she forgot Amy, new hat and all. The world was warm and comfortable, the past nothing but a cold and empty dream. She knew that she had no pride, to be so abjectly thankful for a man who had lately been crazy for another woman, but drowned by a wave of happiness, the thought had no power to sting. Who cared for pride, when the moon had dropped into one's empty hands?

Colonel Stroud came in glistening like a fondant from his walk in the heat. He was followed by Mr and Mrs Richards, on whose heels came Mrs Oliphant, clutching a sheaf of papers and wearing an enormous hat. Miss Margetson and a friend took up modest positions farther back, and began to talk with their heads close together. Mr Heron approached the table and leaned over to Colonel Stroud.

'Just seen Mr Grey,' he said.

Colonel Stroud ceased from mopping his brow and looked interested.

'Poor feller, poor feller. How does he seem?'

'Not too bad,' said Mr Heron, hissing faintly. 'He's going away for a few days.'

'The best possible thing. But he'll be back. All his roots are here. And I hope,' said Colonel Stroud viciously, 'if he marries again – as he should – it will be a good, honest sensible gal, not a ...'

Remembering Dinah in time, he swallowed the word which had sprung to his lips, and cleared his throat violently. To her amazement, Dinah was conscious of a sudden pity for Laura Grey, gone, and, as it seemed, regretted by none. Unless Ralph Grey mourned, he had loved her but so had others whose love had died. "All lovers young, all lovers must consign to thee, and come to dust." Her eyes pricked momentarily with tears. It wasn't fair that love and joy should so inevitably decay. She met Brian's eyes again across the room, and the thought was banished. After all, said a voice in her heart, we're here, we're young ...

'Queer affair, altogether,' said Colonel Stroud, lumping together Ralph's marriage, Laura's behaviour, and her violent death. 'Not the kind of thing we're used to at all. God bless my soul!' he added, staring.

'What?' asked Mr Heron, rather surprised.

'Here's that feller from Corpse Path Cottage. Just come in.'

'He's a member. He paid his subscription,' said Dinah.

'No doubt. Somehow, though, I thought he'd be leaving the place. Don't know what he came here for in the first place. Don't know what he's doing here at all.'

At the moment, Endicott was committing the blameless act of seating himself beside Miss Faraday, who greeted him with heightened colour and a tremulous smile. Mrs Richards turned massively in her seat and gave him a gracious nod. Mark was cleared now of all suspicion; what was more to the point, he was also connected in the mind of Mrs Richards with a charitable and courageous act on her own part for which her husband had warmly commended her. Therefore Mrs Richards was gracious, and Endicott inclined his head courteously in reply.

Colonel Stroud rose and introduced the speaker of the evening, Mrs Oliphant, naturally using the phrase that good wine needed no bush. The lady's subject was, not surprisingly, poems and poets, and as no false modesty hindered her from quoting freely from her own works, her address was at least original, which can scarcely be said for all such efforts. Mark, who looked tired but not unamiable behaved well throughout. When the poetess sat down, however, he turned to his neighbour.

'Is this why you asked me to come? Your note led me to expect something new and strange.'

'Wait a bit,' said Amy in a strangled whisper. 'You'll see.'

He observed her attentively, noted the change in her appearance and the fact that she was shaking with nervousness. Funny little thing, thought Mark, with a kind of affectionate amusement, what the deuce is she at now?

He was not left to wonder long. As the thanks to Mrs Oliphant died, Amy rose, and caught the chairman's eye. Colonel Stroud, who had never before seen Amy on her feet at any meeting, blinked. Another poetess?

'Ah h'r'm. Miss Faraday?' he said warily.

'Mr Chairman,' said Amy faintly. 'I have something to say.'

'Contributions by our members,' murmured the Colonel automatically, 'are always welcome.'

Dinah looked at the little face under the pretty hat and thought

– of all the dark horses! The Reverend George Richards turned to smile encouragingly. Endicott murmured, 'Attagirl!'

'It is not a contribution,' said Amy, twisting her fingers together. 'It is a confession.' She gulped, and added, with an admirable economy of words, '*How Does Your Garden Grow*? I wrote it.'

There was a stunned pause. In the utter silence, every eye turned on the unhappy authoress, who felt a veritable Hester Prynne, with the scarlet letter blazing on her breast. Colonel Stroud, utterly at a loss, stared helplessly. Dinah blinked, and wondered if she dreamed. The voice of Mr Heron broke the silence.

'Well, I'm damned,' he said.

As if at a signal, the gathering exploded into speech. Amy sat down rather suddenly. The colour had left her cheeks. She was not sure whether this had been a mistake, or a far, far better thing than she had ever done, but it was certain that virtue had gone from her.

'Bear up, sister,' said the voice of Mark in her ear, 'the worst is past.'

He sounded amused. Of course, it would be merely a laughing matter to him. She had made a fool of herself yet again, and to no purpose. Tears pricked her eyes.

'It's all right, I tell you,' said Mark reassuringly. 'They won't cast you into outer darkness. You'll see.'

She looked at him, unconvinced but vaguely comforted.

'It seems,' said Colonel Stroud, rising, 'that we have entertained angels unawares. May I congratulate you, Miss Faraday?'

Amy's startled ears were assailed by a rattle of applause.

Everywhere smiling faces greeted her. Mr Heron shook his head, but smiled with the rest. Miss Margetson leaned across.

'Oh, Miss Faraday,' she said breathlessly, 'if I brought along my copy, would you autograph it for me?'

Agreeing in a dazed voice, Amy became conscious that Mr and Mrs Richards were standing before her.

'I don't, as you know, like your book,' began Mrs Richards.

'Neither do I,' said Amy sadly.

'But I admire your ability, which, I trust, may one day be put to better use.'

'And my wife and I,' added Mr Richards, 'both admire your courage, which is very great.'

So he understood she must have made it plain to everyone, but she told herself that she did not care.

Colonel Stroud rose again. The Richards returned to their seats.

'This,' said the Colonel, beaming around him, 'is a day which adds new laurels to our society. Already with a poetess in our midst' (Mrs Oliphant modestly drooped her head) 'we now find that a novelist, too, has been blushing unseen amongst us. What further revelations await us—'

'Ask Mr Endicott. He writes,' broke in Mr Richards.

'Very well,' said Colonel Stroud, rather taken aback. 'Would you have any objection, sir, to telling us in what direction your own literary ambitions lie?'

Mark rose with an unholy light in his eye.

'Since revelations seem to be the order of the day, none,' he said cordially. He looked around him modestly. 'I,' he said, 'am Annabel Lee.'

He was still smiling to himself as he turned the corner into the lane. The rabbit had stood not upon the order of her going, but she would not escape him by running away. There were things to be said. He saw the figure approaching him, and the smile left his lips.

'I've been wanting to see you,' said Ralph Grey.

Mark halted, with a strong feeling of discomfort. The position was a foul one, say what you would. The other man looked quite normal, though very tired, but he could certainly find no pleasure in a meeting with himself.

'That day,' began Ralph, with an effort, 'I behaved like a fool. Sorry.'

'Nothing to be sorry for,' said Mark gruffly. 'Any man in your position would have thought the same.'

'Good of you to say so. And, of course, then I didn't know ...' He broke off again.

Mark looked away. Poor devil, the worst part of it had been his. And what in God's name was there to say?

He muttered, 'It wasn't as bad as it sounds, you know. She hadn't heard from me for nearly a twelvemonth – no means of knowing whether I was alive or dead.'

Ralph said nothing.

'The devil was in it that I should have come here. I didn't know – I should have left as soon as I realized, but I was too pigheaded. I had bought the cottage, and it would have seemed like running away. That day she came it wasn't because of any feeling for me – it was only because she was afraid.'

'I know. It's all been a miserable tangle, and none of our talking will set it right. I only wanted to say I was sorry.'

'I'm sorry, too,' said Mark.

There was a pause. Ralph glanced at his watch, with obvious relief. 'I must be off. I'm going away for a few days, but I shall be back. Like you, I don't run away.' He smiled suddenly. 'Thank the Lord, there's always work.'

They shook hands, and Ralph limped away. Mark watched him out of sight.

'Poor devil,' he said again.

Amy wandered into the garden. She was hot, and the house seemed airless. The buzz of comment and laughter which had followed Endicott's statement still echoed in her ears. She was glad that Dinah was out, and that she herself need talk no more. An immense weariness engulfed her. She sat down on the grass and gazed vacantly into space.

The gate clicked. She started, and looked up.

'Oh,' she said unwelcoming. 'It's you.'

'In person,' agreed Mark. 'May we join you?'

Without waiting for a reply, he came across the lawn and sat down beside her. James greeted her politely, wandered along the hedge, and was lost to view.

Endicott sat in silence for a moment, then he said, 'Went well, didn't it? Plenty of good clean fun.'

'You didn't expect them to believe you, surely?'

'Why not? It happens to be the truth.'

Amy gaped. 'But – but I thought you were joking!'

'And you had many to bear you company. If you want to keep a secret, tell the truth. It's true enough, my dear. Before the war I had been turning out that tripe for years.'

'I didn't think it was tripe!'

'Neither did a large and appreciative public. But can't you understand how sick I got of it? "So my lady leaned upon my arm, and we took the road – together." Muck. Slush. Infernal sentimental bilge. If I could write one – only one – worthwhile book before I die I might forgive myself.'

'That's why you came here?'

'Yes. Not to follow Laura.' He took a deep breath, and looked away. 'We were married, you know,' he said.

'I ... didn't know,' said Amy, in a small voice.

'Nobody did. And she naturally wanted it kept quiet afterwards.'

'But I don't understand.'

221

'She probably thought I was dead. A bit of a shock for her when I turned up. And, to be fair, just as big a shock for me.'

Amy was silent. She was recalling Laura's face that evening at the hall, and the expression of fear she had read on it. She had not been mistaken, after all.

'I wanted to tell you before,' said Mark, 'but we haven't had much chance of talking lately.'

'No.'

'And I am telling the truth. I had no idea that she was here.'

'I hadn't doubted it.'

'Then what are you thinking?'

'Only that I suppose you'll be going away now.'

She was quite certain of what his answer would be, but she did not look forward to hearing it. And he was taking long enough to find the words. Probably, since she had made such an abject fool of herself, he was afraid of hurting her.

'I would go,' said Mark slowly, 'if it weren't for one thing.'

'Your book?'

'No. You,' said Mark.

The colour swept painfully to her face.

'You needn't try to be funny,' she said in a choked voice.

'I wasn't being funny.'

'Well, you were making fun of me. You've always done it,' said Amy passionately, 'ever since we first met. And tonight, when I told them the truth, you didn't understand. You only laughed.'

'I laughed,' said Mark, 'but I understood.'

Miss Faraday found that his arm was around her, and her head resting on his shoulder. She was somewhat surprised, but extremely comfortable.

'You funny little rabbit,' said Mark, with his cheek on her hair, 'do you think I don't realize that you did it for me, and what it meant to you?'

'If I'd told the truth in the first place,' said Amy in a muffled voice, 'they might never have been so ready to suspect you.'

'That's sheer nonsense. You've got the whole thing out of proportion. None of my troubles were in the least degree due to you. And anyhow, it's all over now.'

'Yes,' agreed Amy drearily, 'it's all over now.'

She lifted her head from its resting place, but Mark did not remove his arm. She saw that he was smiling.

'You wouldn't misunderstand me, would you?'

'I ...'

'I didn't mean that this was all over. On the contrary. I have hopes that it's only beginning.'

'I don't know what you mean,' said Amy faintly.

'Don't you? Couldn't it be arranged for Tom Pinch and Annabel Lee to live happily ever after? I think it would answer, you know.'

Amy sat very still. He's fooling – he's always fooling. Don't let him think you've swallowed it.

'Will you?' he asked.

'Why?'

'There you go again – always wanting chapter and verse. Because I think we could make a do of it, that's why. I believe we should hit it off. Quarrel, no doubt, but never a dull moment. Why, we might have a family—'

'You know I'm too old! Besides, you want someone pretty and gay.'

'Oh, no I don't. I want you. And how the devil old are you, anyway? Not much over forty.'

'I am thirty-eight,' said Amy coldly.

'There you are, then. what's all the fuss about? Damn it,' said Mark querulously, 'you don't have to make difficulties!'

'If this is a proposal ...'

'Lord save us all, of course it's a proposal. What did you think it was, a penny reading?'

'They do it better in those books of yours,' said Amy viciously.

'Oh? Well, there's one thing they don't do better in books,' said Mark, tightening his grip and bending his head towards her. 'Come here!'

'No,' said Amy, resisting.

'You'll like it,' said Mark encouragingly.

Miss Faraday did.